# Never a Sinner

## by

## Lynn Shurr

*A Sinner's Legacy, Book Four*

**Never a Sinner**

Cover Art by *Diana Carlile*

The Wild Rose Press, Inc.
PO Box 708
Adams Basin, NY 14410-0708
Visit us at www.thewildrosepress.com

Publishing History
First Champagne Rose Edition, 2017
Print ISBN 978-1-5092-1627-7
Digital ISBN 978-1-5092-1628-4

*A Sinner's Legacy, Book Four*
Published in the United States of America

### He almost missed her,

the girl laid out on the exercise table closest to the door. A female trainer massaged and worked her patient's legs, but Teddy only noticed the beauty of the face surrounded by a halo of light brown hair, long and sun-streaked, surrounding a complexion too pale to have gone outside to attain those highlights. That perfect oval contained closed eyes perfectly made up with subtle liner and shadow beneath deftly shaped brows. Her nose was pert, her lips full, but not too heavy, candy pink outlined in a darker color. Not a single blemish marred its surface. Her hands lay crossed under her chest. Their nails, lacquered pale pink, had white tips. A French manicure his sisters called it. Gold and black running shorts showed off her still shapely legs, and the U-necked matching top revealed some cleavage between two full breasts. An old man rehabbing his knee on the next table ogled her, and other guys in the gym definitely noticed, but weren't as blatant about it. Maybe that's why she kept her eyes closed.

"Jessica," Teddy murmured.

She must have heard him because her eyes opened. They were green-gray hazel flecked with gold, large and luminous. Her lovely lips opened. "What are you staring at, jerk?"

Teddy had been stared at plenty in his life. In fact, he headed home to shower because he hated the jock atmosphere of the men's locker room. He did know how it felt to be gawked at, but he wasn't gawking. He worked his crutches to her side.

## Praise for Lynn Shurr

"Shurr is a wonderful storyteller"

~*The Romance Studio*

~\*~

"Lynn Shurr's delightful New Orleans Sinners series is sure to please both non-sports fans and sports fans alike. Do yourself a favor and dive into the world of the Sinners."

~*Farrah Rochon, USA Today best-selling author of the New York Sabers football series.*

~\*~

"The author has created a family full of surprises with the Billodeaux bunch. After reading just one book, I am eager to read more about this colorful family."

~*Rachel's Willful Thoughts, The Romance Reviews*

~\*~

"Very easy reads, well written, combined with conflict, believable plots and secondary characters that make the plot come alive."

~*Jane Lange, Romances, Reads and Reviews*

~\*~

"I love how deep and well-written the characters are."

~*Juliette Brandt, Paperbacks and Frosting*

## Dedication

For all those who spend their lives in wheelchairs.

## A Sinner's Legacy
The Children of Joe and Nell Billodeaux
who fulfilled the prophecy that they would have
twelve offspring, this way, that way, all ways.

Dean Joseph Billodeaux—Joe's illegitimate son by a one-night stand with a woman who planned to shake him down for money. He is adopted by Nell who believes she cannot have children of her own. Current Sinners quarterback. (*Wish for a Sinner*)

Thomas Cassidy Billodeaux—a redheaded son who enters the family through an open adoption with a teenage mother. His birth father is Joe's no-good cousin. He is a kicker for the Sinners. (*Wish for a Sinner* and *Kicks for a Sinner*)

Jude Emily Billodeaux—twin of Ann, conceived by in vitro fertilization using eggs purchased from Nell's sister, Emily. (*Wish for a Sinner*)

Ann Marie Billodeaux (Annie)—Jude's quiet twin. (*Wish for a Sinner*)

Lorena Renee Billodeaux (Lori)—first of Nell's little frozen babies to be born, one of the triplets. (*Kicks for a Sinner*)

Mack Coy Christopher Billodeaux—second of the triplets to be born. (*Kicks for a Sinner*)

Trinity Billodeaux—youngest of the triplets and named for the Father, Son, and Holy Ghost, smallest of the three and in need of powerful saintly help to survive. (*Kicks for a Sinner*)

Xochi Maria Billodeaux—child of Joe's no-good cousin by a young Mexican woman. She is Tom's half-sister and is adopted into the family after the terrifying deaths of her parents. Her name means "blossom" in Aztec. (*Kicks for a Sinner*)

Teddy Wilkes Billodeaux—a child with spina bifida abandoned by his mother at Nell's health care center and adopted by the family. He believed himself to be Joe's natural son. (*Paradise for a Sinner*)

Anastasia Marya Polasky (Stacy)—daughter of Nell's sister, Emily, and a bogus Polish prince. She becomes a ward of the Billodeauxs upon her parents' deaths, but is never adopted by her own wish. She arrives on their doorstep the same day as Teddy. (*Paradise for a Sinner*)

Edith Patricia Billodeaux (Edie)—a normally conceived child, twin of Rex. (*Love Letter for a Sinner*)

Rex Worthy Billodeaux (T-Rex)—Edie's twin brother and future Sinner's quarterback, maybe. (*Love Letter for a Sinner*)

~*~

**Other books by Lynn Shurr**
**available from The Wild Rose Press, Inc.**

The Sinners Series: *Goals for a Sinner, Wish for a Sinner, Kicks for a Sinner, Paradise for a Sinner, Love Letter for a Sinner*

A Sinner's Legacy Series: *Son of a Sinner, She's a Sinner, Sister of a Sinner*

The Mardi Gras Series: *Queen of the Mardi Gras Ball, Mardi Gras Madness, Courir de Mardi Gras*

The Roses Series: *The Convent Rose, A Wild Red Rose, Always Yellow Roses*

Single Titles: *A Trashy Affair, An Ashy Affair, A Will of Her Own*

Chapter One

Nell Billodeaux palmed her car keys and picked up her travel mug filled to the brim with rich, dark coffee. Should be decaf, but it wasn't. She paused for a moment relishing the utter peace and quiet of her enormous house. As soon as Camp Love Letter closed for the summer, Joe Dean Billodeaux, her famous quarterback husband, had taken himself off to assist with the Sinners training camp at a luxury resort in West Virginia, far cooler and more comfortable than Louisiana. Retired, he still couldn't keep his hands off a football, loved breaking in the rookies with his long passes, and sharing his opinions on the new crop with the coach. More power to him.

Her two youngest children, the last of the twelve remaining at home, traveled to school in the van driven by their ranch manager and bodyguard. Corazon, the housekeeper, rode along to do some grocery shopping, and Nell suspected, to make a side trip and place her hands on the belly that contained their mutual grandchild. Her daughter, Xochi, and Corazon's Junior, married in May and already expecting. Xo seemed in a rush to fill the gingerbread Victorian the couple had purchased in Chapelle with offspring as soon as possible. No wonder with what they'd been through last year. Nothing spurred the urge to reproduce faster than nearly dying.

But now, all sat settled and still at Lorena Ranch. Her children, no matter where they were, seemed happy with their lives. She was ready to resume her volunteer work as a psychologist at the health clinic, to do some good.

Then, the buzzer on the gate sounded in the kitchen. Nell never said shit, but often thought it. She expected no deliveries and feared a paparazzo seeking an intimate interview, never granted, or a Sinners fan who had negotiated the back roads to seek out the ranch and beg for entrance. The buzzer rang again, zzzzzz like a nest of angry hornets being poked with a stick. Someone laid on it hard.

Nell peered at the small video screen of their upgraded security system. A pale face with a small, lightly freckled nose pushed up against it. Large blue eyes and a fringe of corn silk blonde hair filled the view. She couldn't see the mouth, but it spoke loudly into the box.

"Ella Sue Smalls to see Teddy Wilkes Billodeaux." Nell hadn't heard a twang like that in Cajun country since Teddy came to live at the ranch, and his accent had faded considerably over the years.

"I'm sorry. Teddy isn't home, and I am on my way out. Could I take a message?"

"Figures. I spent my last dime on a taxi to get out here. It's hotter 'n the devil's arse at eight in the mornin', and I'm about to die of thirst. Got no way to get back into town, neither."

Nell had heard it all over the years and did not relent. "Teddy no longer lives here. Now, I have an appointment to keep."

The girl stepped away from the camera and put her

hands on her slim hips, which made the bulge of her pregnant belly straining the seams of a thin cotton dress all the more outstanding. "Well, I gotta talk to him. Think I'm gonna faint." Ella Sue swayed and gripped a wrought iron upright of the gate keeping her out of Lorena Ranch.

Teddy? Her adopted son crippled by spina bifida? He'd be the last of her boys Nell would suspect of putting a girl in the family way. Not that he wasn't capable of having sex or siring children. They'd done the tests years ago to reassure him. He carried no genetic flaw to pass along either. She guessed Joe had taken care of seeing that Teddy lost his virginity. Her husband had contacts from his old days as a playboy, but she'd never asked. Now if it had been Mack, tearing through women in Dallas according to the tabloids, she wouldn't be surprised—but sweet, gentle, courageous Teddy?

"Ma'am, I ain't had no breakfast neither, and I'm feeling wobbly." Her knees buckling, Ella Sue slid down the gate and landed on the ground, sending up a small puff of dust.

"Oh, for heaven's sake, I'll be right there and see you get back to town."

Nell abandoned her coffee, grabbed a bottle of water from the fridge, and snatched a handful of Corazon's homemade oatmeal raisin cookies from the jar. She kicked the door shut behind her and raced for the modest little Toyota she preferred driving to the big ranch vehicles. The lane to the road was long and curving, lined with live oaks and hung with Spanish moss, but she made the trip in record time, punched the remote to open the gate, and stopped just short of the girl's now prone body. She cracked the water bottle as she jumped from the car.

Working a hand under the pregnant woman's shoulders, Nell raised her head and held the bottle to her pallid lips. Ella Sue latched on like an infant to her mama's breast and drained the contents dry. "Thank you, ma'am."

"Let's get you into the car."

"Don't forget my suitcase." She pointed at piece of old, blue Samsonite that looked like it might have been purchased at Goodwill, no wheels or pull bars, but solidly packed. Nell heaved it into the back seat and settled Ella Sue in the front passenger seat.

"We'll stop by the clinic where I work and have you checked over, then find a place for you to stay."

The girl gave her a sideways glance. "I figured on staying at the ranch with Teddy."

"As I said, he has his own place now in Lafayette. I'll be contacting him about you."

Ella Sue nodded and eyed the cookies shoved into a drink holder. "All right if I eat these?"

"They're for you."

The unexpected guest wolfed them down. "You got anything else? Seems I'm hungry all the time."

"Expecting will do that to you." Nell watched the girl brush the cookie crumbs off her belly, but a few clung to the top of her protruding navel poking against the fabric of her dress. They approached the Mickey D's that had sprung up on the outskirts of Chapelle to the delight of the cheeseburger and chicken nugget lovers of the town, who no longer had to drive out to the highway to satisfy their cravings for fast food. At the drive-up, she ordered a breakfast sandwich with eggs, cheese, and ham.

"Get me a pop with that, a co-cola," said Ella Sue.

"We'll want milk and an orange juice, too. Yes, that's all. Thanks."

Her passenger had recovered enough to make pouty lips.

"Better for the baby," Nell said as if she had to explain this simple fact.

"Guess so, but pop is cheaper." Regardless, the girl ate every bit of her meal, picked a small blob of cheese off the wrapper with her fingernail, and sucked it into her mouth.

They arrived at the clinic, a low-slung brick building with a wing for medical exams linked to a section for dental care by a small pharmacy. Nell parked in her reserved spot and led Ella Sue inside where the air conditioning blasted an almost arctic chill. "Feels good," the girl remarked. "Never gets this hot where I come from."

"Miss Nell, your nine o'clock is here. I put him in your office," said the long-term receptionist, though the woman's eyes followed Ella Sue toward a chair where the girl plopped down, her legs splayed apart by the weight of her belly.

"Thanks. I'd like Dr. Bullock to give this young woman a prenatal exam. Please work her in as soon as you can." She accepted a clipboard full of papers for Ella Sue.

The girl scanned the top sheet. "Easy—name, sex, birth date, no current address, no insurance. Can't pay nothing." She flipped the page. "No diseases. I'm only takin' some big ole vitamins I can hardly swallow, and some other pills because of the baby."

Thank heaven for that, Nell thought. "It's a community clinic. People pay what they can."

"All righty, then."

"They'll call me when you're done."

That seemed okay with Ella Sue. She picked up an old copy of People and leafed through the lives of movie stars and athletes. The famous Billodeaux family had appeared in it more than once. Nell went to meet her patient, but paused in the hallway outside her office door to place a call to Teddy. It went to voice mail. "Call me as soon as you can. Important. This is your mother speaking." She always felt compelled to add that along with "Love you" and this time, "No matter what."

Chapter Two

Teddy Wilkes Billodeaux, formerly named Teddy
Bear Wilkes by his adolescent birth mother for being so
cuddly, strained to complete another round down the
lane between the parallel bars. He'd completed his
upper body strength training and his core work, but
always left this most hated task for last. With the aid of
his well-developed arms and his thighs where he had
some feeling, he carefully placed his braced legs and let
his feet flop down, trying to get them to line up in some
kind of natural manner.

Thanks to keeping up his exercises, he'd been able
to walk across the stage using his armband crutches in
high school to receive his diploma, and stand long
enough to deliver a short speech as one of four
valedictorians who maintained a perfect 4.0. In college,
he'd done that walk again and graduated top of his class
in Communications. Couldn't give up now.

Balancing carefully, he paused a moment to mop
his face with the towel hanging around his neck.
Outside the rehab center, a recuperating runner sped
past the window with a parachute device attached to his
torso creating drag and increasing his strength. Off to
one side of the bars, a jumper squatted and hurled
himself upward to the top of a three-foot padded block.
Another injured athlete worked the long ropes, making
them jump across the floor like waves in a mighty

ocean. At least, Teddy could do that one for a while. The pros and cons of having access to a facility used by university athletes was on rare occasions he could do the same exercises, but mostly not.

Teddy caught a view of himself in the long mirror some people enjoyed working out in front of, but not him. His fine blond hair lay plastered against his brow so sweat-soaked it appeared brown. His normally pale face burned red with exertion. He took a deep breath, expanding his chest built up from the strength training. There, that was better. He straightened his body to its full five-foot-six frame, that courtesy of a number of operations involving cracking open the heavy scar on his back to allow him to grow. He'd never be six feet tall like most of his brothers and heck, one of his sisters; he'd never play for the Sinners football team like two of them, but he was grateful for what he could do, thanks to a caring family.

"You stuck, Teddy? Do you need your chair?" asked one of the PT trainers.

"Nope, only resting a minute. One more round and I'm done for the day." He turned awkwardly and started down the lane again, focusing on his crutches waiting at the end of the course to give him some relief. Goal attained. Teddy placed his arms in the bands of his sticks and made his way to grab his hoodie from a rack, not that he needed it to go outside. Louisiana in early August required no extra coverage. The humidity ran so high sweat didn't dry off the body.

He almost missed her, the girl laid out on the exercise table closest to the door. A female trainer massaged and worked her patient's legs, but Teddy only noticed the beauty of the face surrounded by a halo of light brown hair, long and sun-streaked, surrounding a complexion too pale to have gone outside to attain those highlights. That perfect oval contained closed eyes perfectly made up with subtle liner and shadow beneath deftly shaped brows. Her nose was pert, her lips full, but not too heavy, candy pink outlined in a darker color. Not a single blemish marred its surface. Her hands lay crossed under her chest. Their nails, lacquered pale pink, had white tips. A French manicure his sisters called it. Gold and black running shorts showed off her still shapely legs, and the U-necked matching top revealed some cleavage between two full breasts. An old man rehabbing his knee on the next table ogled her, and other guys in the gym definitely noticed, but weren't as blatant about it. Maybe that's why she kept her eyes closed.

"Jessica," Teddy murmured.

She must have heard him because her eyes opened. They were green-gray hazel flecked with gold, large and luminous. Her lovely lips opened. "What are you staring at, jerk?"

Teddy had been stared at plenty in his life. In fact, he headed home to shower because he hated the jock atmosphere of the men's locker room. He did know how it felt to be gawked at, but he wasn't gawking. He worked his crutches to her side. "Teddy Billodeaux. We went to high school together and college, though I didn't see you around much there. Different majors, I guess. I studied communications."

"So what." She turned her head away, closed her eyes again as if blocking out all around her.

Teddy remembered her as one of the nicer cheerleaders. He'd interviewed Jessica Minvielle for the high school paper years ago. She'd been self-deprecating about her gymnastic abilities, asking who could make a career out of leading cheers. Best of all, she hadn't treated him like a dweeb or a freak, simply spoke naturally about her life. Her father coached the football team at UL, the local university they'd both attended. Her mom taught physical education at a public school and coached the girls' basketball team. Jessie came by her athleticism naturally—until the accident early this summer, a jet-ski collision reported in the newspaper, her fiancé dead, herself paralyzed from the waist down. Tough all the way around.

"I just wanted to say I'm sorry about your accident and what happened to your boyfriend."

Her head rolled back his way, and the hazel eyes blazed at him. "Troy Gilbert was my fiancé. We were going to be married in October. He played football for the Cowboys with your brother, Mack. You should have known that."

"I guess I did, but I didn't know him personally."

"You want to know what my major was? Phys. Ed. I wanted to be an athletic trainer, and I was for my dad's team until this happened. Now, I'm only a burden and this is pointless." She gestured to the therapist working her useless legs. "Just go away and leave me alone!"

"Okay." Teddy started back toward the peg holding his hoodie, then stopped and did a rather smart pivot on his sticks. He didn't raise his voice, but spoke firmly. "I've been handicapped since the day I was born. The only time I felt like a burden was when my mother abandoned me at the free clinic because her boyfriend didn't want me around. I've had more operations than I can count simply to be able to stand upright on these crutches and reach a normal height. The reason for being here is to stay healthy and keep our muscles strong in case a medical miracle comes along and we might be able to walk normally. When I look at you, I see a bright, beautiful woman who still has a lot to offer and can learn to take care of herself. Too bad she can't see that."

He didn't bother to wait for a reaction, but stumped to the rack, seized his hoodie, and pushed through the door bearing the prominent sign No Cell Phones Allowed to the lobby. Teddy continued on to his low-slung, red Honda Odyssey mobility van with the hand controls, ample room for his wheelchair and a ramp if he needed it. He stowed his sticks in the passenger seat and lowered himself behind the wheel, swinging his legs in afterward. Cranking the A/C halfway, he paused a moment to cool off both mentally and physically. Taking his cell phone from a slot, he checked for messages.

One from his adoptive mom: the best woman on earth as far as he was concerned. He frowned over the urgent need to reach him, smiled at her telling him who called as if he wouldn't recognize her voice, and puzzled over the odd sign off, "Love you—no matter what."

Teddy returned the call immediately. It, too, went to voice mail. Probably with a patient. "Been at the gym. On my way home. Catch you later. Love, Ted."

Fairly sure no one had died, but also certain that one of the Billodeauxs, most likely the troublesome Mack, had some kind of issue possibly requiring a family team meeting, he put the van into gear and headed to his apartment. Whatever had happened, it could wait on a hot shower.

Chapter Three

Nothing came easy to Teddy, not even taking a shower. He arrived at the accessible college apartment he once shared with a roommate entirely wheelchair bound, but now had the place to himself. The university let him stay on since he called the football games for them, and he continued to pay the housing fee. Though he'd never be a Sinner, he knew the game inside out because of his sports-saturated upbringing. That gig led to providing color and analysis for the Sinners' home games—or maybe his dad's influence had, but he excelled at what he did, and it paid well during the football season.

Using his sticks to get to the side of his van, he wrangled his wheelchair from the interior, not bothering to use the lift. He'd selected a side loader, hating to be discharged from the rear like cargo if someone else drove. Teddy slammed the sliding door and sank gratefully into the chair. Crutches stowed into a sling, he pushed himself up the handicap ramp from his parking space and all the way up the longer incline leading to his first-floor front door.

Inside, he rolled past his living room and dining area, by a small kitchen with cabinets and counters lowered to wheelchair height, and one of the bedrooms to the spacious bathroom off the hall.

With the wide shower stall flush to the floor and

loaded with safety bars, Teddy entered to adjust the water temperature, reversed, and shucked his workout clothes. His legs emerged from the braces as if he were a molting crab. He sat in the sliding shower chair and shuttled himself into the stall. Using the handheld sprayer to wet his body, he took the bottle of liquid soap from a caddy and scrubbed away the sweat of his exertions. Next, a good shampooing of his fine hair that looked limp if not washed daily.

He used his sticks and upper body strength to get back to the wheelchair. Toweling off his bottom and privates before sitting, he reapplied his braces. Time to change his ostomy pouch, the bag that collected his waste, though he probably should have done that first. Accidents did happen and were hell to clean up. He added deodorant drops to the pouch and slapped his nude body with a light cologne in case the danged thing seeped and smelled. With no need for modesty, Teddy wheeled to the bedroom and took underwear, wide-legged jeans that covered the apparatus on his lower legs, and a T-shirt from a low, built-in dresser and got himself clothed. All that finished, he returned to the bathroom to hang the damp towel and put his gym clothes in the hamper. No excuses for being a slob, Mama Nell always told him.

The cell phone he'd left on the counter informed him she'd called again. "Teddy, we're at the clinic. Get here as soon as you can. Love you."

The clinic—had his youngest brother, the ever leaping and climbing T-Rex, broken something? Maybe his littlest sister ran a high fever? But Nell wouldn't call him for assistance. Despite Joe being gone, she had a nurse in-house at the ranch and plenty of other help. A terrible thought poked to the surface of his mind. Had Xochi miscarried, and the clan been summoned to give her support? He'd be the one most easily reached. His recently married sister had blossomed with excitement over the baby. What if it had been taken from her? That spurred him to his van. Teddy dealt handily with the rigmarole necessary to get back behind the wheel and sped south thirty miles to meet his mom.

As usual, by this time of day on a Monday, he found the clinic parking lot jammed and all the handicap spaces taken. Teddy blew off his wheelchair and hitched himself along on his crutches. Sweat from the heat gathered on his forehead before he reached the door and hit the button to open it automatically.

"You can go on back, honey. Your mom is between patients," said the receptionist.

He swore Marvelle had been sitting behind the desk since before he'd been left at the clinic. She simply grew grayer and wider in the beam over the years, but always greeted everyone with a broad smile.

He hiked past a clutch of noisy children playing with toys from the box in the corner, a pregnant teenager who looked about to pop, and an old black woman nodding off in her wheelchair as an aide read a magazine by her side. Thought he heard his name called, but kept going. No time for friendly clinic chitchat if the very beloved Xochi needed his comfort.

"I'm here!" he announced, opening the door with the plaque, Nellwyn Billodeaux, MS, LPC, attached. "Is Xo okay?"

His mom looked up from a chart. "As far as I know. We're supposed to have lunch together, but I'm not so sure now. Something has come up. Sit." She gestured to one of the comfortable overstuffed chairs that encouraged people to relax and spill their concerns into her ears. "Does the name Ella Sue Smalls mean anything to you?"

Caught off balance in more ways than one, Teddy fell into a chair. "It—ah—might."

Disappointment washed over his mom's face. They'd never intended for Mama Nell to know about their computer searches for information about lost family members, he and Xochi and Stacy. Not that they thought the Billodeauxs tried to hide anything, maybe just soften the past when they were younger. But as teens the three housed at the end of the hall in the mansion near the elevator Teddy used had done their best and found little. Xochi came up with her birth record from a Texas hospital learning only her mother's appallingly young age and a Mexican surname so common it led nowhere. Stacy attempted to track down her father's Polish relatives, supposedly royalty, but finally had to accept that the noble Polaskys were a fictional construct as Nell had gently tried to tell her.

He'd been more successful. Maydell Wilkes Smalls had given birth to a six-pound, five-ounce baby girl in Bristol, Tennessee, the sister she'd told him she expected with so much joy. Everything would be fine now with Newton Smalls, her boyfriend, who wanted a child of his own—a normal child who wasn't so much trouble, though she didn't say that. Evidently, Newt did finally marry her and headed farther north looking for good work as he constantly said he would do if not for being stuck with this handicapped kid who needed special care the local community provided. More than once when drinking as Maydell worked her waitress job, he swore he'd chop Teddy's head off and leave it in the drive for her to find if he had to clean up another mess made by the boy. Teddy shivered in the depths of the overstuffed chair just remembering.

"Well?" said Mama Nell. "How do you know her? Because she is out in the waiting room very pregnant and looking for you."

"It's not what you think." He'd done all right in college tooling around in his flashy red wheelchair showing off his chest and shoulder muscles in tight tees. Some girls could get into that and found the penis ring he used to sustain erections cool and exotic. Eventually, the novelty wore off. Still, no matter what his disability, he followed Daddy Joe's rule number one: always use a condom.

Cheeks burning because he couldn't seem to overcome his childish blushes, the curse of the pale, Teddy said, "I think someone named Ella Sue Smalls might be my sister. That was Newt's last name."

"Oh, Teddy, forgive me for suspecting the worst." Nell made use of the box of tissues she kept on her desk for clients and dabbed at her doe brown eyes. "I didn't make the connection, and you look so much like her. Your mother never revealed the name of your father, or of the baby she carried when she left."

"Newt wasn't my dad. She wouldn't talk about the man who got her pregnant with me when she was so young. Best let lay, she'd say. We had Granny, and Granny took care of us until she died. Then, along came Newt who carried us off to Louisiana where he said he had a job. His jobs didn't last long because he drank."

"When I counseled her, I simply could not convince Maydell she was in an abusive relationship.

17

My failure." Nell wiped her nose of the drip the tears brought on.

"My good luck she left me behind when Newt took off again. Since I'm not the daddy, what does my half-sister want?"

"I imagine money as she made a point of telling me how broke she is and a roof over her head while she waits for the baby to come. Maybe more."

"Let's bring her in here and find out." He said the words oh-so-casually. As part of the Billodeaux family, he didn't lack for interesting and involved siblings, ten of them plus their ward, Stacy, but a tinge of excitement passed through him at the thought of a real blood relative, one who could tell him what happened to his birth mother. Newt hadn't lingered long in Bristol before he moved the family again, and they disappeared from the records.

Nell contacted the front desk. "Marvelle, would you send Ella Sue Smalls to my office?"

Not long before Ella Sue filled the doorway with her belly. "Please sit down. Teddy tells me you might be his long-lost sister."

"That's right. I am." She sank into the other chair.

Teddy stared at the gravid teen he'd passed in the lobby. She possessed the same light complexion, blue eyes, and pale blonde hair his mama had, and him, too. Nothing of the brutal Newt in her. Though he hadn't said a word yet, his sister got her back up immediately, a white cat spitting.

"I know what you're thinkin'. She's too young, but I'm eighteen and got my GED diploma after being mostly homeschooled since we moved so much. I'm plenty old enough to be on my own and have a kid."

"I was thinking you look just like Mama. How is she?" His voice shook a little.

"Dead." Ella Sue didn't pretty up the news any. "Passed last year of breast cancer. No mammograms for her. Daddy said he couldn't afford it and wouldn't take no charity when the clinic offered them free. Stage Four. She went fast, but not before all her hair fell out and was nothing left of her but a bundle of bones. Only decent thing Daddy did for her was take her back to the hollow where she grew up, and plant her beside her own mother in the graveyard. Had her cremated so we only had an urn to put in the ground. Cheaper that way, he said. Her Uncle Merv paid for the marker."

Teddy closed his eyes tight for a moment. He'd nearly reached for a tissue himself. After his initial bewilderment, fear, and anger over being abandoned receded, he'd taken what Mama Nell said to heart. His mother left him in a safe place—even if she did knock down the door by claiming her son belonged to Joe Billodeaux, a total falsehood.

"I'd like to go there sometime and visit their graves."

"Not much to see. There's a little white Baptist church that been there forever by the cemetery. Bunch of rundown cabins and some trailers. Merv owns the gas station and convenience store, about the only business in town besides the Dairy Queen. He let us stay in Granny's old place since Daddy was between jobs again."

"Nice of him," Teddy managed to say.

"You think? That place was a dump. We worked days fixin' it up. Now it's good enough for Merv to rent."

Teddy didn't remember the cabin that way. Not that the small house was anything special, but it had been warm and dry, full of handmade quilts and good home cooking. The church members built a ramp to the porch for his wheelchair and held bake sales and raffles to pay for his needs. He, his mom, and his granny rocked in a swing on that porch in the evenings. In fact, he had a photo of the three of them someone had taken. He'd found it wedged into his favorite of the Harry Potter series, The Goblet of Fire. No doubt his mother had placed it there to be discovered when he reread the set as he did over and over. He could have asked Mama Nell for a frame because she'd understand, but instead he left it exactly where Maydell laid it for him to find. He could almost feel the touch of her fingers as she pressed the picture between the pages when he handled it, the same way she'd tested his forehead for fever from his many illnesses.

Ella Sue continued on oblivious to his pain. "Merv give me a job in the store and had Daddy fixin' flat tires and doing oil changes and such at the gas station."

"Generous guy."

His sister curled her pink lips. "Ha! Minimum wage pay, and he'd play grab ass every time I passed. He's quick for a geezer. Merv the Perv I called him. I quit and moved on over to the Dairy Queen. The woman who owned that place said my looks would bring in the young men. She was right. They lined up for soft serve."

And maybe something else, Teddy declined to say.

Nell took over the conversation. "Is your father still living in the cabin?"

"Doubt it, but don't know. He kicked me out when

I started to show. Asked if the baby was Merv's kid like Teddy. I think he believed he could get blackmail money out of him if that was so. Sorry, Daddy. I wouldn't let that creep touch me for all the world."

Nell studied Teddy's face. "You've gone whiter than white. Are you ill, son?"

Since he was prone to infections, she'd posed a reasonable question, but Teddy felt sure she'd caught the reference about Merv being his father. Now he knew what everyone suspected—Teddy Wilkes Billodeaux was a child of incest, an ugly truth.

Ella Sue caught on quick. "Didn't know, huh? Well, Mama told Daddy, and when we went back there, he said he thought Uncle Mervin was too old to get it up now, but to be shy of him if he got handsy."

Teddy still had no words. Nell filled the gap. "Would you care to tell us who the father of your child is?"

"My baby daddy was a local boy who loved chocolate-dipped soft serve. I stayed with him for a while, but he wasn't into the whole fatherhood thing. I got to thinking I have a brother out there who's done pretty well for himself. Mama always said so. How you'd landed in clover. We followed you in the magazines, and she'd say, 'Look at my Teddy Bear at that fancy wedding. Don't he look good?' She talked about you all the time when Daddy went to work. Anyhow, maybe you'd give me a place to stay until the baby comes."

Teddy's words came out as feeble as his legs. "I have a spare room at my apartment. It isn't far from the University Medical Center and its clinics."

"Is that a charity place? Because I don't want my

baby born in no charity place. Besides, I figured I'd be staying at that famous ranch. Took all the money my boyfriend give me to get there. I almost perished by the side of the road. Did Miss Nell tell you?"

"We hadn't gotten that far in discussing your situation." Nell's intercom buzzed. "My next appointment must be here."

Marvelle's mellow voice announced, "Your eleven o'clock just cancelled."

Nell shook her head. "Why do the ones who need it most always cancel? It appears I am free for an early lunch."

"Great, because I'm starvin'. Eatin' for two." Ella Sue patted her bulging stomach.

"I'd planned to dine at my daughter's house, just the two of us. Let me call and see if she has enough to go around. If not, we'll go out. Would you mind waiting in the lobby, Ella Sue?"

"Fine by me. Either way is good." After two tries, the pregnant girl heaved herself out of the chair and headed for the lobby.

Teddy also rose, steadier now that he'd had a few minutes to think. "Stay a minute," his mother said. "Do you really want your sister living with you in Lafayette? We have plenty of room at the ranch."

"Yes, I think that was her intention, to sponge off of you and Dad. If all she really wants is a place to stay, mine should do. You'll have Xochi check her out, right?"

"Oh, absolutely."

Chapter Four

Teddy followed Nell and his sister to Xochi's house in his van. The tall Victorian stood on the other side of the bayou bridge. With enough fancy fretwork hanging off its eaves to give it a wedding cake appearance, the house possessed a deep wraparound porch and a long yard running down to the water. Old rambling roses rather tired in the August heat, draped the white picket fence. Formerly the home of a prominent attorney, it had a small frame building to one side that had served as his law office before he retired to Toledo Bend to do all the fishing and bird watching he ever wanted.

That structure proved to be a selling point when Xochi and Junior began house hunting. Now it held herbal medicines and her worktable for concocting them, along with space for her clients to sit when they sought her skills as a folk healer, a traiteur in the Cajun parlance. She charged no one and accepted no thanks for whatever comfort she could provide. The house also sat only a short walk across the bridge and down a block to the riverside restaurant in which Junior had purchased a share. That man always thought ahead.

They parked and entered through the front gate rigged with a small bell on its chain to sound a visitors' alert. "Ain't it pretty," Ella Sue gushed as they passed along a short walk lined with clumps of dark green aspidistra.

Dressed in sunny yellow that became her tan skin and long black curls, Xochi came out to the porch to greet them. She hugged Nell and turned to Teddy as he mastered the last step on his crutches. "Not handicapped accessible," he teased.

"Yes, we'll have to do something about that. So good to see you, hermano. You don't visit often enough." Xochi wrapped him in a warm embrace.

"I see you've already done something about all that white paint you hated."

"Yes, now the neighbors are calling this house the King Cake instead of the Wedding Cake. I'm not sure that's a compliment. I guess they expected two people with Mexican blood to live in an adobe, but I love it!" She held out her arms toward the slender pillars now sporting narrow stripes of purple, green, and gold top and bottom. The fish scale shingles in each apex of the roof glowed with similar colors, one light green, the other lavender, a third a pale blue like the inside of the porch roof, very eye-catching and not so traditional in the area.

"I see we have a guest."

"Yes, Teddy's sister dropped by. This is Ella Sue Smalls. Do you have enough food or should we dine out, my treat? We can go to the Down by the Riverside restaurant." Nell stared at her aura-seeing daughter as if trying to send a psychic message.

Teddy watched the exchange. Xo's brown eyes went wide, but she didn't hesitate to move forward and offer the girl her hands, clasped top and bottom rather than shaking.

Ella Sue said, "Nice to meet you," and pulled from

her grasp. "Warm handshake you got there."

"So people tell me."

Ella Sue looked her up and down before saying, "Ain't you the sister who was chosen to be a human sacrifice? I seen your picture in the paper." Teddy knew exactly the kind of papers she mentioned, the ever-inquisitive tabloids.

"Obviously I wasn't sacrificed." Xochi moved on as she had with her life. "I have plenty to eat for all of us. Junior filled the freezer with casseroles before he left for training camp, as if I'd starve without him to cook for me. I thawed out a turkey tetrazzini. There's salad from a bag, a dozen warm rolls I got from the Riverside because theirs are the best, and cookies Corazon brought from Pommier's Bakery when she visited this morning. Between my husband and my mother-in-law, I'm only a little over three months and already showing." Xochi smoothed her dress over her belly to show a tiny baby bump.

"I'm pregnant, too." Ella Sue stated the obvious.

"So I see. I bet you'd like to get off your feet. When is your baby due?" Xochi held the door open for her guests. They paraded into the cool, dim hallway.

Ella Sue peered down at her belly. "Not sure. Soon I guess."

"Didn't your doctor give you a date? Mine said the end of January. Before the Super Bowl, I hope." Xo guided them into her parlor once full of large and dreary Victorian pieces, now hosting comfortable floral-covered sofas and chairs and a large TV wall-mounted over the fireplace instead of a painting displaying dead rabbits amid vegetables to make a stew. She took them through the pocket doors, always left open, to the dining room, once formal, now casual with a big, distressed oak table and mingled chairs and benches for seating. A large ceiling fan churned the air where once a crystal chandelier hung. Opening a glass-fronted cabinet, Xochi gathered two more place settings and utensils to set the table for the extra guests.

"Do you want to sit at the head, Mom?"

"Not unless you have several cushions or a telephone book for me to sit on," her petite mother answered. "That's Junior's chair. He might be called Junior, but he is king-sized, Ella Sue."

"I know. I follow the Sinners—trying to catch a look-see at Teddy in the stands sometimes. Mama did the same, always saying how well he was doing." She turned the conversation back to herself. "To answer your question, I did have a doctor for a while, and he said end of September for me, but I feel like it might be sooner. He gave me iron pills on a kind of me being peaked, and those big vitamins full of folic acid because I told him I had a brother with spina bifida. Supposed to prevent that from happening again. But I've been on the road a lot since then." Ella Sue plopped down on a bench, taking the load off.

Teddy felt obligated to sit next to her. Nell sat across by Xochi's place. His sister went through the door to the kitchen to get the casserole and prompted them to pass the salad and rolls. She'd embellished the bag-o-salad with slices of boiled eggs, a ring of cherry tomatoes, and a pinch of fresh chopped herbs making it bright and pretty like her, Teddy thought. Returning with the main dish, Xo sat it on a trivet in the center of the table close enough for everyone to serve themselves.

Ella Sue gouged a large portion from the casserole and began shoveling it down before the rest got settled. "This is real good. Lots of cheese. I'm not too keen on sweet peas, but the sauce kind of covers them." She mopped the plate with her roll, didn't touch her salad though she'd taken a small amount. "You got anything besides iced tea to drink?"

"Water? Or milk for the baby?" Xo questioned.

"Pop?"

"I try not to keep much of that around unless we're having a party, but I'll see if I have anything left over." Xochi left her own meal cooling to accommodate Ella Sue and returned with a glass full of ice and a canned drink. "Cream soda okay?"

"Yes, ma'am. One of my favorites."

"Junior loves it, too—along with lots of cheese."

"See, now that's something I didn't know about the Sinners. Junior Polk loves cream soda and cheese."

Not joining in, Teddy kept his eyes on his plate. His mom and Xochi had warm hearts and wouldn't judge Ella Sue by her grammar or her table manners, but Stacy and Jude, another of his sisters, or someone like Jessica Minvielle might. Why had Jessie come to mind when his thoughts were already confused by this sudden sister and what she'd revealed about his mother and Uncle Merv? He shook his head free of the image of the pretty face with the paralyzed body. His mother was right on him.

"Are you okay, Teddy? Not an ear ache or infection coming on?"

"No, nothing." He made a try at conversation. "I saw Jessica Minvielle at rehab today. She's in a wheelchair because of her accident and not adjusting well." Why had he chosen that topic above all others?

Concern alit on Nell's face. "I'm sure her family is taking care of that, but if not, I'd be glad to see her at the clinic."

"I'll tell her if I talk to her again."

Ella Sue piped up. "She an old girlfriend or something 'cause you're going all red."

"No! We went to high school together is all. She was engaged to a football player who died in the same accident. What would she want with me?"

"Teddy Wilkes Billodeaux, only the shallow would judge you on your disability and not on your personality, brains, and talent. Teddy was class valedictorian," Nell added for Ella Sue's benefit.

"Smart, huh?" His sister gave him a sidelong look as if doing a reassessment of her brother.

"Very," Xochi said. "I know it's hot out, but would you like to have dessert on the back porch? It's shady, and I'll turn on the fans. We have such a nice view of the bayou from there. Anyone want coffee?"

"Not me. I'll bring along the rest of my pop. How do we get out there?" Ella Sue scanned the room for an exit as if she were casing the joint. The others agreed it was too scorching for hot coffee.

"Look, this is cool." Xochi went to one of the very tall windows letting light into the dining room. She tugged on the sash and raised it higher than her head. "You can walk right out. Refill your glasses with tea and take a seat. I'll bring the cookies."

Nell carried drinks for herself and Teddy while he made his way to a wicker settee with wildly colored cushions. Carrying her soft drink, Ella Sue sank into a cane-seated rocker that groaned a little under her weight. Xochi came out with the plate of cookies: peanut butter and chocolate chip with a heap of powered-sugar-coated Mexican wedding cakes in the center. Ella Sue took one of each on a paper napkin and tuckered in to eat. Teddy savored a chocolate chip already melting a little in the heat.

"It's right nice out here," Ella Sue declared. "Wish I had a place like this to live."

No one said much after that. They simply watched the bayou flow by. A small flotilla of ducks, white Pekins deserted after Easter, warty-faced Muscovys, and a smattering of mallards and mixed breeds noted their presence, came ashore by the gazebo, and waddled their way up the lawn.

"Can I feed them some of the leftover rolls, Miss Xochi?"

"Just Xochi. I'm not that much older than you."

"About ten years, I figure, but can I?"

"Certainly."

Ella Sue ducked through the still-open window and returned with a handful of rolls. She eased down the porch steps and did her own waddle to meet the ducks halfway. They mobbed her with attention, and she gloried in it, dispensing the bread like royalty throwing coins to the peasants.

With his sister out of earshot, Teddy asked, "What do you think, Xo?"

"She's healthy and so is her baby. I saw no signs of disease."

"Not really what I meant."

"She's not evil, Ted, but she is a deceiver, smart and ambitious despite the country girl exterior. Her aura is muddled, not pure. I'd be careful what you offer her because she'll take all she can get, and you are a white knight in a wheelchair who might try to give it to her."

"Ahhh, normally both you and Mom would be the first to give her a place to stay considering she's hinted pretty hard at that. She wasn't so enthusiastic about my apartment, but I feel she's my responsibility, not yours. I should see her through the birth and recovery, then help her find a job and her own place to live. She'll have more opportunities in Lafayette."

"We're here to be your backups in case that doesn't work out." Nell patted his hand.

"I went sort of wild buying maternity clothes the second I found out I was pregnant and don't really need them yet. I'm about the same height as Ella Sue even if I do have more up top and behind, but I doubt that will matter much. Let me pick out a few things to see her through to the end. I'm afraid she'll split the seams of that dress any minute now." Xochi rose to do the task.

"You two are the best, you know that," Teddy said as Ella Sue, out of bread, trundled toward them trailed by the still-hopeful ducks.

She took Xochi's empty chair and piled cookies into a napkin. "Mind if I take some of these along for an afternoon snack?"

"Take as many as you like," Xochi said. An aggressive Muscovy fluttered up the porch steps. Xo flapped her skirt at him. "Vamanos, pato! You are not going to poop on my porch. Back to the bayou."

Ella Sue held her stomach as she laughed. "So where are we going, brother?"

"Allons a Lafayette," Teddy told her. "I'm taking you to my place in the city."

"Huh? I thought we was going to the ranch." Ella

Sue's disappointment showed.

"Before you go, I have some gifts for you." Xochi watched the girl's smile return.

"I like surprises!"

"Don't we all?" Xo went inside to sort through her maternity clothes.

Maybe not everyone. Teddy certainly hadn't enjoyed being suddenly abandoned, searching for his mother and sister, and then having Ella Sue find him out of the blue. Not quite what he'd expected.

They left a half hour later toting half the casserole, a bag of cookies, and a huge shopping bag in his van. Yes, they were on their way to Lafayette for better or worse.

Chapter Five

Ella Sue appeared unimpressed with his university apartment on the very edge of the campus, but she did help with his wheelchair and carried the bags and her suitcase inside. The aroma of the pork roast he'd put in his crockpot before leaving for the gym that morning filled the air. She sniffed. "That smells good, but seems like all the furniture is made for Munchkins."

"For people in wheelchairs actually. I'm making pulled pork sandwiches for dinner. Got some buns and coleslaw from the deli." Teddy steered her down the hall to his spare room. "It's pretty basic, but you do have plenty of room for your clothes, a bed, and nightstand. Bathroom is across the hall."

Teddy assessed what he had to offer. Thanks to his mom, the bed had a nice spread: blue and white patterned with curtains at the single window to match, good white sheets that could be bleached in case of accidents, but no carpet or throw rugs that just made life harder for the wheelchair bound. It wasn't a dump, but Ella Sue's next words sure made it sound that way.

"Well, not like Daddy Joe's place in New Orleans, huh. I saw once in a magazine he had a crystal chandelier in his bathroom." Ella Sue flung the shopping bag on the low-slung bed and began rooting through the contents. "I thought your sister was giving me used stuff, but look here, these jeans still have the tags on and a pouch in the front for a baby belly. I been wearing mine unzipped with men's shirts over the top. Must be a half-dozen tops in here and a couple of dresses good enough to wear to church." She held up a modest blue number that matched her eyes.

"Lafayette has plenty of churches if you want to go."

"I didn't say that, did I? Full of nosey, judgmental people, that's what my daddy says. Even that tiny Baptist church in the hollow is full of old biddies watching your every move. I don't miss that place at all. You got scissors to get these tags off?"

Teddy fetched a pair from a drawer in the kitchen. Ella Sue snipped the price tags and folded her new clothes into a drawer. She added her own underwear, shamelessly explaining that since her bikini pants slipped under her belly they weren't getting stretched out, but she'd had to buy new bras for her bigger boobs.

"I'll let you get settled and go check on the pork roast." Teddy hastened to the kitchen before his sister could share any more pregnancy tidbits. Poking the meat with a fork, he considered it done enough and transferred the roast to a cutting board. Another fork in-hand, he pulled the pork into shreds, dumped the mound of meat into a bowl, and doused it with Connor Riley's Sweet and Mild Barbecue Sauce. Truth be told, he hadn't developed a taste for his dad's brand, Joe's Hot and Spicy. Regardless, sales of both went to their charities. He worked the sauce into the meat, covered the bowl, and put it in the fridge until dinner. Ordinarily, a roast lasted him for days, but he wasn't too sure that would be the case with the voracious Ella Sue around.

Making a pork roast in a crockpot symbolized independence to Teddy, as did this apartment. He could have stayed at the ranch and commuted to the local college in the nifty red van with the hand controls he'd gotten for graduation, but he wanted to prove he could live on his own. Going to LSU would have been more daring still, but knowing his mom and Nurse Shammy lived only thirty miles away instead of ninety bolstered his courage. The smaller campus was easier to navigate, and he often ran into kids he'd known in public school, unlike the bigger university where Xochi said you never saw anyone you grew up with because of its size. Rarely Jessica Minvielle, though. He'd made a good choice that suited him, wanted to be responsible for himself—and now he'd made the leap to taking care of another person.

Ella Sue ducked her head into the kitchen. "I think I'll get a shower, then a nap. This being on the road wears a person out, not to mention getting pretty ripe." She sniffed her armpits. "Yep, time for a bath."

"Towels are in the hallway closet nearest the bathroom."

"Gotcha."

He wheeled after her to make sure she found them okay, but Ella Sue had an armful by the time he got there. She disappeared into the bathroom. On his way back, he glanced into his sister's room. The large shopping bag lay on the floor making a hazard for his navigation. He entered, picked it up, and folded it for further use. His sister had left her vitamins and iron pill containers on the low dresser. He picked up the prescription bottle, filled last week at a pharmacy in Tennessee. She hadn't been on the road all that long and might have hitchhiked. Deceitful, but still needy. He'd have to watch his step with her—if a guy in a wheelchair could do that.

The next day, Teddy spent most of the morning finding an obstetrician for his sister, not something most women did in the last six weeks of a pregnancy. He finally got her in with a doctor who delivered at the University Medical Center, helped her fill in the copious paperwork, and put himself down as being responsible for her bills. On the way back, they stopped at Albertson's for the fresh fruit and vegetables he felt his sister needed. She wheedled a cream puff out of him at the bakery counter. "Please, please, pretty please."

Yesterday, Ella Sue complained about the lack of snacks in his apartment. He explained Mama Nell didn't believe in junk food, and he hadn't been raised to crave it. Besides, he didn't need more weight to lug around on his crutches or to watch his bottom spread in the wheelchair. She spent the afternoon snarfing down the giant cream puff with a glass of milk, and watching soaps on what she referred to as his "itty-bitty" TV. The obstetrician confirmed Dr. Bullock's assessment that Ella Sue was in good health, about six weeks out, and carrying ten more pounds than she should. He didn't think that likely to change even with his refusal to buy soft drinks for her.

The following morning, his sister roused herself enough to make scrambled eggs mixed with chopped ham and cheese from his cold cuts drawer. Teddy usually stuck to whole grain cereal with blueberries or a sliced banana on top as being quick and easy, but she'd turned up her nose at that. "Breakfast is always eggs," she said. He recalled Newt making a similar statement to his mother who got up to cook for him no matter how tired or nauseated from carrying a new baby.

"I'll make biscuits later on. Give me something to do. We need bacon."

"We're near the park if you want to take a walk. That's supposed to be good for expectant mothers. You can explore the campus, too. They have an alligator pond and a union where a person can get coffee and sit all day if they want. Fast food places are on the main road, but we have plenty of pork and tetrazzini leftovers right now. There's an indoor pool and a great library, but I'd have to get you cards to use those."

Ella Sue put her hands on her hips, framing her belly. "Seems like the only thing free is the walking."

Teddy, getting ready to leave for his workout, shelled out two twenties. "Here, go to the coffee shop or get something to read. The park has ducks you can feed."

Ella Sue regarded the twenties as if it were counterfeit. "Won't go far. A debit card would be better. Say, what do you do for a living besides announce Sinners' home games?"

"I call the games for UL, too. Otherwise, I write sports articles for the newspapers. I'm a stringer for Sport Illustrated, too. They pay well, but the local papers are often by the word count so I submit to a wire service. Just before football season starts again, my finances can get a little slim." Gym bag on his lap, he wheeled a little closer to the exit.

"A rich man adopted you. Mama said she left you in a safe place where you'd be taken care of real well. Seems you got the short end of the stick what with Xochi being able to afford that fine house and two of your brothers playing football for the Sinners and makin' plenty."

Teddy glanced down at his braces. "I can't exactly play football, but I'll take you to watch one of my sled hockey games when the season starts."

"I don't guess you get paid for that."

"No, it's just for fun." He pressed the button to open the door.

"What's this here red button for?" She fingered another mounted low on the wall.

"Emergencies since this is a handicapped suite. It calls the campus cops in case someone inside needs help, say if they'd fallen."

"And can't get up." Ella Sue snickered.

"Yeah, like the old television ad. Leave it alone."

"You gonna give me a key to this place? Otherwise, I'm pretty much trapped here."

"I'll have one made. My mom has the other in case of emergencies."

"Now ain't that sweet, your mom still lookin' out for you. Wish our mother was alive to see to me now livin' with my famous brother." Ella's face held onto a smirk.

"It's nice to have a family who cares—most of the time. Sometimes, they can get on your nerves. I'll be gone a couple of hours. Maybe we'll go out somewhere for lunch when I get back."

Teddy escaped into the blazing summer sunshine, loaded the van, and took off for the gym, entering that space cautiously. His eyes found the therapist who had been working on Jessie when he interrupted on his last visit. He thumped over to her and apologized.

"Sorry, I shouldn't have spouted off to your

patient."

The therapist ruffled her short, brown hair, showing off a strong bicep as she did so. "I wish I could talk to some of them that way, but all I can do is encourage. You did her some good, though." She jerked her head toward a corner of the gym where Jessica Minvielle pulled a set of cables that lifted some light weights. "I have her scheduled for water therapy, too. Before, she didn't want to put on a bathing suit."

"That's great, but I'll stay out of your business now."

He warmed up with his core exercises and moved on to the hated trek up and down bars he usually saved for last. He'd do his weights when Jessie left the area. While slogging through the reps, he mulled what Ella Sue had said about his getting the short end. He'd been born with a disability, and his adoptive parents spent thousands on his medical care. Still, he was the only one of the brood of twelve not related by blood to the Billodeauxs in any way. They'd taken in the illegitimate boys, a niece and a cousin, had babies by IVF with an egg donor, and naturally. Only he had been left in their care like an unwanted kitten. Never had they made him feel that way, but he'd often thought he had to be super good or be put out in the early days, especially when Stacy got him into trouble. He did not whine about any of the mild punishments doled out for misbehaving like some of the others. Teddy guessed he could have lived at the ranch the rest of his life and been taken care of, but he'd needed to make his own way. Mama Nell, though worried about him, supported that decision. Unlike Ella Sue's situation, his parents remained his safety net if he failed even if he didn't want to consider that. Maybe he should cut her some slack.

Reaching the end of the row, he did some step climbing, up and down, up and down, turned and started back. Bent over to mop the sweat stinging his eyes, he heard a soft voice over the groans of rehabbers and the clank of exercise machines.

"Teddy, I'm sorry I was rude." Jessie, beautiful as always, sat in her chair almost speaking in his ear. "You were right. I'm trying harder now."

"Good, that's good." He had the most terrible urge to sniff his armpit as Ella Sue had done the other day. Jessie smelled like a whole bouquet of wildflowers.

"I want you to teach me how to be independent. My parents run around trying to do everything for me, especially my mother. I want to scream at them to let me alone. You know how to do this. Show me."

She leaned so close to his bowed head that a tendril of her honey-toned hair stuck to his cheek. Teddy brushed it gently away. "There are professionals who can help you better than me."

"Yeah, I've gone to some of them. None are in a wheelchair. Just talk to me about your life. That's all I'm asking."

"I still have my weight work to do. It's important not to blow off your exercise. I come here three days a week. That's my first tip for you."

"I am sure my tormentor can find something for me to do while I wait for you."

Teddy raised his head and stared into her gold-flecked eyes. "Another piece of advice, your therapist is trying to help you. Sometimes it hurts or gets embarrassing. Say thank you once in a while."

"I didn't mean it." Jessie stared at her useless feet. "Meet me at the juice bar, please."

He should say no, but didn't. She wheeled away happy. Teddy rushed his weight training and drew a comment from one of the male therapists. "Hey, Ted, you should do those slowly to build muscle, not that yours aren't looking good. Got a hot date?"

"Sort of." He put the weights aside and headed for the dreaded shower.

He had street clothes in his gym bag, but usually went home in the workout gear he'd worn under them. Choosing a stall with bars for the handicapped, he shucked his gear just outside, drew the curtain, and let the water pour over him head to toe, wishing he'd brought soap and his cologne, nervous as a guy on his first date.

Okay, so he'd had a slight crush on Jessie since he interviewed her for the high school paper. After that, he'd always said hi to her in the hall, and she always answered even if she walked with a gang of the popular girls or her athletic boyfriend. She often added, "How's it going, Teddy?" With a wide smile, he'd reply, "Great," whether it was or not. Once, she told her friends he won the award for upbeat guys. He tried hard to deserve that accolade.

Just thinking of her face so close to his moments ago began to cause a little action below the waist. He pressed up against the cool tile wall to discourage its growth. Just in time, too. Someone muttered, "Who the hell left all their stinking clothes in a heap on the floor?" and ripped open his curtain. Teddy fumbled for the towel he'd looped over one of the bars and secured it around his waist. Now all the intruder could see was the heavy scar on his lower back.

"Oh, it's you, Teddy." One of the UL football players doing some last minute rehab before the first game of the season looked a little shamefaced. "Want me to put them on a bench for you?"

"No, I'll do it. I shouldn't have left them there." In truth, he'd wanted to get into the shower before anyone came along to stare.

The guy bunched up his shorts, top, and smelly socks, and moved them anyhow. "There you go." He offered his hand, withdrew it quickly when he saw Teddy take up his crutches, and settled for an introduction. "I'm Xavier Hopkins, tight end for UL. Transferred from junior college. Remember to pronounce that X-avier, not Zavier when you call the games. I think you'll need to say my name a lot."

"I'll remember," Teddy answered as if he didn't already have the team roster with notes on how to say everyone's names. There were some doozies. Teddy managed a grudging thanks for the favor he didn't want before the fellow walked off and left him alone to dress. People damaged his pride when they did simple tasks for him and dented his feeling of autonomy. They meant well, he knew, and tried to bear it.

He dried off with another towel, then putting his crutches aside, sat next to his gym bag and pulled out relatively fresh socks. Step One done. Step Two: drew up his underwear beneath the towel and over his pouch. Got his braces and boots back on. Step Three complete. Worked his legs into his khakis and whipped off the towel. Step Four finished. Put on his polo shirt and stuffed the dirty clothes into the bag. C'est finis, as the Cajuns would say. He forced his feet to take him to the juice bar, not his van.

With a pretty tempting smoothie sitting in front of her, Jessie waited at a table for two. She waved as he bought a bottle of water—as if he'd ever enter a room and fail to notice her instantly. He took a seat across from her and leaned his crutches against the table. "That looks good." Teddy nodded at her drink.

"Banana-strawberry. Want some?" She offered him a second straw, and he took a sip.

"Good, but I'll give you another piece of advice. Be careful of too much fruit juice, high in sugar, and it can lead to accidents, but the fiber in the banana is good for you. I don't know about yours, but my plumbing is as complicated as the city sewer system." He felt the scarlet rising up his neck. Had he just mentioned bowel movements to her?

Jessie's cheeks burned red, and she ducked her head. "Catheters, stim, and suppositories every other day," she whispered like a dirty confession.

Too busy with her own embarrassment, she didn't appear to notice his. He rushed to salvage the conversation. "You have a great figure and want to keep it, so watch the calories exactly like you would otherwise."

"Men don't notice my body anymore, only the chair."

"Give them one of your smiles, and they'll forget all about it."

Her smile burst forth like the sun coming out from behind a raincloud. "I guess I haven't been using it lately."

He answered it, always cheerful Teddy. "You should."

"I wear makeup every day hoping people will look at my face instead of my wheels. I try to keep my hands pretty and let my nails grow out. I kept them short when I worked as a trainer. I guess that's some small compensation for this." Jessie gestured to her legs. Her smile faded.

"Me, I rely on my beautiful baby blue eyes as a diversion." Teddy fluttered his pale lashes at her—and she laughed, a good sound, low and throaty, maybe a little rusty from lack of use.

He went for two. "And my studly body with my six-pack abs and bulging biceps." Teddy rolled up his shirt to his armpits, struck a masculine he-man pose, and waited for a giggle. Nothing. "Sorry." He covered his chest again.

"Don't be sorry, Teddy. I think you are living proof of the power of regular exercise."

He had a light build, and despite his dedication to strength training, had been scrawny in high school. Wheeling around the college campus built him up some and since he'd matured, so had his body, filling out nicely to his surprise, but he didn't consider himself in a league with most athletes.

"You should see some of the guys in the sled hockey league, really macho." He went for the modest answer as usual.

"Sled hockey?"

"Yes, hockey for guys like me. Some have lost their legs or been paralyzed in combat. We can get pretty intense."

"I'd like to see one of your games."

"Sure, when the season comes around. We have to wait for the arena to be iced for the regular hockey team first. Then, we set up a schedule." He appreciated that Jessie showed a hundred-percent more interest than Ella Sue. Ella Sue—back at the apartment waiting for lunch, probably raiding his fridge by now. "Say, I have to get going. This has been fun."

She corrected him. "This has been real. My mom should be along soon to pick me up. She's running a little late. I'm not certain how I'll get here once school starts. She mentioned quitting her job to take care of me, the last thing I want."

"I could pick you up. I mean since we come here around the same time. I have a van with plenty of room for both our chairs." Did he sound too eager?

"We live in Lafayette now, not too far from here. Lend me one of your pens." Jessie pointed at the pocket on his shirt.

Now she knew exactly how dorky he was, but he liked to have pens handy in case he had an idea for an article or interview questions. Teddy turned one over to her, and she wrote her phone number on a napkin as if he'd met her in a regular bar and not one serving juices. He offered his, and she immediately turned on a phone she carried in a pouch on her chair and punched it into her list of contacts. "There, we can make plans."

"Great! We'll work something out soon. Yeah, gotta go." Now, his feet wanted to stay at the table, but Teddy forced himself up and out of the facility.

As soon as he got into his van, he groped for his phone to register Jessie's number and call Ella Sue. Not in its usual place. Fabulous, he'd have to search the floor and elsewhere for his personal lifeline in case of trouble. Maybe he'd left it at home. Only way to find out was to go there. As he pulled out, he passed Mrs.

Minvielle, worry all over her face, driving a little fast for a parking lot. He checked his rearview mirror and noticed Jessie sitting by the door waiting. He wanted to tell her mother that Jessie wouldn't melt if she arrived a few minutes late, though in his opinion her daughter was still very hot.

With Jessie on his mind, he parked at the apartment, did his transfer to wheelchair routine and opened his door. Ella Sue lay stretched out on his sofa with his phone to her ear and her hand in a bag of potato chips. "I'm just fine, Daddy. I'm staying with Teddy in Lafayette, not at the ranch. Yeah, yeah, he just come in, and I don't want to run up his phone bill none. Bye-bye."

"Thought I'd lost my phone. Glad to know it is in good hands," he forced himself to say. Now he remembered being in a hurry to get away from Ella Sue's complaints and leaving it on the kitchen counter. "You ready for lunch?"

"Had mine an hour ago. I got you some Burger King, too, but it's probably gone cold by now. I walked over to that union place and ordered a latte 'cause it has milk in it. Wandered around and found a little grocery that carries the tabloids, bought some reading material and snacks to pass the time. Oh, got the makings for biscuits, too. I'm about broke and wore out from the heat and carrying this baby."

She must have bought every one of those rags since they covered his coffee table. Teddy opened the fast food bag on the kitchen counter. Every once in a while, a cheeseburger and fries wouldn't kill him. "Thanks for getting lunch. It's good you let your father know that you're safe."

"He don't care much."

Teddy hoped her call didn't bring Newt to their door. He remembered the man as being huge and violent. "Did you give him my address?"

"Don't know it yet. Didn't find a scrap of mail around neither to get it."

"I have a box at the post office. Mostly I use email, texts, that sort of thing for my business." He might have been the least of the Billodeauxs, but he did take some precautions, especially since Xochi's kidnapping.

"Yeah, I noticed your computer needs a password. Want to share that with me?"

No, he did not. Considering his sister's taste in reading, no telling what she'd get into online. He evaded her question. "I can log you on when you need it, but right now, I have an article to write and get off to the wire service."

"What about?"

"I interviewed my brother, Dean, about how training camp was going for the Sinners."

"All right. I'll just watch my shows, and let you get at it." Ella Sue flicked on the remote she had within arm's reach. She picked up a tabloid from the stack and handed it over to Teddy. "You might like this one. Ain't that another one of your brothers? He's so handsome."

"Yes, that's Mack, a wide receiver for the Cowboys." Of course, it would be. His Texas beauty queen du jour hung on his arm. Teddy expected he wouldn't have tabloid attention at any point in his life, or a woman like that. An image of Jessica Minvielle rolled through his mind.

"He sure is having more fun than me." Ella Sue

sighed. Her big belly rose and fell, fat as a leech in a swimming hole. Not the baby's fault who it had for a mother.

"More than me, too. He always does. Time for me to get to work."

Chapter Six

Jessica Minvielle sat at the dinner table across from the vacant space where her brother used to make faces at her and generally cause trouble. But he'd grown up, and failing to make it as professional football player, had gone into coaching like their dad at a small college in the Midwest where he hoped to shine and rise in his career, higher than his father. How she wished he still occupied that space, ready to lob a spoonful of mashed potatoes at her as soon as their parents looked away. In their rivalry for attention, she often won. Now, she'd willingly let him have center stage all to himself. Anything to divert their parents' one-hundred percent scrutiny from her.

She needn't worry about getting fat. Her mom taught health as well as gym. Tonight's menu consisted of large grilled-chicken salads with slices of whole grain bread on the side. Probably watermelon for dessert. Her dad, a big block of a man with the start of a middle-aged gut, would eat every bit, then sneak into the kitchen later and make a sandwich from the leftover chicken, adding mayo and more salt. He had high blood pressure, a hazard for coaches, but figured his pills should take care of that for him. Still, her mom tried, as she was doing now with Jessie.

"Once school starts, I can drop you off for rehab at eight since I don't have a homeroom, though it might be eleven before I can pick you up during the lunch break and make something for you to eat. I'll be home by three-thirty, but once basketball season starts, I'll have to stay later for the practices. Are you sure you're okay with that? Maybe we should hire an aide to stay with you during the afternoon. Or I could give up coaching. We don't need the extra money with our children grown." Dale Minvielle raked her hand, fingernails unpolished, through cropped blonde hair. Tall, trim, athletic, the picture perfect of health for women her age, she wanted everyone to be so. Now she had a crippled daughter she didn't quite know how to manage. Doing five more laps or running up the bleachers wouldn't help Jessie's condition.

"Mom, I can still make a sandwich and grab a piece of fruit for lunch. You love coaching. Don't give it up for me. I'll be perfectly fine in the afternoons alone."

Depressed, bored, but fine. Amazing how friends stopped coming around after the initial outburst of sympathy. They simply forgot about her. Who wanted a girl in a wheelchair to ruin their fun? No more Jell-O shots for Jessie or bikinis on the beach during a weekend at Gulf Shores.

"Dale, let her try," her dad said. "You never know if you don't try. Obstacles can be overcome with the right attitude." Jessie knew that speech from the locker room. He ruined the rah-rah spirit of his words by picking a piece of baby spinach from his teeth. His hair might have receded to the point that he kept it shaved close to the scalp to deny balding, but he still owned a great smile when he wasn't raging at a referee.

Jessie inherited that smile, her mom said, along

with the curvaceous body of the Minvielle women that made her daughter more fit for cheerleading than gymnastics after her figure developed. Only growing to five-seven, basketball had passed her daughter by except for recreation, but Jessie tried hard apply her gymnastic skills to cheering, more hazardous than most people thought, and to excel at her job as a trainer, both gone now.

Her mom shot a glance at her dad that could have killed if she'd had laser beams for eyes, but she said, "Okay, we'll see how things go. So about your rehab schedule. Sorry you'll have to hang around there for an extra hour and go in early."

"Hey, I can get some of my players to take her in and bring her home like doing public service," her dad suggested, his smile now locked in place.

"Will they know how to deal with her wheelchair? Who knows what kind of cars they have," Dale countered.

"Trucks, mostly, I think. Put the chair in the back, lift Jessie into the front seat, and there you go."

"Not such a good idea, Mo."

Morris Minvielle, Mo for short or Meaux if people wanted to go Cajun with his name, seemed perplexed. More accustomed to the crowd shouting, "We want some Mo," than any opposition to his ideas, he questioned, "Why not?"

"They might drop her or—or take advantage of her. She can't run away if they try anything."

"Not my boys!"

They'd been arguing so much more since her accident, mostly about how to proceed with a handicapped child, as if she didn't have ears or a voice and sat there in a wheelchair like a piece of the furniture.

"Stop!" Jessie clanged her fork against her glass of unsweetened iced tea to get their attention. "I know someone who can give me a lift and is completely trustworthy. Teddy Billodeaux. He's already offered."

"Teddy from high school, the one with the crutches?" her mother asked.

"The guy who calls our games, that Teddy?" her dad said.

"Yes to both. Also one of our class valedictorians, and a man with a degree in communications. He has a van all set up for wheelchair transport, and no one knows more about that than he does."

"Maybe we can get the Handicab that goes around to the assisted living places to come for you." Her mother would not give up!

Just what Jessie wanted, to ride the Handicab with the elderly who would most likely treat her sweetly and talk her ears off. "No! I want to ride with Teddy."

"That's imposing on him," Dale decided.

"Seems like a nice guy. He sure isn't going to molest her with all the hardware he has to carry around. Let her try this for a while." Dad, as usual in her corner. "We can chip in for gas money."

"If you don't care about your daughter's safety..."

"I'll be safe with Teddy. He is the nicest guy, really. I'm going to call him right now and set this up." Jessie reversed her wheelchair and turned away from the dinner table. As she left the room, her mom called out, "But we have watermelon for dessert." Anything to stop her forward progress.

\*\*\*\*

Mrs. Minvielle lurked in the window when Teddy turned into the driveway of the rambling ranch style home, easy enough to get around in a wheelchair. She didn't come out to say hello. Jessie waited in the open garage and wheeled to greet him. He came around the van on his crutches to open the vehicle's doors.

"Want to ride up front with me, or we can use the lift to put you in the back, strap your chair down, and off we go?"

"Up front, please, if it isn't too much trouble."

"Okay, here we go." He braced himself against the side of the van, got his arms under her, and slid her into the front seat. "Buckle up." He put her chair in the back next to his and off they went.

Jessie suppressed the desire to shoot her mother the bird. At a red light, they stopped next to a car in the turn lane. One of girls she'd cheered with in college sat in the driver's seat.

"Tap your horn for me, Teddy."

He did. She waved madly and put on that dazzling smile all cheerleaders were supposed to wear along with their sexy clothes and shaking pom-poms. Her former friend waved back, then focused on the light as if praying for it to turn green. Jessie enjoyed the moment, feeling nearly normal with her chair nowhere in sight and making one who had deserted her since the accident squirm. Then, back to reality as they arrived at the rehab facility, back to her wheelchair and the grueling exercises, but not nearly as grueling as what Teddy accomplished.

As she lay on an exercise table having her legs massaged and stretched, she watched him sweat through his routine. Her therapist had her working on her upper body strength by the time he struggled down the path between the parallel bars and back again. His blond hair flopped across his forehead in a boyish way, but his arm muscles were those of a man in very good condition. In fact, Teddy Billodeaux was cute and kind of sexy. Why had she never noticed that before? Easy. The handicapped were often overlooked. Still, she remembered most from high school his cheerful smile and blue eyes, sunny as a summer's day. Pausing before beginning his step work, he looked her way and offered that same smile, encouraging her no end.

They finished about the same time, and Jessie suggested going to the juice bar again to sit and talk. He turned her down, the first guy to do so. That proved she'd lost her appeal to men, and it hurt more than she expected. "I guess you have other things to do."

For a communications expert, Teddy seemed to struggle with his words. "I have another obligation, and frankly, I prefer to shower at home."

Jessie wondered what might happen if she offered to take a shower with him, if she suggested she sit in his lap on the stool, and they soap each other up and down every cleft and crevice of their bodies. He'd blush in that boyish way he had and turn her down flat she supposed, so she merely replied, "Me, too."

Without saying much else, he delivered her home. Now, her mom made an appearance, waving her arms like a referee calling a foul. "Don't get down. I know it's hard for you," she called, and Teddy reddened. Dale rushed to the van and extracted the wheelchair, helping her daughter back into the prison of its seat. She thanked Teddy for the ride, tried to press a twenty on him for gas, which he refused, and finally made a gesture that said she'd given in to her daughter.

"In case I'm not home, you should have this." Mrs. Minvielle presented him with a garage door opener. "Jessie can manage once the door is up."

"Yes, I certainly can."

"See you Friday, Jess."

"Absolutely."

## Chapter Seven

Teddy's obligation lounged on the sofa. He couldn't believe he'd passed up a chance for another heart-to-heart talk with Jessie for his sister's company, but he chided himself for thinking it. After all, if he'd been raised by Newt Smalls, he might be just as conniving and rough around the edges as she was. No, he'd be dead. One way or another, Newt would have gotten rid of him. Ella Sue had survived a weak mother and a harsh father by using her wits and being tough. He should admire that, not criticize it.

Ella Sue's eyes brightened the second he entered the apartment. Her often sullen lips curled into a smile. She shoved herself up on her elbows. "Where we going for lunch? I get to pick the movie afterward, right?"

"Yes, your choice. I thought Subway or Panera."

She wrinkled her nose. "Don't know about that Panera place. Subway is okay. Even Merv the Perv's gas station had one. About the only place to eat out in the whole town."

Deciding she'd be better off with the familiar rather than Panera's vast menu and great selection of baked goods, he nodded. "That's where we'll go then."

He should have known she'd get the meatball sub, a bag of chips, and a cola. Ordering a carved turkey on whole wheat with a pile of veggies on top, he shared his little sack of apples with his sister. At the theater, she begged for popcorn and another soft drink. Might be worse. Same with her choice of shows. Ella Sue decided on a children's animated feature—in other words a cartoon with dogs acting like people. Glad she hadn't chosen anything violent, Teddy found he enjoyed laughing along with her and watching her belly shake. At one point, she put his hand on her stomach right on top of a strongly kicking foot. "I think all this laughing woke the baby." Or maybe all the caffeine she consumed.

Regardless, they had a good afternoon. Maybe he could invite Jessie along next time. Back at his place, Ella Sue said she needed a nap and started for her room. "You make supper, okay? I cooked up a big breakfast and washed the dishes."

She certainly had: fried eggs, grits, bacon, and fresh from scratch biscuits. Teddy added glasses of orange juice. He watched her mix her runny yolks with the grits and shovel them down, then make a biscuit sandwich with the whites and strips of bacon. Plenty of grits and biscuits leftover for tomorrow, she said. She'd add grated cheese to perk up those grits and scrambled eggs.

"Sure, I'll get something on the table."

"Or we could order pizza." So much hope in her voice.

"No, I'll cook. You rest."

His easy thirty-minute or less chili coming right up. He took a pound of hamburger and an onion from the fridge, nuked the meat with salt and pepper while he chopped half an onion. When the microwave dinged, he drained the fat from the hamburger and put in the onions for a couple more minutes. Opening a can of tomato soup and another of kidney beans, he dumped the contents into the bowl when the meat finished cooking. Added a tablespoon of chili powder and stirred it all together. Heated the mixture again and let it sit in the refrigerator until suppertime. He'd shake some salad mix into bowls and offer crackers with the meal. Done.

Now to get back to work on his notes on the major UL players, going beyond the publicity releases. He planned to interview them all eventually, usually catching them by phone in the evening after practice. X-avier owned a pit bull named Rage, not because of its temperament, but to honor the college team he played for, the Ragin' Cajuns. Another guy had eight siblings and was the first of his family to go beyond high school. Doing his own research, that made his commentary special. Anyone could read the statistics. He portrayed each player as an individual. They liked that.

Teddy went in search of his phone to make sure he'd charged it. Lately, he'd been mislaying it frequently. As he wheeled past Ella Sue's room, he heard her speaking softly, maybe talking to the baby. Sweet. He didn't interrupt. Now where had he put the damned phone?

It turned up, low on power, after dinner hiding in the sofa cushions. He plugged it in to do his interviews in his bedroom while Ella Sue watched The Bachelor on the TV. She'd preferred biscuits to crackers with her chili and now balanced a bowl of ice cream on her belly. Having grown up in a noisy household with so many brothers and sisters, he kind of liked having another person in the apartment with him. Too bad it wasn't Jessie Minvielle.

Thursday, he walked Ella Sue to the park and gave her a bag of bread crusts to feed the ducks from the small bridge over the pond. From there, he steered her across campus, a barge to his wheelchair tugboat, and bought their lunch of a fried shrimp po-boy at the Olde Tyme Grocery, a modest frame building with bold red trim and a snowball stand in the rear. One large sandwich served to feed the two of them, though Ella Sue scarfed up any stray shrimp that dropped from his half of the loaf.

Back at the apartment, she claimed, "You run me nearly to death. Easy for you in that wheelchair to just roll along."

Not actually, but he didn't argue. His sister settled in for an afternoon nap, again talking to her baby for a while. Peace reigned long enough for him to polish a couple of articles he hoped to sell and work on his notes for the UL opener.

Unfortunately, Ella Sue woke peevish. "What's for dinner?"

"Spaghetti and meat lumps with a salad. I cook the hamburger in the microwave, chunk it up, and pour the jar of tomato sauce over the top. Basic but filling."

"Why we always gotta have salad?"

"Good for all of us." Teddy pointed at her belly, which appeared to ripple in agreement.

"What are we gonna do tomorrow? This waiting to hatch goes really slow. Maybe we could visit the ranch?" Ella Sue lowered herself onto the sofa and picked a tabloid off the stack by her side.

"No one home right now. The youngest started private school this week, my mom is working again, and Dad is out of town. Besides, I have PT in the morning." Funny how he looked forward to that task since Jessie had become so friendly. He'd make plenty of spaghetti, enough for lunch tomorrow to feed Ella Sue. Then, he could spend some extra time at the juice bar.

"Take me with you to the rehab place. It's soooo boring here. I could watch you exercise."

"No, you can't. Family and drivers have to stay in the waiting room."

"They have a bigger TV with lots of channels in the lobby?" Ella Sue gestured toward his modest and obviously inadequate set.

"No, there's one in the juice bar, but I think you have to ask the guy behind the counter to change channels. They offer free coffee in the waiting room."

"Be better than sitting here alone. You know this place ain't much better than a doublewide trailer, and some of those are nicer."

"Maybe, but this apartment represents independence—something you need to work on after the baby comes."

Ella Sue's face went from sullen to sour lemon. "You sayin' I'm lazy? You try hauling this belly around all day. It's work."

"I guess it is. Okay, you can come with me and hang out in the juice bar until I'm done. Maybe you'll find someone to talk to while I work out."

"That'd be good."

"Be ready by eight-thirty. I give a friend a ride."

"Sure, anything to get out of these walls."

Her eyes strayed down to the half-naked guy on the front of one of the magazines. He hoped it wasn't his brother, Mack, this time. She talked like his place was a maximum-security prison, not seeing that here he could take care of himself, a burden to no one, and make his way in the world. Maybe he could teach her that, maybe not.

## Chapter Eight

Jessie waited in the driveway for Teddy's arrival. She checked her watch. Running a little late, but she didn't worry. He seemed utterly trustworthy, not like her fiancé Troy, often late and never apologetic. She'd learned about his cheating with a Dallas girl from the merciless tabloids not long before the accident. He asked her forgiveness, claiming the affair to be a brief one. She'd given it, but the niggling doubt remained. The wedding date had been set, the church and hall reserved, the cake on order, and her dress purchased. Jessie decided to go through with the ceremony. Not a problem now.

Once in high school, she'd ditched her boyfriend for carrying on with a fellow cheerleader behind her back, the word being that the other girl put out and Jessie did not. She'd broken up with him just before the prom. Another lovely dress hung in her closet unused until her father invited one of his freshmen players to be her escort. Not wanting to disappoint her dad, she put on the sparkling blue gown and her best game face. Troy Gilbert, handsome and beefy in a way that made most of the boys seem scrawny, was a college man and every cheerleader's dream. Her social stock on the high school exchange rose higher and higher. Honestly, she wished she'd stayed home and escaped seeing her old flame dancing with his new girl while she'd laughed and smiled at her date, a guy she barely knew.

The red van swung around the corner, down the street, and into her drive. Jessie rolled forward to the front door of the vehicle and discovered the passenger seat to be occupied. A pale but pretty face surrounded by wispy blonde hair peered out at her. The window slid down, and the girl put out her arm as if to shake hands, drew it back as she realized she sat too high up. "I'm Ella Sue. I guess you're this person Teddy told me he had to pick up."

"Yes, Jessica Minvielle. We went to high school together."

"That so. Were you both in special ed?"

"Ah, no. My injury is recent."

"That's right. Teddy mentioned you once before when we was talking to his mother. Anyhow, we need to get going. You're making him late." The window slid shut.

This morning, having convinced her mother to go and get her classroom in order for the start of public school next week and allowing Jessie to wait alone, she'd felt as if she'd made a small move toward independence. Was she a burden for Teddy? Evidently, his passenger thought so. Why did she simply assume he had no other life than the gym and his job? They'd both been out of college for a while. Why shouldn't he have a jealous girlfriend? Jessie had to admit to herself she'd assumed being handicapped also crippled his social life. It certainly ended hers.

Teddy opened the side door, lowered the wheelchair ramp, and made sure he settled Jessie carefully in the rear of the van with her chair secured. "Sorry," he murmured. "Ella Sue got bored at the apartment."

More likely, Ella Sue didn't want to share Teddy's attention. At the rehab facility when he came around to help her down, the girl, much younger than Teddy, opened her door and held out a hand for his assistance. Perhaps, she had a physical problem, too? Jessie noted immediately what it was—an almost obscenely pregnant belly about ready to pop. Even a trendy pair of distressed maternity jeans and a cute navy blue top edged in bright yellow appliqued daises did little to minimize her bulk.

"Oh, you're expecting!" Jessie said, as soon as Teddy extricated her from the van.

"Pretty obvious unless you're blind as well as crippled," Ella Sue snapped.

Teddy winced. "If you can't be polite, I won't bring you along again." He said that like he meant it, and the girl backed down.

"I'm sorry. You're so pretty, and I'm all fat and ugly right now. The heat gets to me even this early in the morning. Don't it ever get cold around here?"

"Not until the end of October, if then. Let's get into the air conditioning." Embarrassed for both of them, Jessie wheeled away.

A fairly new relationship, then, less than a year if she didn't know when Louisiana weather cooled. Teddy didn't wear a ring, nor did Ella Sue. Maybe they cohabited. He did strike her as the kind of guy who would stand by the mother of his child no matter how crude or bitchy. Ella Sue trundled along behind her still making conversation to Jessie's back.

"Won't be long until I'm shut of this load. Teddy signed us up for childbirth classes at the hospital, but I

63

told him I want drugs, lots of drugs, just put me out and wake me when it's over."

"I told you they won't give you anything until you are five centimeters dilated, and they won't knock you out either. It's best to know how to cope with the pain. Didn't you read the pamphlets the doctor gave you?" Teddy's voice frayed with frustration.

"You're the brains in the family. I guess you got it figured for the both of us."

Teddy deserved better, so much better. How had a nice guy like him ended up with an Ella Sue? Too nice maybe, easily taken in by a woman willing to have sex with him, perhaps unaware he could get a girl pregnant. Why did this make her so sad?

Troy made it clear he didn't want children right away. First, he needed to gain free agency before marrying in case his career dictated a move away from Dallas. Though they'd gotten engaged right out of college, he wanted the marriage postponed for those three years in order to concentrate on his game. She agreed, maybe wondering if their relationship would last that long.

After the prom, she'd been surprised when he called again for another date. Troy, a Lafayette native, hung around the Minvielle home that summer, eating the coach's barbecue and getting pointers for his sophomore year, hoping to be a starter. He took her crabbing, boating, and to the movies, made no sexual demands. Her dad watched his every move. They'd stayed together all through college, eventually climbing into bed, Troy always using a condom, she never forgetting her pills.

A swat of cool air as the automatic doors opened

and the slight bump as Jessie wheeled across the threshold brought her back to the present. Ella Sue still whined behind her like the mosquitoes at Cypremort Point and puffed as if she'd trekked from the far reaches of a Walmart lot instead of the short distance from the handicap parking.

In a voice brusquer than usual, Teddy handed the girl a ten and pointed the way to the juice bar. "Wait for us there." Once she was out of earshot, he said, "I apologize for Ella Sue. She's kind of rough. Her family drifted around, and she didn't get much education. Smart enough since she passed her GED. Right now, I'm all she has."

"How long have you been together?" Curiosity and pity made Jessie ask.

"A week or so. Seems longer." The red rose in his cheeks. "That sounds ugly. I guess all pregnant women are difficult."

"She's not your—girlfriend?" Somehow the term baby mama seemed wrong when it came to Teddy.

"Oh, no, no! Ella Sue is my sister, half-sister actually. She showed up at the ranch recently looking for me. We'd never met before, but my birth mother died and my stepfather isn't a good guy. He tossed her out when she got…did you think it was mine? Because it could be—if she weren't my sister. I mean, I don't know what I mean. Forget I said anything." His tongue tangled like crisscrossed crutches. He blushed and studied his toes. "You'd better sign in since we are late, Ella Sue's fault. She couldn't decide what to wear because she wanted to look cute. Xochi gave her a big sack of new clothes since she didn't arrive with much. And you don't need to know all this."

"I don't mind listening. I'd help if I could." Jessie meant that when she said it, but regret came on fast. Whatever could she do in her condition?

Teddy's baby blue eyes brightened, worry washing away as if an autumn rain just passed. "You could be her friend. Maybe offer her some pointers on how to act that would give her a better chance to find a decent job in the future. Talk to her about girl stuff."

"Okay, I'll try." Jessie's therapist appeared and summoned her to the hell of her exercises. The whole time she wondered what she might have in common with Ella Sue. Watching Teddy flex his muscles lifting weights barely distracted her from the task ahead. For a change the workout passed quickly, too quickly, and they were off to the juice bar to join his newfound sister who sat having a smoothie and watching the TV tuned into a game show.

"Melungeons!" Ella Sue shouted. "That's what they call these mixed-race people in the Tennessee mountains. Can you believe they put up Melon Heads as another answer? That's really insulting. I know a few Melungeons, and some are a real nice people," she explained as Teddy and Jessie joined her. "I coulda won five-thousand dollars. Wouldn't that be nice?"

"Yes, it would. You're from Tennessee then?" Jessie tried for general conversation while Teddy got bottles of water for both of them.

"Born there, ended up there, but traveled around in between, and now I'm here. Pineapple-mango." Ella Sue slurped the very last of her smoothie from the cup. "I could drink another one."

Teddy handed Jessie her water and sat down. "One is enough. We'll be having lunch soon." He sounded more like her parent than a brother.

Ella Sue studied Jessie's hands. "I sure like your fingernails. That hard to do?"

"Not too difficult. I do them myself instead of spending money on an expensive mani-pedi. Lots of time to kill now and no income." Hard to accept she had to rely on her parents again for spending money, another reason to stay home and avoid going out.

Ella Sue mulled that over. "Sounds exactly like me. A mani-pedi. The stars are always getting those. I'd love to have one before the baby comes so my hands and feet would look all nice in those childbirth classes." She glanced sidelong at her brother, waiting for him to take the hint.

Before Teddy opened his mouth, Jessie dove in to save him. "I could do that for you for free. I have everything we need. When I was a cheerleader, the girls would get together and do each other's nails. We had fun."

"I could use some fun. Teddy?"

"That would be great. When and where?"

"I really need to go home, clean up, and get some lunch." If she'd told the complete truth, PT took a lot out of her, and she wanted to rest. "No PT tomorrow. Why don't I come over to your place, and we will beautify your hands and feet?"

"I'd like that. Teddy?"

"I'd like that, too. I'll pick you up at one, okay?"

"It's a date." There, she could be a help to Teddy in his predicament and not simply a burden, a bundle in a wheelchair to be transported to and fro.

## Chapter Nine

With her manicure kit in her lap, Jessie waited in the drive for her date with Teddy, or she should say Ella Sue. The second the red van pulled up, her father lumbered outside, waving and shouting as if Teddy were deaf, that he didn't have to get down. He'd put Jessie in the front seat and stow her chair. There went a chance for getting the smallest of thrills from Teddy lifting her and belting her in ever so tenderly.

Her dad leaned into the van once he dealt with his daughter and the wheelchair. "Say, I'm grilling tonight. You and your sister want to come eat with us? Just the family, no other guests."

"We'd like that, sir. Can I bring anything?"

"Only yourselves. Have a good afternoon now." Coach Mo closed Jessie's door and pretended not to notice her glare as he trotted back to the house.

He'd sprung this on her out of nowhere. Maybe because she refused to come out of her room when the Minvielles had the football team over for a cookout a few weeks ago. "The guys are asking how you're doing, Jessie. Please make an appearance," Mom begged. Her answer: turning her wheelchair toward the wall, turning her back on her mother. Yes, she knew many of the guys on the team. No, she did not want them to see her this way.

Her dad was setting her up neatly as a volleyball,

exactly the way he had with Troy back in high school. He wanted to foist her on Teddy Billodeaux; Jessie knew it because no other man would want her. She'd thought Teddy deserved someone better than Ella Sue, but not an ugly-on-the-inside person like her. Anger and bitterness still resided deep like a hidden abscess. Much as she liked Teddy, she wouldn't be good for him.

Troy and his juvenile stunt had left her this way. Playing chicken with another couple on a Ski-Doo, he'd headed straight for their machine, daring the other guy to veer first. His rival tried to turn at the last moment, but Troy rammed into them, sending both flying. Jessie catapulted off the rear, hitting the edge with her back hard, and ending up in the water. Blacking out, she came around with her legs dangling like bait for the sharks beneath her and her life jacket holding her head above water. Ever confident Troy hadn't been wearing his, not that it mattered. He died instantly of a broken neck. She considered him the lucky one.

"Nice of your dad to ask us over." Teddy broke into her thoughts with that cheerful voice of his.

"Oh, he loves cranking up the grill and feeding a bunch of people. I've been putting a damper on that since I'm not much fun to be around anymore." She didn't expect his response.

"Not if you sit around feeling sorry for yourself. You can still talk, can't you? Make conversation, tell a joke, ask about their interests and their families, enjoy a burger."

"You don't understand."

"Really?" His pale brows rose. "I've been doing it all my life. Make an effort for your own sake. After a while, it comes easily."

She wanted to cry and rage at him, but took a deep breath and said, "You're right, I should."

"Good. Practice on Ella Sue."

The girl waited eager as a hound dog puppy for them at Teddy's apartment. She held the door open and led the way to the sofa. "How do we start?"

"First, I'll clip and shape your nails. I should have brought something to soak them in. Do you have any olive oil, Teddy? I guess that's not something guys normally have around." She knew he'd insist on struggling out to buy some and would have kicked herself if she had any feeling in her legs.

Instead, he got a bottle from a low cupboard and found a small bowl. "You don't know my mother well if you think she'd let me cook with anything but olive oil."

"You cook?"

"I absolutely do. But I admit it's nice to get out of it tonight. Ella Sue has been serving breakfasts big enough to make me skimp on lunch. I put a little ham and cheese in one of her biscuits and have some fruit. That's all I need. Here, you two get started. I have some work to do on the computer. Have fun." He left them alone.

"Nice what he said about my cooking, but sometimes he is so happy he's downright depressing. You know what I mean?"

"I think I do."

"Not that Teddy don't have a testy side. Try asking him for junk food or money."

"I'll be sure to avoid doing that." Jessie clipped and filed Ella Sue's nails into pleasing ovals. They weren't long, just slightly above the tips of her fingers. Jessie soaked them in the olive oil and used an orange stick to push back the cuticles.

"This is just like a real manicure, ain't it?"

"Certainly. Let me get the pale pink coat on. While it dries, I'll cut your toenails."

Ella Sue kicked off a pair of orange flip-flops and put her feet into Jessie's lap without a minute of hesitation. "I can't see my toes anymore, but I want them to look nice."

"Don't we all?" Jessie could see her own feet strapped into a pair of cute white sandals her mother picked out that morning. The nails hadn't been polished in a long time. "Maybe you could do mine next?"

"I'll give her a try." Ella Sue lounged back into the cushions. "I don't suppose you give foot rubs, too. That might feel good considering the shape I'm in right now."

"Not my area of expertise. I'll put the polish on, then get back to your nails to do the white tips and a clear coat." That done, Jessie took a template from her kit and used it to make perfect white crescents on Ella Sue's nails.

Waiting for the lacquer to dry, Teddy's sister admired Jessie's work. "You could do this for a living now that you're in a wheelchair and can't do much else. Go to beauty school, maybe. I might want to try that—have nice nails all the time."

"I suppose that would be an option." One Jessie Minvielle had no desire to take. Doing this kind of job once in a while for a friend qualified as fun. Fooling with people's hands and feet day in and out, not so much. "Manicurists aren't paid well. They depend on good tips to get by. I've never seen any with fancy nails."

"That so? Hey, Teddy," Ella Sue hollered. "Can I give Jessie a tip?"

"No!" he shouted from the depths of his room.

"See what I mean about him being cheap? Still, he's a good guy to take me in. Sometimes I feel bad about what I'm doing here. Thought I'd be living in luxury at the family ranch. You been there?"

"No. Let me put the clear coat on to keep your nails from chipping."

Ella Sue extended the hands she'd been waving in the air to help the drying. "They got a chandelier in the master bath and a huge swimming pool, lots of horses to ride, and servants to wait on a body hand and foot. I can't figure why Teddy lives in this place."

"I understand the Billodeaux children are expected to make their own way."

"Bet they have a big, cushy safety net if they don't."

"Probably. Finished. Do you want to try to put a clear coat on my toenails? You'll have to lift my legs onto the sofa for me."

"Let me put down some papers so I don't mess up this ugly brown couch." Ella Sue spread some of her tabloids over the upholstery, hiked Jessie's feet up on the sofa, and unstrapped the sandals. "Cute shoes. Seems a shame you'll never wear them out. Wish I had cute shoes. Xochi gave me some maternity clothes like this top, but nothing for my feet. Now there's a lucky girl. She married a football player who bought her a great big house."

That explained the stretchy red top that hugged

Ella Sue's belly so tightly it resembled an overripe tomato sitting atop the same distressed jeans the girl wore to the gym. From what Jessie saw of her around town, Xochi Billodeaux didn't know the meaning of the words pastel or neutral. Xo could wear hot shades though. The bright color wasn't good on the pallid girl. Jessie didn't really know Xochi, but other than criticism of how she'd painted that house, most people thought her kind and generous. Jessie felt she had to clarify a few things for Ella Sue.

"Xochi speaks several languages and has her own business doing translations. She isn't totally dependent on Junior. Besides, those two grew up together. She didn't hunt him down for his big bucks."

"I guess that's real romantic, but a woman should marry rich if she can." Ella slapped some clear coat on Jessie's toenails. Kind of a sloppy job, but the polish did give them a nice glow. The girl probably did the best she could. As she'd so bluntly pointed out, Jessie had a closet full of shoes she'd barely use. "Try on the sandals. See if they fit."

Ella Sue made as great an effort as Cinderella's stepsisters to get them on, but failed. "My feet is all swolled, and they're too long anyhow, but kind of you to offer."

"Maybe we can go shoe shopping one day."

"With what? I don't have cash or a debit card. Teddy isn't willing."

"I have debit card." Her parents had forced it on her, hoping she'd take it to the mall with some of her old friends or at least go out to lunch with them. Painful to be so dependent after several years of earning her own way. "Maybe we could go shopping Sunday afternoon. Summer shoes should be on sale."

"Hey, Teddy!" Ella Sue bellowed. "Can you take us to the mall on Sunday afternoon?"

"Yes! Then maybe I can get some work done."

She lowered her voice to a volume for Jessie's ears only. "See, also tetchy about his work."

"I can understand that. Let's not interrupt him again." Jessie recalled Teddy asking her to improve his sister. "Say, why don't I do your makeup, too?"

"I'd like that."

Jessie thought she had enough cosmetics in the backpack on her wheelchair to do a decent job. A light foundation to cover the freckles, a hint of blusher on the cheekbones, the pallid eyebrows darkened a little with the feathery touch of a brown pencil, a thin application of dark blue eyeliner, and a brush of soft gray on the lids from a palette of colors and done. Jessie added the last touch with a splash of glossy pink lipstick. Ella Sue pushed off the sofa and trundled to the bathroom.

"Lookit me! Just lookit me. Teddy, you gotta see." She interrupted her brother's work again.

"Very nice." He accompanied his sister back to the living room. "I guess I'm done for the day. Is it too early to go back to your house for the cookout?"

"Not a problem. Right now my mother is assembling healthy snacks to offset the wad of cholesterol my dad is grilling."

"Sounds very much like my parents."

Jessie held out a small makeup bag to Ella Sue. "You can keep these and practice doing your own makeup. Stay away from the bright blue eye shadow no matter how tempting."

"Oh, I will! I promise." Ella Sue took the little bag

to her room to squirrel away, leaving Jessie with Teddy for a moment.

"I really appreciate what you did for my sister today. If I can pay you for…"

Jessie waved her own nicely manicured hand in his face. "For used makeup and a couple of bottles of nail polish, I don't think so. I enjoyed doing something helpful."

"Okay, then. Off to the barbecue."

\*\*\*\*

Teddy could have pegged to the backyard of the Minvielle home on his sticks, but he elected to use his wheelchair to keep Jessie company. He navigated the wide flagstone path edged with monkey grass around the side of the house with ease.

Mrs. Minvielle waved him into a shady spot by a low patio table as if she were landing an aircraft. Jessie alit by his side.

Not standing on ceremony, Ella Sue plonked onto a chaise and put her feet up on the cushions. Her toes, so grubby in the same flip-flops as on the day they met, now shone with polish.

Coach Minvielle stood by an immense stainless steel grill, one Joe Billodeaux would not have despised, gripping a platter of raw meat. "Now that you're here we can start these beauties."

If Teddy had carried a ruler with him, he judged the steaks would measure three inches thick. Foil wrapped potatoes big enough to serve two already nestled on the grid and a pot of baked beans bubbled on a side burner. Mrs. Minvielle passed around sturdy plastic plates and pointed out the bowl of hummus surrounded by baby carrots. A fruit platter with a yogurt dipping sauce and chunks of cheese between the strawberries and melon balls sat in easy reach on the table. "To keep you going until the steaks are ready."

Ella Sue put her feet down long enough the load up on cheddar cubes and strawberries. "What's the brown stuff?"

Teddy intervened as quickly as he could. "Hummus, a Middle Eastern dish made with ground chickpeas. We often have it at the ranch."

"All righty, then." She cautiously dipped a carrot. "Not bad."

"Iced tea, lemonade, or a soft drink?" their hostess inquired.

"Co-cola for me." Ella Sue rushed to put in her order before Teddy said milk. Jessie selected iced tea.

Teddy started to say the same when Coach Mo spoke up. "Dale, offer the man a beer. None for the little mama naturally."

Teddy considered his choices: drink with the coach or seem a little wussy. One thing he'd learned in college. A drunk cripple with a leaking ostomy bag led to a disastrous night. He finessed his way out. "Just one beer. I'm driving."

Coach Mo delved into the ice chest at his feet and came up with a dripping long neck. He popped the top with an opener on the side of the grill and delivered it to Teddy. "A man after my own heart, and careful too. Should have invited you sooner after all that time you spent announcing our games." He returned to his steaks, deftly flipping each one with a long hook. "You don't want to puncture the meat and drain away the juices."

"That's what my dad says."

"Great man, your dad."

Ella Sue giggled, but kept her mouth shut about his true paternity. If the Minvielles knew, would he be so welcome at their cookout or hanging around their daughter? Teddy prayed Ella Sue could keep a secret. He thought she might be good at it. Jessie spoke hardly a word, and he wondered if he'd offended her in some way, or if his sister had told her about Merv the Perv as they bonded over nail polish and makeup.

They moved to a picnic table with the bench removed from one side to accommodate Jessie and Teddy as the steaks came off the grill with a nice brown crust and pink nearly all the way through. Ella Sue eyed hers with suspicion. "I'm not accustomed to my meat being this raw."

"I can give yours a few more minutes," the coach said, clearly a little disappointed with her reaction to his grilling skills.

"Sophisticated people eat it this way," Jessie said. "Try a piece and if you don't like it, Dad will char it for you."

"Like the movie stars, huh? Why, it's real good this way."

Teddy cut his steak in half with a seriously serrated knife designed for the purpose, same with the potato. He helped himself to toppings from the lazy Susan on the picnic table, low-fat sour cream, chives, grated cheese, and bacon bits made from soy. He took one small scoop of beans and nursed his beer.

During a quiz of the coach on the prospects for this fall's team, X-avier's name popped up several times. Teddy respectfully asked if he could write an article for the local papers to be vetted by Coach Mo before he sent it in. Maybe not the best of journalistic ethics, but he had no wish to alienate the man. Permission granted.

As for Mrs. Minvielle, Teddy showed an amazing interest in girls' basketball, mentioning that he knew Riley Bullock who played in the WNBA. "Do you think she'd come speak to my team when she's in town?" Mrs. Minvielle asked.

"I'll ask." There, he'd netted a three-pointer with Dale. Teddy searched Jessie's face for some indication that she listened and learned how to make people unaware of the chair. She appeared more interested in poking her straw into the lemon floating in her tea to release its bitter acid taste.

"We should get some pictures of this occasion," Mrs. Minvielle said, all bright and chirpy, nothing like the way Teddy remembered her as a coach urging her girls on or arguing with a ref when he'd covered those games in high school. She held up her phone and started clicking.

"Please, Mother! No!" Jessie protested. "Let me see those."

Teddy watched as Jessie deleted two shots showing the two of them side by side in their wheelchairs. She left the one of only their faces even though her expression read as pissed off and his held a goofy grin. Jessie slapped the phone back into her mom's hand as if it were a sharp-edged surgical instrument capable of causing great pain.

"Let's get one of you sideways by the fence to show off your baby belly. Someday, you'll want to tell your child how it grew inside you, and this will be the proof," Jessie's mother continued with false cheer.

A tinge of disgust pinched Ella Sue's face, but she buried it deep under a smile. "That would be right nice of you." She posed with her hands at the small of her back and her stomach jutting out like a shelf from a wall.

"Cute." Mrs. Minvielle bought the phone to Jessie and Teddy to share. "I can send these to your phone if you have it handy."

Teddy groped his hip pocket and came up empty. "Must have left it at home, but here's my contact information." He fished one of his business cards from a case in the bag that hung on the back of his chair.

Mrs. Minvielle studied it. "Teddy Wilkes Billodeaux—freelance writer and sports commentator. Does this pay well?"

"I support myself." He tried hard to keep the edge from his voice and do the happy, happy guy for her, another lesson for Jessie's sake. "My independence is important to me." That was a lesson for her mother.

Coach Mo, who had mostly stayed out of the mess, asked, "What's for dessert?"

Dessert turned out to be lime sherbet. "Nice and light after a heavy meal," Dale said.

When their hostess returned from the kitchen with leftovers wrapped in foil to take home, Teddy took that as the cue to say thanks and leave. He asked Ella Sue to carry the sack of food and gave her a nod in the direction of the van to get her going.

"Jessie, why don't you see our guests to their car?" Mrs. Minvielle suggested.

"Good idea. You're on the guest list for next time." Coach Mo pointed a thick finger at Teddy as if daring him to resist.

"I appreciate that. Wonderful dinner, great steaks—but I can find my own way out."

"No, I'll go with you." Jessie followed him to the driveway where Ella Sue waited. Teddy beeped her into the van. She scrambled into the seat without assistance and slammed the door. Jessie gripped his hand before he could move to get his sticks and stow his wheelchair.

"You know what they're doing, don't you?"

"Being nice to me and Ella Sue?"

"So wrong. They're pushing us together exactly the way they did with Troy and me for the high school prom. Daddy handpicked him as a guy with a future to take me out."

"Oh, everyone assumed you'd just done better than the jerk you were dating. For the whole week you were unattached, I harbored this thought I might ask you to go with me. I consulted my mom about it. She told me to go for it, but if you turned me down, I should consider some of the girls who rode the handicap bus with me. They'd be thrilled and excited to go."

"I recall you brought Polly Oubre, the girl with cerebral palsy. You pushed her around in her wheelchair in time to the music. So sweet and kind. You didn't ask me."

Teddy felt a flush creeping up his neck. "I tried. I stopped by your locker and wondered if you'd gotten another date. You had."

"I'm sorry, I don't remember. A lot of fellows asked me that week. I wanted to stay home, but Dad came up with Troy. I remained with that man all through college and the start of his career because he seemed to have my father's endorsement, always over at the house, became like one of the family. But in many ways, he was as big a dick as my high school steady. I should be grieving for him, but all I can feel is anger that he put me in this chair."

Jessie squeezed his hand so hard he felt pain. "My mother said if you want to talk to her about your accident, just to call the clinic. She's a good psychologist if you don't already have one. She won't tell me a word you say."

"You think I'm that messed up, Teddy Billodeaux?"

Her fingers—her lovely manicured fingers—dropped away from his. He'd blown it. "No, just struggling a little. We all need help some time or another even if we are reluctant to take it."

Ella Sue saved his bacon by leaning on the horn and shouting out the window he'd lowered for her. "I need some AC. I'm about to die in here like a baby left in a car seat."

"Pick you up Monday?" he asked, dreading Jessie's answer. Would she tell him to drive his bright red van straight to hell?

"No."

His heart clenched as if her fingers had squeezed it instead of his hand. He'd gotten close to the girl he secretly admired in high school, and they were already over without having gone on one real date. His big mouth. His fault.

"Aren't we going to the mall tomorrow?" Jessie asked.

"We sure as hell are. You promised, Teddy," Ella Sue chipped in.

"Look, I am messed up. At least you aren't susceptible to my damaged charms and my parents' schemes. See you then." Jessie reversed, turned, and rolled down the garden path.

"Uh, right." He spoke to her back. Not susceptible to her charms. He wished.

Chapter Ten

Teddy sat in the mall café with an Americano at his elbow and his laptop open. Young mothers passed, guiding baby carriages with one hand and a toddler with the other. A gaggle of giggling teenaged girls strutted their stuff in incredibly short cutoffs and tight tops. A pack of boys their age prowled after them, prodding each other with elbows and dares to cut one from the flock. As for Ella Sue and Jessie, he had no idea where they'd gone, but between the grossly pregnant belly and the wheelchair, he'd spot them at a distance when they came his way. While working on his article about Coach Mo's team, no one noticed his disability, though he'd stowed his crutches on the next chair.

Satisfied with the piece, Teddy saved it and sent a copy to the coach's university email address for his approval. Then, he opened a file holding the start of a book for boys not good at athletics who still made a difference for their teams. In the back of his mind, he held dear an idea for a series in the vein of his favorite Harry Potter books about a kid with a disability who uses magic to transform into a superhero, kind of like the old Wheels of Fate video game that made local billionaire, Jonathan Hartz, his first million. That would be nice. For now, he stuck to inept guys who simply did the right thing at the right time to save the game.

Engrossed, he nearly missed the sight of Jessie wheeling along, her lap covered by shopping bags as if she were a grocery cart. Ella Sue marched beside her clad in a voluminous white T-shirt with a swirl of brilliant tie-dye colors that seemed to center on her protruding navel, one of Xochi's offerings. Below the maternity jeans, her feet slapped the tile floor in a pair of low-heeled, white strappy sandals Teddy had not seen before. When she tossed her fine blonde hair, he realized she'd had it stylishly cut into layers that made her seem less a child and more of a woman. As she passed Auntie Anne's booth, her freckled nose sniffed the air like a Bluetick hound. A moment later, she sighted her brother and abandoned Jessie to get to his table first.

"Did you see they got them soft pretzels like in Philadelphy and New York? I'll bet they taste as good as they smell." Taking the hint, Teddy opened his wallet and handed her a ten.

"I'll get enough for all of us." She paddled off to get in line.

Teddy wrenched a fourth chair from the table to make a space for Jessie. He gave her a crooked smile and kept his wallet in hand. "What's the damage?"

"A sore bottom and tired arms. I really have to do more weight work."

He unburdened Jessie of their purchases, placing them on the seat that held his crutches. "I meant what did this shopping spree cost? I might have to transfer funds into your account. Somehow, I don't think I have enough cash to cover it. That haircut alone…"

"My treat. My parents gave me a debit card after my paid sick leave at the university ran out. I haven't used it. The salon in the mall takes walk-ins, and the beautician did a cut for a very reasonable forty dollars. A more sophisticated style will give your sister confidence. We bought three pairs of shoes for Ella Sue: those sandals, some low heels for dressy occasions, and new athletic shoes she'll probably get the most use out of, all on sale, and another pair of maternity jeans. Those distressed ones are fashionable but wear out quickly. We bought makeup in Macy's since she told me she was saving the stuff I gave her for special, but I want her to practice putting it on. Then, we built a bear for the baby. I think I have just enough left for coffee."

"Let me get that."

"No, thanks." Jessie pivoted toward the line at the coffee shop where the two customers ahead of her parted to let her go first over her protests of, "Really, I can wait my turn. I'm the one sitting down." The elderly woman said, "Bless your heart, honey." The young guy went ahead and placed his order but insisted on paying for Jessie's beverage as well. He carried it to the table for her. She thanked him with a lovely smile Teddy wished he'd earned.

As soon as her benefactor left, striding on long legs effortlessly toward the exit, Teddy shrugged. "Being crippled hath its privileges, but I'll bet he wouldn't have paid for my drink. I'm not pretty enough."

"Frankly, I'd rather do things for myself, but thanks for the compliment."

"Now you've got it. You deflected their pity with a small joke up at the counter and graciously accepted that you are still beautiful. You've got Ella Sue's number, too. Tell her the Hollywood stars eat their meat rare, and she'll gobble it down. But Jessie, don't let her take advantage of you financially. My mom and Xochi both think she's out for all she can get, and they usually don't judge people harshly."

Jessie imitated his shrug. "You're not as naïve as you look, Teddy Billodeaux—and neither am I. But I enjoyed helping someone else. God knows I won't be wearing out my own shoes, and all she has is a pair of flip-flops."

"Actually, she has sneakers that smell to high heaven and a pair of red stilettos she can't wear right now. I saw both in her closet."

Ella Sue approached with two pretzels and a jumbo soft drink. "Not quite enough for three pretzels, but we can share, one plain, one with cinnamon sugar." She ripped off an ear of the cinnamon sugar and offered the rest around the table. "Yep, as good as they smelled. Bet the ones in Philly are better though."

As soon as she sucked the sugar off her fingers, Ella Sue put her feet into Jessie's lap. "I love these shoes you got for me, but I'm rubbing a blister big as an egg. Can you trade 'em out for my flip-flops? Hurry 'cause I gotta pee. I always gotta pee."

Jessie managed the transfer of shoes and watched Ella Sue hurry into the café, making a ponderous dash for the restroom. "You know, I kind of like that she isn't afraid to take advantage of me."

"May I?"

"May you what?"

"Take advantage."

"Are you flirting with me, Teddy?" She watched his blush bloom.

"Not exactly. Next weekend I have to go to New

Orleans to announce the Sinner's first preseason game. It's a long drive, and I usually stay overnight at Junior's condo. Could you stay with Ella Sue in case she goes into labor or something? Call an ambulance if you must."

"Hey, my first sleepover not at the hospital. I'd love to do that for you."

"That's a load off my mind. No telling what trouble she could get into, but I can trust your good sense."

"Yes, that's me, sensible," Jessie said, as if she'd hoped for something else.

Ella Sue returned from her pit stop. "I'm beat. Let's head back to the apartment." She loaded her loot onto Jessie's lap again, but pushed the chair this time.

After dropping Jessie off, Ella Sue squirmed in her seat. "Step on it, Teddy. I need to pee again."

"Ever think that giant soda might be part of the problem?"

"Everybody knows pregnant women have to pee all the time."

"Right."

She didn't wait for Teddy to maneuver to their front door. By the time he got inside, she'd made use of bathroom and went outside to collect her packages. Dumping all on her bed, she stretched out next to the bags and curled around her belly. "Shut the door, would you, Ted?"

He did this small service for her and went to take care of his own bathroom needs. Passing her room later, he heard her talking to the unborn child again. "Oh, baby, if you could see me now!"

## Chapter Eleven

Teddy spent the week making sure Ella Sue would be fine in his absence. He took her to her weekly checkup. All was well. The baby had dropped, which accounted for her awkward shape, but no dilation as yet. Granting that the first class hadn't gone well, he forced her to go to the birthing class again. On the previous occasion, the instructor assumed him to be the father, introducing them to the group as "our new couple, Teddy and Ella."

"He's my brother," Ella Sue corrected in her hillbilly accent.

Someone in the group barked a short laugh. Teddy sputtered, "I'm the baby's uncle. The father isn't in the picture. I'll see Ella through this."

A woman with a long black braid down her back already seated cross-legged on a floor mat, reached up and patted his hand. "Bless you, no woman should have to go through this alone."

He'd come in on his crutches and faced the awkwardness of lowering himself to the floor. As Teddy rubbed his sister's belly and encouraged her to inhale and puff out, hee-hee-hoo, he felt as if he wore the stain of Merv the Perv on his T-shirt. He had to ask for assistance getting up, but one of the dads, a big fellow yearning for a son, heaved him up by circling Teddy's chest from behind much as he had his rotund wife who weighed lots more according to his helper.

Unhelpful that the next session began with a graphic film on natural childbirth that bared all, including an impressive muff on the woman who had not been shaved for the occasion. The big-headed baby emerged like a raccoon pushing through a forest thicket while the mother screamed in her last ditch effort. All the way home, Ella Sue whined, "I want drugs!"

"You'll get the epidural, but you have to be prepared for pain before that happens. I've told you before. You want to go to the gym with me and Jessie again tomorrow?"

"Nope. Boring waiting for you two to finish. I'll hang around the apartment."

"Okay, but don't be alarmed if someone comes. I have a cleaning lady twice a month to do the bathrooms, change the sheets, and dust."

"Won't be a problem. I'm not shy. I could use some company."

On the way home, Teddy swung by the grocery store and stocked up on milk, salad, fruit, and cranberry juice, especially since Jessie should be drinking that to keep her bladder clear of infections. Eggs, too, since they appeared to be using them faster than a hen could lay. He tried to think of what else Jessie might want to survive an overnight with Ella Sue and finally left pizza money on the counter.

The next afternoon, Jessie's father insisted on driving her to his place. When they got inside, Teddy noticed the coach checking out the apartment as if dropping off a teenage babysitter for the first time. With little guile, he asked to use the bathroom, and came out after a flush and the sound of running water smiling.

"Wish we had as good a setup at home. Now, Jess, call if you need any help."

"My number and the obstetrician's are on that card on the counter." Teddy checked his pocket. "Yes, I've got my phone which seems to be playing hide and seek lately. I'll be at Junior's place tonight. The game is at noon and should be over around three. I'll get on the road as soon as I can, but it might be seven or even eight if traffic is bad. Help yourself to anything in the fridge or order a pizza."

"Teddy, I have your number in my phone. Dad, thanks for the lift, but you can leave now. We'll be fine." Jessie made shooing motions toward the door. Both men left with the greatest reluctance.

This wasn't her first babysitting gig, and Ella Sue's care certainly fell into that category since she tended to be wayward as a child and just as outspoken. Jessie put on a bright smile. "It's too hot to go outside. Want to binge watch Pride and Prejudice? It's the best one with Colin Firth as Mr. Darcy." She rummaged the set of CDs from the backpack she'd brought along and let Ella Sue examine it as if she'd presented her with porn—which maybe Teddy's sister might have preferred.

"I guess. He's a good-looking dude. Dresses like Prince though."

"It's a costume drama, the Regency period." All of that lost on Ella Sue.

"I'll give him a try."

They viewed half the set before hunger came calling. "This baby needs something to eat. You want to call for the pizza, or should I?" Ella Sue launched herself off the sofa. "We got to use your phone since

Teddy took his. Guards that thing like it was made of gold and diamonds."

"It's his lifeline. I know how he feels. But why don't we make chef salads tonight? Better for all three of us. When I checked for cold drinks, I noticed Teddy has lots of cold cuts and cheese, bags of salad, too."

"Yeah, mostly we have sandwiches and fruit for lunch. He sure pushes the fruit. I'm surprised he left us that six-pack of unsweet tea. Usually, it's milk, milk, and more milk."

"He's thinking about your health. Can you boil a couple of eggs and find a big bowl for me?"

"I guess." Ella Sue wore her disappointment over not getting pizza like a holy martyr with a hair shirt, but she did put two eggs on the stove while Jessie poured salad into the bowl and julienned ham, turkey, roast beef, and Swiss cheese into strips, plus adding a handful of cherry tomatoes to the mix.

"As soon as the eggs are hardboiled, we can eat. Meanwhile, what did you think of the movie?"

"I don't understand all that's going on. It might be nice to have a sister like Jane, but the rest are trouble, and that Caroline is a bitch. Mr. Darcy is a real prick, but handsome enough and so rich I'd let him lay me any day."

Jessie blinked. Not a comment she ordinarily received on Pride and Prejudice. "He's nicer than he seems, but yes, very rich." One of the eggs cracked in the boiling, and the hot water overflowed the pot. "Would you turn down the heat, please?"

Ella Sue obliged. She waited for the eggs to finish cooking, ran cold water over them, cracked and quartered the eggs according to Jessie's instruction.

Jessie divvied up the salad and garnished it with the eggs, placing club crackers on the side. Taking a bottle of low-fat Thousand Island dressing from the fridge, she added a couple of dollops to her share and passed along the bottle to Ella Sue who made a pink moat around the greens. "Covers the taste," she told Jessie.

They ate in front of the TV while watching the rest of P&P. Ella Sue tended to doze off during any scene where Mr. Darcy failed to appear, but in the end, she said she'd liked it well enough. Her final pronouncement was, "Her little sister was an idiot to go off with Wickham, but Mr. Darcy is sure fine. Say, could I use your phone to call my daddy?"

"I thought the two of you were estranged, um, don't get along." Jessie didn't want to talk down to Ella Sue, but couldn't be sure what the girl understood most of the time. Ella had gotten the gist of Pride and Prejudice though.

"Now that I'm not his problem anymore, we can talk without fightin'."

As soon as Ella Sue got the phone in her mitts, she took off for her bedroom and shut the door, leaving Jessie to clear the bowls and forks and get them in the dishwasher herself. Laps came in handy when a person didn't have functioning legs. She'd taken care of her daily maintenance routine and bathed at home before coming over, but took advantage of Ella Sue's privacy issues to cath herself before bedtime, brush her teeth, and wash her face. On the way to the bathroom, she heard Ella's laughter. No strain in her voice considering the circumstances, but then, the girl had managed to shift her medical bills from her old man to Teddy, something to celebrate, Jessie guessed. The way Ella

Sue chattered, she also guessed the call wouldn't end until the phone ran out of juice and needed recharging.

Might as well get ready for bed. Jessie came prepared to sleep in her clothes rather than ask Teddy's sister for help changing. She went into his bedroom and parked close to the bed conveniently the right height for her to slide from her chair to the mattress. Lifting one leg across the other, she took off her athletic shoes with a rip of Velcro and placed them on the night table for easy retrieval. She left the socks in case her toes got cold, not that she'd know if they did, stacked the pillows, and transferred to the bed. Jessie unfastened her jeans, wiggled them off her hips, and bent low to draw them off her legs. Of course, they bunched around her ankles, and kicking them off was not an option. Trying to pull one leg up and remove them with her hands only tangled them more. So let them stay there. Her oversized T-shirt served well enough as a nightie, and the jeans would still be there in the morning. The hell with them. She pulled a paperback from her backpack, a Regency because that is what she was in the mood for, and settled in to read.

Before Jessie turned out her light, Ella Sue rapped on the door and entered, sheepishly holding out the phone. "I used up all your bars," she said.

"No problem. The charger is in my backpack. Just plug it in."

"I meant to help you clean up, but we got to talkin'."

"I didn't want to leave a mess for Teddy. His place is pretty tidy for a guy's."

"Oh, he don't like clutter to get in the way of his wheelchair. He got a woman who does for him twice a month, too."

"Really?" For some random reason, Jessie's brain turned that statement into sexual content. Teddy had a regular date scheduled with a—prostitute, call girl, willing college student earning her tuition? The thought shouldn't cause her any pangs, but it did.

"Yeah, she cleans the bathrooms and changes the sheets and some other stuff. Must be nice to have someone do for you."

Oh, a cleaning lady! "You know I'd rather be able to do those things myself."

Ella Sue's gaze glided down Jessie's legs. "How about I get those jeans the rest of the way off and promise to make breakfast and clean the mess since I ran up your phone bill?"

"Deal."

Ella Sue not only handled the jeans and folded them beside the shoes, she tucked Jessie under the covers. "I took care of my mama some when she was dying and got so weak."

"I know you loved her."

"A bunch, but I think she always loved Teddy best."

"I don't believe that's true."

Ella Sue hunched her shoulders. "Whatever. See you in the mornin'."

\*\*\*\*

Jessie woke to the aroma of bacon sizzling and pancakes made from a batter perfumed with vanilla. She'd slept late and let Ella Sue get the jump on her. Good thing the girl wasn't a toddler intent on getting the Cheerios off a high shelf. Her mom claimed that was how the Minvielles discovered Jessie's gymnastic ability. She pushed that memory aside and maneuvered into her chair to do the bathroom routine. Jeans and shoes later.

"Smells delicious," she told Ella Sue when she arrived in the kitchen.

"Hot and ready to serve. All I could find to drink was this cranberry juice and milk unless you want more of the ice tea."

"Cranberry juice is good. I have some every day. Let's eat."

The girl kept her word and did the cleaning. She went out to fetch the newspaper from the rack under the unused mailbox by the door. "Look here, what Teddy wrote at about the UL team."

"He did a good job."

"Hard to imagine anyone can make a livin' that way. Don't know what I'll do after the baby comes."

"You could certainly cook at a restaurant with some more training."

"Or maybe one of those LPNs that help people like you. Let's get your britches and shoes on. I thought maybe we could go over to the Burger King and spend some of Teddy's money for lunch."

Jessie noticed the two twenties had vanished from the counter. Not her business. "We could do that, but let's get the food before the Sinners' game starts. I know it's only preseason, but I'd like to watch it." And hear Teddy's warm voice with that tinge of a twang that made Ella Sue's accent seem like a large-stringed instrument. She'd heard him call games in high school and college, never taking much notice, always busy with cheerleading, but now she realized she missed it on days they didn't have PT together or time to talk going to and fro.

"Fine by me. We can get chicken fries and chocolate shakes." Which would leave Ella Sue plenty of change to pocket.

Though she wasn't hungry after the big breakfast, Jessie allowed Ella Sue to lead her out into the sweltering summer morning around eleven to get the game provisions. Perhaps out of respect for the Lord's day, Teddy's sister had donned a wildly floral, high-waisted dress with cute cap sleeves and a scooped neck. She padded along in her new white sandals like a bloodhound on the scent of chicken fries, breathing in the smoky smell of the restaurant on the corner.

Traffic ran heavy from the Episcopal and Presbyterian churches side by side releasing their worshipers for Sunday dinners and late brunches. The light turned yellow as they approached the intersection. Ella Sue simply kept walking, trusting to the good Lord and the kindness of strangers to get her to the other side. Jessie, more familiar with Cajun drivers running through red lights, stayed on the sloping curb and watched the girl disappear into the Burger King.

Finally, she got the green and rolled into the crosswalk, pushing hard, glad her exercise was paying dividends. She rarely went out on the street and never alone, unlike the courageous Teddy, who knew each inch of the campus from a wheelchair. Safe on the other side, Jessie searched for a sight of Ella Sue. The view from the front window showed a line queued up for burgers, but not Teddy's sister. Maybe the bathroom since the girl couldn't hold it for long in her condition.

A small boy held the door for Jessie and received a commendation for being a gentleman from his grandpa.

She headed straight for the ladies' room and shoved the door open wide enough to call, "Ella, are you in here?" No answer, though a guilty middle-aged woman emerged from the handicap stall and murmured, "Sorry," on her way out. Jessie reversed in the narrow corridor and went outside again. There, behind the big dumpster enclosure in the back of the lot, she sighted a not quite hidden belly swathed in a tropical floral print. Jessie rolled that way.

A man, deeply swarthy with black curls hanging to his shoulders, stepped into her path. "Need some help, honey?" he asked, showing strong, white teeth feral as a coy dog.

Jessie tried to classify his face, not black, his features too sharp and defined, the cheekbones high. Probably not Hispanic either. The campus had its share of students from India and the Middle East, but he lacked the foreign accent, his from somewhere in the South. For no reason at all, she felt vaguely threatened as he discarded the butt of a cigarette and ground it out with the toe of a battered work boot.

"No, thank you. I'm looking for someone."

Ella Sue stepped out behind him. "I guess that would be me. Sorry, this feller needed directions to Olde Tyme Grocery. Teddy took me there so I know where it's at."

"I believe they're closed on Sundays. Lots of places in Lafayette are."

"Thanks for the information, ma'am. I'll try elsewhere." He loped off with his worn jeans hanging low on lean hips and his none-too-clean white tee clinging to his sweaty shoulders.

"Ella, you shouldn't talk to strangers like that. In

your condition, he could have knocked you down and taken your money."

"Got it in my bra. Besides, Teddy is always saying how friendly folks are around here. I ain't a child, in case you haven't noticed." Ella Sue's lips, glossed pink, pouted.

"I don't think he's from this area. Please be careful when you aren't with Teddy."

"Like either of you could stop an attack from happening."

Jessie shivered in the ninety-degree heat because the girl was right. "Let's go inside and order before it gets any hotter."

No argument from Ella Sue. As they returned to the apartment with enough chicken fries, French fries, ketchup packets, and dipping sauces for four in a greasy bag, the girl asked, "How come you call me Ella instead of Ella Sue?"

"Oh, I think it sounds…"

"Less hick?"

"More elegant."

Ella Sue mulled that as she waddled along sampling fries from the bag. "Yeah, more elegant. I'm gonna ask everyone to call me Ella from now on."

Back at the apartment, Jessie sipped unsweet tea, but Ella sucked her chocolate shake and laid out the food on the coffee table. Most women this far in their pregnancy would have had heartburn from the fried food, but not Teddy's sister. Jessie envied her, an unwed teenager with poor prospects. How could she? Here she sat in a wheelchair, close to a decade older than the girl, with no hope of bearing a child, and the meal still upset her stomach.

Game time! Despite the small size of the television, Teddy carried a full sports package, and they had no trouble getting it. As usual, his brother Dean, the star quarterback, played only the first quarter before retiring to the bench to save his arm for more important games. The rookies got a workout, and Coach Buck watched for weaknesses to be corrected. The final score came to an unimpressive fourteen-nine, the first touchdown having been thrown by Dean and the other team's scores being three field goals. That spoke well of the new defensive players.

Mostly, Jessie listened to Teddy's commentary. He usually did the color: stats, bios, the interesting facts, though he could do play-by-play as he had sometimes in high school. She remembered him struggling up the treacherous stairs to the high school booth on his crutches, giving her a quick thumbs-up when he achieved the platform. She shook a pom-pom his way and promptly forgot about Teddy Billodeaux in the excitement of the game. Rah-rah-rah! Now, she admired him more than she could say. How bravely he lived, but he would probably say he simply lived as well as he could. He'd taken on Ella Sue, no easy task.

The girl asked to use her phone again when the game ended. "I'm calling Daddy, then gonna take my nap. I swear I won't run down the battery."

"Sure." Jessie turned over the phone ready for some quiet time herself, reminiscent of the times when the babies she sat for went to bed for the night and let her binge on old movies deep into the night. The ring of the doorbell woke her from a doze in her chair. Maybe Teddy had returned. She straightened from her slump and checked her chest for ketchup stains.

Ella Sue already stood at the door accepting a pizza delivery. "I called since you had yourself a little nap going on. Say, I'm kinda short. You have any cash?"

"Here." Jessie dug in her backpack for her wallet and forked over the twenty her parents insisted she carry.

The money disappeared into the hand of the delivery guy who groped for change. "Keep it," Ella Sue said magnanimously.

The fellow grinned. "You tip better than Teddy."

"Don't I just know that." She shut the door and carried the box and a bag with two salads to the table. "I ordered from that Alesi's place since Teddy had their menu stuck up on the refrigerator. They already knew the address and his regular order, but I got the special pizza for two 'cause it come with salads. I figured you'd want that. We can save the other one for Teddy. It says this pizza is for two in love or one hungry. I'm the hungry one, and you and Teddy are the other."

"I wouldn't say that."

"Come on. You know he's sweet on you."

"Me and Teddy? No."

"Why, because my brother is crippled? Well, so are you. Seems like you fit together real good." Leave it to Ella Sue to be blunt and tactless.

"With both of us being handicapped, it's probably not a good idea. I can't imagine how we'd cope."

"What? With sex? Where there's will—and both of you got will—there's a way. Or don't you think he's good enough because you were engaged to some football player? Let me tell you, my brother is good, maybe too good."

"We can agree on that. Let's eat."

They shared the pizza, leaving a couple of slices for Teddy in case he arrived home hungry. Jessie ate her anchovy salad, and Ella Sue saved hers for her brother. They watched a second game with little interest until Teddy opened the door and cruised in at seven happy to accept their leftovers.

"Lucked out with light traffic and happy to see my girls," he said.

His girls, they were his girls. Jessie felt a warmth that wasn't connected to blushing. "Did you have a good time?"

"I always do. I love my job, and Junior is good company. Xochi drove down for the game though he only played in part of it. We had a late dinner on Saturday."

"How's she doing with her baby?" Ella Sue asked.

"Showing a little more and proud of it."

Everywhere, women her age and younger were having babies. Jessie's mood sank. "I should get home. I'll call my dad. You'll be tired from working and the long drive."

"No, just let me finish eating. Speaking of which, my family is having a Labor Day picnic at the ranch, the last big to-do since the regular football season starts that week. You are both invited."

Ella Sue's face brightened. "I get to see Lorena Ranch at last! You think your mom will show me the bathroom with the chandelier?"

Teddy smiled at her obsession with celebrity bathing. "I'm sure she'll give you a tour if you ask, but really, it's just a big house with a lot of bedrooms."

"And a movie theater and a gym and a great big swimming pool."

"Yes, all of those things. We'll have to get you a swimsuit since I don't think you'll be playing volleyball or riding the horses, Ella Sue. Jessie, bring yours, too."

"Ella," his sister said. "I want to be just Ella now. It's more elegant."

"Okay." Teddy eyed Jessie to see if this was her doing.

She merely gave him a slight shrug and tried to hide her discomfort about the whole idea of going swimming. Once she'd been a strong swimmer, a person who fearlessly dove off the board into deep water. No more. Well, she could simply forget to bring a suit. "I'd better get going."

"Right. Let's get you loaded."

Jessie took a moment to savor life when Teddy braced himself and lifted her into the front seat of his van. A warm chest and strong arms around her once more. He clicked her seatbelt with caring hands. She didn't feel like talking, but that hardly stopped Teddy.

"How did you and Ella get along overnight?"

"She's a strange combination of ignorant and insightful, cunning and naïve."

"If you'd been raised by Newton Smalls, you'd be that way too. My birth mom and I spent most of our time trying to read Newt and not set him off. Didn't matter. When she went to work, he'd slap me around for no reason but pleasure and tell my mother I fell out of my wheelchair. We lived in terror of him."

"I'm so sorry!" Jessie gripped his arm as he carefully steered the van and felt the tension in his muscles.

"Don't be. As Ella would say, I landed in clover. I think she resents that."

"On the good side, she helped me get out of my clothes at night and ordered a pizza she thought I'd like—then hit me up for the cost."

"Jesus, how much did she roll you for? I left plenty of food in the fridge and enough cash for a couple of fast food meals. Get my wallet out of my hip pocket. Take out eighty for the pizza and your time."

"No, it's fine. I was helping a friend, not hiring out my services. You did leave enough money for food. I think she kept the change from Burger King and didn't want to use it. She escaped me when we crossed the street, and I found her talking to a shady character behind the dumpster. For a minute, I was afraid he'd propositioned her, but he went on his way when I showed up looking for her."

"In her condition?"

"Ella seems to think where there's a will, there's a way when it comes to sex."

"You talked about things like that?"

"Only briefly. She wasn't rattled by the man. Said he'd asked for directions." Jessie failed to tell him she'd been fearful of the guy. Perhaps she should have, but they turned into the Minvielle driveway.

"I'll tell her to be more careful."

"Just honk the horn. My dad will come out and get me."

"Hey, what kind of man doesn't walk a woman to the door?"

She wanted to say one who struggled for every step, but held it in. Fortunately, her father kept watch, probably an anxious watch, because he came out immediately. With no choice left, Teddy unlocked the van doors, and Coach Mo got to work setting up the wheelchair and shifting Jessie. "Have a good time?" he asked, very casually.

"Super," Jessie claimed.

Teddy leaned toward the still-open car door. "I've invited Jessie to the ranch for Labor Day if that's okay with you."

"From what I've heard, Joe puts out quite a spread."

"Always plenty. You and your wife could come if you want."

The coach took time to consider before answering. "Not this time. I think Jessie needs to go places without Dale and me hovering over her."

"It's going to be amazing for her. I have lots of stuff planned she'll enjoy." As if Teddy had read her thoughts, he added, "Be sure she brings a bathing suit."

"Will do. I'll tell Dale."

Jessie managed only a feeble wave as her dad slammed the door. Teddy promised her amazing, but she was fairly certain amazing experiences were no longer part of her life.

Chapter Twelve

Labor Day arrived far too quickly in Jessie's opinion. Since the remaining two of the Sinners' preseason games took place away, Teddy hadn't called on her to stay with Ella again. At the gym, she worked extra hard to build her strength as if someone in the famously athletic Billodeaux family might challenge her to arm wrestling. It could happen.

Jessie argued with her mom about the bathing suit, refusing to use any of the bikinis in her dresser because they reminded her of Troy and summers spent in the sun and sand, cavorting in the water, and then, ultimately the crash. Her skin, after staying inside from May to September she could only describe as plucked-chicken white. At best, her legs, regularly massaged and exercised for her hadn't deteriorated much. In the end, they found a one-piece suit at a specialty shop that carried swimwear all year round. Black, sleek, and unadorned, it wouldn't draw any attention, though she wished it flattened her breasts way more than it did.

She decided on jeans and boots, a black Sinners' T-shirt with the cute, little red devil logo to go with the flow of what she thought most people would be wearing, and a high ponytail to keep the hair out of her face. Jessie spent time in front of the mirror getting her makeup exactly right, natural but enhancing, not too dramatic. She did her nails in red and didn't bother to ask her mother to do her toes. Her backpack hanging from her chair was stuffed so full of items she thought she might need that the large yellow beach towel hung out of the top like a penalty flag.

When Teddy drove up, he smiled. "We aren't backpacking in the high country. I swear the ranch has towels and anything else you might need." Ella, she noted, brought nothing but herself adorned in the tomato red top extended over her belly like a circus tent, the distressed jeans, and new sandals.

"Brace yourselves. There are a lot of Billodeauxs. No need to remember all their names the first time at the ranch. We know we are overwhelming."

Ella bounced in her seat, making the springs creak. "I know them already from their pictures in the papers."

Jessie saw the family members around town; everyone did, but the children had gone to private schools, all except Teddy. She couldn't claim any acquaintance. Mostly, she felt nervous, unlike the elated Ella.

They weren't the first arrivals by far. Teddy opened the wrought iron gates with his device and waved to their ranch manager/guard as he passed. He let Ella and Jessie down by the barn before parking the van amid mixed rows of SUVs, big manly trucks, luxury vehicles, and a few economy cars. He worked his way back to his girls on his sticks, covering the uneven ground with alacrity.

"Why don't you take a seat in the shade, Ella? Brinsley will be by to take your drink order if he doesn't have anything on his tray you want."

Ella Sue nudged Jessie's shoulder with her elbow. "They got a butler who brings whatever you want on a silver tray. See him over there in the Bermuda shorts, white socks, and sandals." She waggled a finger in his direction. The finger switched directions. "Lookee, two Sinners players side by side." They were easy enough to pick out by their size alone, and most wore some type of team regalia.

Jessie fit right in wearing hers. Sigh of relief. "Yes, everyone in Chapelle knows Brinsley by sight. I think he's the only butler in the parish. But Ella, you shouldn't point. It makes people uncomfortable." Jessie took the opportunity to offer a small lesson in deportment. Probably the Sinners were used to gawkers, but the butler would be appalled by such bad manners.

Ella clamped her hands behind her back. "You think someone will show me around?"

"Xochi is right over there with an empty seat beside her. Go sit down, and I'll send some of the guys over to meet you."

Ella Sue pivoted so fast toward Xochi—a little more showing, a little more glowing since the last time they'd seen her—that she nearly took a header tripping over the roots of one of the live oaks that studded the ranch. Teddy caught her elbow in time. "Take it easy. Remember the doctor said to rest these next two weeks."

"I will!" Still, his sister walked off as fast as her inflated belly would allow and dropped panting into the seat by Xo.

"I'll go with her, I guess." Jessie started to wheel away, but Teddy stopped her with a firm hand to her shoulder.

"Absolutely not. We're going riding."

Jessie stared at the fenced equestrian arena next to the barn where small children were being given pony rides. "Really, I don't want to be the biggest kid being led around on a horse."

"You know how to ride western, right?"

"I did. My uncle keeps horses and taught me and my brother, but now…"

"Come along." Teddy guided her past the bounce house and the climbing wall, both teeming with children. He paused to ask his brothers, Dean and Tom, plus Junior Polk standing around with beer bottles in their hands, to speak to Ella Sue. Obviously, the Billodeaux grapevine had delivered the news about his half-sister and squeezed all the juicy details out of it because none of them questioned who the pale, blonde, and pregnant girl was. All three touched hands with Jessie who did need an introduction and offered their "Pleased to meet you."

Teddy moved on to the barn where his youngest and smallest sister, Edie, held a big, red horse that looked as if it could run off with her if it chose, by the reins. "He's all ready to go, Teddy. May I leave now?"

"Sure. After you say hi to my friend, Jessie."

Edie displayed her manners and barely gave the wheelchair a notice. The kids at Camp Love Letter came here in them all the time. No big deal, her impatient expression appeared to say.

"Thanks, short stuff." He ruffled her short, curly black hair. She batted his hand away and raced for the rock wall. Teddy turned his attention to Jessie. "This is Rascal, the wonder horse, best mount that ever existed. Daddy Joe bought him especially for me."

Teddy fed the animal a sugar cube from his pocket,

and the horse's graying muzzle nosed for more. "Watch this. Down, Rascal." He added a hand signal. Rascal dropped to his knees and waited patiently. "Slide onto the saddle. I'll help you get your leg over. There we go. Up, Rascal!"

This horse was no small pony, and the ground seemed far away as Jessie looked down at her dangling feet being inserted into the stirrups by Teddy. He handed over the reins.

"You can neck rein him for direction changes and shift your weight, too, but he also obeys verbal commands." To make his point, Teddy commanded, "Walk, Rascal." The horse moved forward to the paddock gate and waited until his master caught up to open it. "Smartest horse ever."

Jessie gripped the horn with one hand, not good form, but she feared tumbling off from her uncertain seat.

"Hands off the horn. This is good for your core," Teddy ordered. "Enjoy yourself. Walk on, Rascal."

She found herself plodding around the ring among the stream of ponies being led. After two trips around, she began to trust her balance and steered the horse more to the center of the area before saying, "Trot!" Rascal took off at a lively pace. After several more circuits, Jessie found the courage to say, "Canter." Rascal picked up his feet and raced by the sedate ponies. Exhilarated, she finally pulled up by the gate where Teddy stood waiting. "That was wonderful! You should take a turn."

"I think I'm more in the mood for swimming since you raised a lot of dust out there." He opened the gate and let her through. "Down, Rascal!"

The horse knelt, and Jessie slid off the saddle into her chair with very little assistance. "I think he deserves another sugar cube." The horse nodded emphatically, making her laugh.

"What do you think, Rascal? Do you deserve a sugar cube?" The trusty steed nodded again. Teddy fished another from his pocket and gave it to Jessie to present. With that treat devoured, Rascal bumped her with his big head.

"He wants to bully you into giving him another, but don't let him. All gone, Rascal." The red head drooped with greatest dejection.

"Oh, I but want to!"

"He's conning you, but go ahead." Teddy provided another treat for Rascal to slobber from Jessie palm. "Okay, that's enough. T-Rex!" he shouted to yet another of his brothers, the youngest son already showing signs of being the next Billodeaux quarterback. The boy led a pony to the fence and lifted a little black girl from the saddle. She scooted over to the bounce house.

"You can use Rascal for the rides, but please give him a good rubdown when he's finished. I'd do it myself, but I have company. This is Jessie Minvielle."

"I don't know how you get such pretty girls, bro," he answered, also showing Joe Billodeaux's eye for women. "I'll take care of old Rascal here, but you owe me."

"Don't I always? I think we need a swim, Jess. To the pool."

"You know I could use a swim, too, the way you kicked up the dust," T-Rex shouted after them, wiping his handsome youthful face with a bandana.

"I'll toss you in the bayou when we have the dragon boat races," Teddy retorted.

Jessie loved it all: the miraculous horse, the banter between brothers, the butler in his Bermuda shorts. She felt as star struck as Ella Sue, and hoped she didn't goggle. They arrived at the pool via a pathway made for wheelchairs after a rough transit from the corral. It was a big one with a deep end, safety bars all around, and a wheelchair hoist. No way could she claim she couldn't manage to get into the water. A fair number of people swam and splashed. One of the Billodeaux twin girls manned the lifeguard station and wielded a mean whistle for misbehavior.

"Must be Jude on the stand. She's pretty strict. Go into the pool house and change," Teddy said. "I'll do the same."

He left her no choice. How did he expect her to get out of a pair of boots and her jeans and slip into that sleek suit without help? Somehow, she must manage. Going into a curtained cubicle, she tried to lift a leg onto her lap to pull off the boot, way harder than sandals or athletic shoes. "Damn it to all to hell! Teddy, the pool, and everything."

She was not alone. A soft voice asked, "Need some help?" The curtain parted slightly. The pixie face that peered in seemed to be the lifeguard, but the shrill whistle sounding again denied that. Seeing the puzzlement on Jessie's face, the woman as curly-headed as little Edie, said, "I'm the other twin, Annie. Both of us are nurses. Teddy said you'd be coming to swim."

"I can't get my boots off." Jessie swiped an eye teary with frustration.

Annie dealt with the boots and jeans with professional efficiency. She let Jessie divest herself of the T-shirt and bra while she got the swimsuit from the backpack and drew it up with practiced detachment. She'd taken more notice than it appeared. "If I had your assets, nice full breasts and a great booty, I'd wear a bikini, one that tied at the sides. That would be easier for you to handle by yourself." Teddy's sister wore a modest red two-piece. She owned small, high breasts, delicate curves, and a lovely smile.

"To be honest, I don't know what I can handle by myself yet. Just look at me, first time in the sun since May. I'm whiter than a snowy egret."

"Sunscreen?" Nurse Annie asked.

"In my pack."

"I'll get your back, and you can do the rest."

"Wrap me in my beach towel, please."

"Are you kidding? Flaunt what you've got." Annie did not hand her the large towel. Instead, she drew back the curtain and beckoned Jessie to follow.

Teddy waited, already in the water, and waved at them. Jessie could see his muscular chest furred with hair so light it was nearly unnoticeable, and farther down below his really loud knee-length trunks, his stick-like lower legs floating.

Annie spoke close to her ear to be heard over the splashes and shouts of children and teens playing Marco Polo or trying to shove their opponents off the shoulders of sturdy boys. "You can use the hoist or go down the ramp if you want, but you look strong enough to just slide into the water and grab onto the bar. After that, it's up to you what you want to do. If you need help, give a shout. My twin hasn't let anyone drown yet."

Jessie nodded, pushed off, let her dead legs take her under. In a brief moment of panic, she thought they'd sink her to the bottom of the pool like a block of cement and make it impossible to rise. She shoved the water away with her arms and came up next to a grinning Teddy.

"Race you to the other side." He took off doing a powerful butterfly stroke, his legs drawn along like the tail of a dolphin.

"Unfair!" she shouted after him as he touched the wall and reversed into a backstroke. "You're showing off."

"Yep. You impressed?" He offered her that Teddy-smile, as full of light as the reflection of the sun off the water.

"I am." Jessie let go of the safety rail. "Breast stroke!" She dipped her face into the water, pushing it aside with arms wide, and reached the far side before him. "I didn't know I could still do that."

"I did, because you are amazing."

"Let me return the compliment." Jessie found herself answering that smile with one of her own and wondered if it was as bright as people used to say about her. Doubtful.

No matter. They did some laps side by side, and once when she lost track of her companion, he came from below and pulled her under, a sneak attack. She began to scold, then thought of a better answer, beckoned him close, and used both hands to duck Teddy in return. He, of course, surfaced laughing. Both pulled themselves out of the pool and sat sunning and talking until the lifeguard blew her whistle several times and announced in a no-nonsense voice, "Clear the pool. Lunch will be served in half an hour. We reopen at two."

Jessie saw Annie herding the smaller children, getting them out, toweling them off, and wondered who would help her skin out of the tight suit now. The deeper voice of a very mature woman sounded behind them. "I brought your sticks and braces, Teddy. Miss Minvielle, your chair is behind you. Feel free to pull yourself into it, or I will assist you if necessary."

Jessie turned her head to stare up at an imposing figure of a nurse clad in a starched white uniform, traditional cap, white stockings, and thick-soled shoes. Gray hair neatly stowed in a bun, face lined by experience, she appeared to have stepped out of a 1950s version of General Hospital.

Jessie knew she sounded ungrateful, but the words spewed. "You hired a nurse to look after me?" That fact wiped away all the marvelous freedom she'd experienced in the pool.

"No, this is Mrs. Clive Brinsley," he said, giving her a very formal introduction. "She's our resident nurse. In fact, she's taken care of most of the Billodeaux kids from childhood, some from birth. Now, she helps with Camp Love Letter, and she'll be standing by when Xochi gives birth. We call her Nurse Shammy since she was previously Miss Haversham." He said the words with so much fondness the woman's stern cheeks rouged with pleasure.

"Call me that if you please. Off we go to prepare for the luncheon." The nurse waited for Jessie to make up her mind about getting into the perfectly positioned wheelchair, and she did so by heaving herself up on the arms and taking a seat on the pillow covered with her yellow towel.

"Let me show you to the shower, Miss Minvielle."

"Jessie, just Jessie."

The rather formidable nurse positioned her on a shower chair in a cubicle ample enough for the handicapped and equipped with a hand nozzle as well as regular shower head, stripped off the troublesome suit, and left Jessie in privacy to wash her hair with a small bottle of shampoo from a handy selection, and scrub with a tiny bar of sweet-smelling soap. Feeling refreshed and relaxed, Jessie called for a towel and managed to dress mostly by herself, though her helper expressed her disdain of jeans. "So problematical to get off and on, but all the young girls wear them, much too tightly in most cases."

"Mine aren't as tight as they used to be," Jessie murmured.

"Still very fetching on a young woman like you, I am sure. I'll leave you to do the rest."

Jess carefully reapplied her makeup, combed out her hair, and made use of one of several hair dryers. By the time she finally left the changing room long after the commotion of the swimmers faded, Teddy waited by a deserted pool. He'd had enough time to return to his van and retrieve his red chair, so much racier than hers. Wheeling close to him, she sniffed his scent of chlorine, sunscreen, and masculinity, realizing he'd only showered off briefly, and she'd kept him waiting. "Did we miss lunch because I took so long?"

"No one misses lunch at Lorena Ranch. There's always plenty, too much really. Let's roll."

They joined the end of a long line, and Jessie

appreciated that no one made her feel inferior by offering to let her go ahead. As Teddy promised, plenty of food remained by the time their turn came. She filled her plate with half fruit and greens, passed on the potato salad and beans, and added a fully dressed huge hamburger with the usual condiments plus coleslaw, a Daddy Joe special Teddy warned her, sure to be spicy.

"I can take the heat," she assured him, but kept a container of chocolate milk handy to put out the flames if necessary. He went for two hotdogs with ketchup, mustard, and relish plus the sides.

"Junior wanted to roast a pig in a pit, but they decided on a simpler menu. If you want to score points with my grandmother, get the bread pudding for dessert instead of ice cream, but it goes fast." Teddy scooped a dollop of the pudding with its mile-high meringue into a paper bowl and added a dribble of rum sauce. He balanced it on top of the rest of his meal. Jessie did the same.

When they reached the screened exit door of the barbecue pavilion, she gratefully accepted the strong arm that opened it for them. The big man, Joe Dean Billodeaux, beamed down at her and offered a hand in the manner of a celebrity who had met a million fans and wowed a thousand women. Despite the steel gray hair, he still exuded charm like athletic sweat. She'd seen him around, naturally, at football games, but never this close.

"Always great to meet a friend of one of my boys. Jessie, right?"

She nodded, too dumbstruck to answer. From behind his big frame, a softer voice said, "Joe, you're letting the flies in. Let the girl move on."

The arm not holding the door shot behind his back, drew his petite wife forward, and tucked her to his side. "Have you met Nell?"

Jessie found her voice. "Not formally, but everyone knows her. She does great work in the community."

"That she does." He turned his mega-watt smile on his spouse and squeezed her fondly.

"Dad, our food is getting cold," Teddy prompted.

"Right. Enjoy that Joe-burger."

As they moved from the doorway, two small white dogs wormed their way in while a large black Lab mix too big to sneak past the guard gazed forlornly at the food on the other side of the screen door. As Teddy and Jess found an empty space at a table and shoved the chairs aside to accommodate them, Nell's voice declared, "Half a wiener for each for you and a whole one for Lil, now get out!"

"Let them have some fun," Joe countered. "Speaking of having fun…"

"Not now! We have a hundred guests."

Jessie glanced at Teddy. "Are your parents always so, so…?"

"Physical, intimate? Yes. Used to embarrass us as kids, but now I keep thinking how great to have a love where the flame never goes out."

That statement forced her to think of Troy. They'd had a flicker, not an eternal flame. She turned the conversation to her parents instead. "My mom and dad are more like a team, hard to get past them when they unite. While I was still in the hospital, they sold their home in Chapelle and moved to the one-story in Lafayette so I could be closer to rehab and hospitals. I had my own place up there before the accident, second floor apartment, no elevator. They closed the place down, put a lot in storage, including my car. I should be grateful. Why am I not?"

"No one likes being dependent. Except maybe Ella Sue." Teddy's blue eyes settled on his sister, her red curtained belly hard to miss, now in animated conversation with Nell. "I think she's begging for a tour of the mansion."

"Probably. I wish I could be so shameless."

"Give it a try."

"Being shameless?"

"Yes."

"Okay. After lunch, I'd like to see your old bedroom." Certainly, she blushed worse than Teddy.

"I'd be happy to show it to you. There, simple." He watched Jessie bite into her burger. Tears came to her eyes. "Dad puts a pool of his extra-spicy barbecue sauce in the center. Just eat around the edges."

"Good advice." She sucked up some chocolate milk. Now nervous, she picked at the rest of her food, but the bread pudding did slide down easy.

"If you are finished, I shall lead the way to my boudoir." He tried for a leer that failed entirely on his open, boyish face. His hair, combed back after swimming, dropped over his brows again. Jessie had the greatest urge to sweep it back into place with her fingertips. They dumped their trash on the way, approached a side door of the mansion, and entered to face an elevator to the second floor. Her tension rose as it ascended.

Teddy's room sat first on the left as the lift opened. Painted a pleasant deep green with a trim of forest leaves, the French doors to the balcony overlooked a canopy of live oaks. Everything, the bed, the dresser, a built-in desk, the bookshelf crowded with paperbacks had been scaled down for a handicapped child. An open doorway revealed a spacious bathroom with a high commode and grip bars in all the right places. The dual sinks hung low in a green veined marble counter cantilevered over open space for Teddy's wheelchair. "Well, this is it," he said. "Where I grew up."

Jessie wheeled easily across the hardwood floor and studied his taste in reading. An entire battered set of Harry Potter novels filled a shelf. She took one down and flipped its pages. "The Goblet of Fire, this was my favorite."

"Mine, too!" he answered with more enthusiasm than most grown men would reveal for a childhood favorite. "Before I came here, well, the bedroom I had in the trailer was a lot like Harry's room under the stairs, but Newton Smalls treated me worse than Harry's aunt and uncle. These books were my escape. When Newt tore one up, my mama went out to library sales and used book stores and got me another, about the only time she defied that man. Lorena Ranch became my Hogwarts."

To Jessie, Teddy had always been the handicapped kid with the bright smile and sweet personality. His origins made her shudder. How could she have considered asking him to have sex with her in this place simply because he'd shown her she could still ride a horse and play in the water, because she wanted to grasp even more of her old life, when his early childhood had been a nightmare?

"I guess we should go now."

"Coming up here was being shameless? I thought

you wanted to get it on."

Not the first time Teddy had surprised her, and it most likely wouldn't be the last. This time his smile truly was devilish.

"I did. I mean, can you? I haven't had sex since the accident, and don't know if this is such a good idea."

"I can, I would, and I will make this a good experience for you, but a little more warning might have been nice. Both of us require some preparation." Teddy searched a night table drawer. "Shit, no condoms. Mom must have cleaned them out when I moved permanently. Be right back. You'll want to use the bathroom first, highly recommended. I'll use the one in Mack's room. He always kept a stash of rubbers under his mattress." He shot out the door and left Jessie to prepare.

This would happen thanks to Teddy Billodeaux. She certainly hoped he knew what he was doing because she did not. Jessie used her catheter and wondered if she should lie on the bed and try to undress. She got as far as transferring to the mattress when Teddy returned.

"Don't start without me," he joked, but he drew the curtains with their leafy pattern that matched the bedspread, locked the bedroom door, and secured the shared bathroom before joining her and depositing a handful of helpers purloined from his brother's room. "Let me undress you."

That took care of the awkwardness of getting out of her boots and jeans. Next time shorts and sandals—if a next time occurred. Teddy stayed in his chair, disposed of the boots, and removed her clothes so tenderly, raising her hips, sliding down the stiff denim and the pair of ordinary cotton red bikini briefs she'd worn with no expectation of this happening, that she bit her lips to keep from weeping. He drew off her T-shirt. She rose up on her elbows to allow access to the clasp of her bra.

When Teddy finished, he sat and stared. "Beautiful," he said, before tearing off his own shirt, jerking the shoes from his feet, and getting out of his slacks. He wore only two things, his braces and a light blue band around his torso like a cummerbund as if they had a date to the prom.

He answered the question in her eyes. "My ostomy wrap. At one point in my childhood the doctors decided I had to go this route, too many infections. I use it for swimming and not grossing out sexual partners since it covers my pouch. Forget about it. You can't hurt me. I've got one in black. It's much more dashing. I'll show it to you sometime." Just that easily, he handled the intimate situation with a clear explanation and humor.

She was grateful and a little ashamed that, compared to Teddy Billodeaux, she remained mostly unscarred and normal seeming. "I'm ready," she claimed.

"No, you aren't, but you will be. I've been reading up. The first time after an accident like yours might be painful. Tell me, and I'll stop." He hauled himself beside her onto the bed and began with a thorough kiss. "Hey, your mouth stings from Dad's barbecue sauce."

Reflexively, she licked her lips, which did feel swollen, either from the sauce or Teddy's prolonged licking, probing, and sucking of her tongue. "That isn't helping me take my time. I could use your assistance now." He held up a black knobby silicon loop from his stash on the night table. "Know how to use a cock ring?"

Jessie swished her head against the pillow.

"Not hard, but it keeps me hard. Best put on in advance of an erection." He showed her how it should fit. "That's good. You get an A in following directions."

Teddy swelled at her touch. "In a minute, you can put on the condom, but first, these breasts need some attention. I had dreams about these babies in high school, pathetic but true. More magnificent than even a writer could imagine, so full and firm, so beautifully peaked with rosy nipples." He applied his mouth to each one, his hands massaging the sensitive sides.

She relished feeling his touch, forgot to be self-conscious and shy about her condition. Above the place where she'd lost sensitivity, he grew hard. "Time for the condom," he said and put one into her hands. She'd done this often for Troy, and startled, realized Teddy could compete with her fiancé below the waist despite his shriveled lower legs. Nothing else shriveled down there, nothing at all. Jessie completed this task, taking joy from participating.

He plucked a small tube from his looting of Mack's room. "Lube since you might be dry." He anointed a finger and swirled it against her clit, her nether lips, around the mouth of her vagina. She felt a tingle, let loose with a gasp.

"Hurt?"

"No, the opposite. Keep going."

Teddy rolled on top of her and raised up on his powerful forearms. He rubbed his erection against her cleft, making sure of her arousal before sinking deep within her and beginning with a slow pace in case she wanted him to stop. Instead, she urged him on with her hands on his buttocks, her nails digging in. He increased his rhythm. She wanted badly to arch against his body, but the familiar feeling of tightening built. The orgasm came on so fast she cried out.

He stopped moving. "Pain?"

"No, no, keep going!" She could do this! Experience all the joy of sex she'd thought gone forever. The build began again, more slowly. Could this man, this wonderful, extraordinary man give her two?

He grinned when he did. She opened her eyes just in time to see, wanted to tell him he was far better than Troy—and doubted he'd believe her.

He reached completion too, and rested his head on her breast until his heart rate lowered, finally rolling aside to let the sweat dry on their bodies. "I could stay here all afternoon."

"I'd like that." If only they could do that, free of Ella and all intrusions. Maybe they might try again—with her on top and some hip action from Teddy. A whole new world of possibilities opened for her today thanks to this man lying next to her.

It was not to be. They heard footsteps approaching and Ella Sue's unmistakable twang. "This place is a real palace. Lookee at this bedroom all lilac and ruffles. This is the room I'd like best if I stayed here. Bet the bathroom is as nice as the others. Does it have a chandelier?"

"The room belongs to our daughter, Lorena, who is in Australia right now. The bathroom is handicapped accessible for Teddy, whose place is on the other side. No chandelier."

They both heard the strained patience in Nell's

voice.

"Oh, can I see anyhow?" The bathroom latch rattled.

Panicked, Jessie sat up and searched for her T-shirt, but Teddy put a finger to his lips and shook his head. He shouted, "Hey, I'm using it. Ostomy accident. It's messy, and it stinks. Give a guy some space, Ella. Go outside and find Jessie." As he spoke, he unfastened the penis ring and laid it on the table. The deflated condom wrapped in a tissue followed. Jess clamped a hand over her mouth to stifle a giggle.

"Sorry, Teddy. I just wanted to see your room too."

"Nothing to see. Mom, aren't the dragon boat races starting?"

"Yes. You'd better get moving. You and Jessie are committed to Dean's boat."

"I'll be there. Look around for Jess. See you once I clean up."

"Ella, we can ride down in the elevator," Nell directed the girl.

"Oh, I'd love that. Imagine a house with its own elevator."

They moved away. The lift hummed into action.

"All clear. We can get dressed at leisure."

"You certainly handled that well. Do you use that ostomy accident often?"

"Often as needed. Sometimes, it's true. At this end of the hall, three sisters surrounded me, all of them bathroom hogs. I did what I had to do to get some privacy. I always lock the doors. But I have to admit Lorena was pretty nice about having to use a mirror for the handicapped. She's tall and had to bend over to do her makeup. Good sport, Lorena. Hope you get to meet her someday."

"Me, too." She dealt with her bra and lowered her T-shirt over her head. "Wait a minute. Dragon boat races?"

"Sure, we're rowing for Dean's team. With our upper body strength, we'll be awesome. Let's move it, Minvielle." He finished raising her panties and jeans. "Leave the boots off. You don't want to get them wet or have them drag you down if the boat overturns."

"Does that happen often?" Jessie shifted to her chair, set her feet on the rests, and put the boots in her lap. She tried to keep the anxiety out of her voice.

"Rarely, but I made the mistake of leaving my braces on one year when we had a collision, and I got trapped under the boat. I won't wear them this time. Both of us are strong enough to swim to the bank if necessary. You proved that in the pool this morning, or I wouldn't have signed you up to row."

Teddy pocketed the cock ring and flushed the condom. He shook out a green afghan with a border of brown bears crumpled on the end of the bed and drew it over a damp spot in the spread. "Old Madame Leleux crocheted that for me before I arrived here. They said she had second sight and could peer into the future."

"I've heard of her. I wonder if she foresaw what we just did."

"Disturbing thought, but maybe she knew we'd get together one day."

Satisfied with the cover-up, he called the elevator and delivered them to the alcove by the exit. "You go out first. Pretend you're looking for me." Teddy held the door for her escape.

Five minutes later, he caught up with her on the

bank of the muddy brown bayou where Xochi and Ella sat on lawn chairs to watch the races among a crowd of other viewers. Jessie took her cue from his nod. "There you are!"

"Well, I told you he had an accident, didn't I?" Ella insisted.

"Thanks for spreading that around, Sis." He flushed, but not for the reason everyone thought.

With a clipboard tucked under her arm, Nell walked up to the group. "Time to load the boats. Get your life jackets on. Right over there where Dean is standing. He'll help you get into position, Jessie."

Jessie wheeled off first. Teddy trailed with his mother, who said very casually, "You didn't fool me Teddy Wilkes Billodeaux, not for one minute." Fortunately, Nell didn't elaborate. Jessie, glad her back was turned, felt the surge of red to her face.

"Don't sweat it. We only do this for fun." Dean fitted her vest and pulled it tight. God, up close he was his father come again to devastate the ladies, but didn't do so according to gossip. Having a wife and two kids probably helped with that. He set her boots on the shore and lifted her easily onto the rowing bench of the long narrow boat with the tail of a dragon and a gaping, bulging-eyed head on the bow.

Still on shore, Teddy shucked off his braces, found a PFD that fit from the pile, and accepted Dean's help getting settled next to Jessie. "Sure you don't want to be the drummer?"

"No, let Trin have a turn. I think Jessie and I are well matched as rowers," Teddy answered, giving his usual position to his short and intellectual younger brother. "Who are we up against?"

"Tom and his crew."

"We can take them."

"Tom is at the tiller, but Alix is rowing. They won't be easy to beat."

"Yeah, she's a real Amazon, but we have Jessie with us."

"Right. I'll get the rest of the crew settled." Dean called the names for a motley group of teens and younger Sinners players. Tom's group matched theirs fairly evenly.

Jessie's throat went dry. "I'm supposed to row as well as the Sinners' famous female punter? You have more faith in me than I do."

"I think so, but win or lose doesn't matter here. It really is being in the game."

"What do we win?"

"Glory and a cheap trophy. Sometimes we have leis flown in from Samoa, but not this time. Afterward, we get leftovers to take home and second desserts."

Jessie mustered a smile and tried to borrow some of Ted's confidence in her. "Hey, I'll row as fast as I can for more of that bread pudding."

"If any is left. Remember, dig deep and follow the beat of the drum."

Dean blew a whistle and mustered his crew into position at the starting line. Redheaded Tom, guiding the other boat, shot a competitive grin their way before one of the Billodeaux grandchildren shot off a toy cannon to start the race along the straight length of the bayou before it took another looping turn near a grove of knobby-kneed cypress trees.

Jessie's heart raced to the beat of the drum, pumping her full of life. She glanced to her side to find herself neck-and-neck with the blonde Valkyrie, Alix Lindstrom Billodeaux, her lean, white arms strangling the paddle, her somewhat wide shoulders hunched with effort. Jess realized that while the punter had formidable legs, her own arms might have more strength. The drummer upped the pace. Their boat surged ahead. Tom's boat answered the challenge. Dean's crew put in an extra effort to cross the finish line by a flick of the dragon's tongue. Exhilaration, that's what Jessie felt, buoyant as the foam they'd stirred up in the bayou water.

Nurse Shammy waited with the two wheelchairs and Teddy's braces. Dean helped his brother out first, then Jessie. "You made all the difference. You're welcome to row my boat anytime," he told her and seemed to mean it. The quarterback moved off to congratulate the rest of his crew.

"Do you think I really did, Teddy? He wasn't just coming on to me a little?"

"Mais, yeah, you made a difference," Teddy said, the Cajun expression sounding odd with the remainder of his twang. "Dean is too straight-laced to lie or flirt. If he gives you a compliment, he means it."

"Bread pudding," she said. "I need to refuel."

"Race you back to the barbecue pavilion before the others get there." Ted took off, adeptly handling the rough terrain in what Jessie thought of as his racing chair. She did her best to keep up and suspected he could go faster, but had mercy on her.

Alas, all they found in the pavilion was Mawmaw Nadine, his stately and steely-haired grandmother, marking large brown bags with names: Tom, Dean, Teddy, etc. She lowered a container of coleslaw into each one.

"No more bread pudding, Mawmaw?" Teddy asked.

"One pan hidden in the back of the refrigeration, but you better hurry, my baby. Junior was headed to the kitchen. You and your girlfriend enjoy." She kissed the top of Teddy's head. "You don't forget your leftovers now you got that sister to feed, you hear?"

"Thanks, I won't. Quick, to the kitchen!"

They arrived to find Junior Polk, the big cornerback, digging into the deep meringue with a tablespoon while his mother, Corazon, beamed by his side. "What did you do to deserve that?" Teddy challenged.

"Won my heat while you were among the missing, Teddy-O. Help yourselves. There's plenty." He handed over two spoons. Junior rolled his big, brown eyes with the pleasure of the moment. "I have to get Mawmaw's recipe for this before she dies, but she's not giving it out yet."

"Not planning to die before she turns one hundred."

They ate from the pan, though Junior thoughtfully put aside a small square for Xochi. Towing Ella along like a kite full of wind, Nell found them there. "Award ceremony in fifteen. Be there," she said. "Everyone's leaving right after. Be sure to say goodbye to your grandmother."

Ella eyed the dessert. "That looks good. I only had chocolate ice cream before." Evidence of that dribbled down the tomato-red top. She reached for the square on the paper plate.

Junior firmly pushed her hand aside as if he'd

straight-armed another player. "That's for my baby. You eat out the pan like the rest of us." He forked over another spoon. Ella wasted no time devouring her share, leaving meringue caught in the corners of her mouth. Finished, Junior gave his mother a bear hug and trooped out with the serving of the pudding balanced carefully in his large hands. The others followed to the casual ceremony where the prizes turned out to be miniature dragon boats sent from American Samoa by Adam Malala, the retired cornerback Junior had replaced.

"I'll treasure this," Jessie said, a trinket marking the day she came alive in so many ways.

"Want to drive home?" Teddy asked.

"Me with hand controls?"

"It's easy. It's independence, Jessie."

"Then, yes."

"Ella into the back. I have to sit next to the driver."

Ella's pouty lip poked out full force. "How come you don't teach me to drive it?"

"Because I can't afford to lose the van, or you and the baby at this point. Maybe after the birth."

"Everything's after the birth. Can't wait for it to be over."

Jessie suspected Teddy felt that way, too, but would never divulge it. She got settled behind the wheel and turned on the ignition.

"Steering knob here. Push the bar forward for gas, pull it back for brakes."

Eyeing the live oaks as if they were out to get her, Jessie took the red van sedately down the long drive. With the gate wide open for exiting guests laden with leftovers, she made a slow turn onto the crumbling, potholed country road running before Lorena Ranch and inched along. Some of those behind her passed with good-natured waves. Even the locals in battered pickup trucks showed some respect for Teddy's van.

Jessie breathed deep and took on the ramp to the highway. She maintained at fifty, as fast as she felt safe going, let out her breath when they arrived in Lafayette and turned off toward her parents' home. In the driveway at last, she unclenched her fingers from the wheel, leaving sweaty prints behind. Her father stood at the door before she turned off the ignition. He wrangled her chair for her, but let her slide in by herself.

"Well…driving, I see."

"Kind of tense, but I think I could get the hang of it."

"I bet you could! We'll have to look into it."

Teddy transferred to the driver's seat, but asked the coach to stay a moment. "Need to ask you something about the upcoming game."

Jessie had wheeled ahead, but waited for her dad to catch up. "What did Teddy need to know?"

"Just some team stuff. How was your day?"

Jessie wondered about their conversation, but she gave the only answer she had. "Amazing, truly amazing."

Chapter Thirteen

Teddy insisted that Jessie drive his van home from rehab. He wanted to give her the gift of confidence—among other things. He broached the subject carefully. "Are you busy this weekend? I mean I have to be in the booth for the UL game Saturday night, but the Sinners have their opener on the west coast. I won't have to go down to New Orleans."

Jessie bit her lip, concentrating on the heavy flow of traffic along Johnston Street, getting plenty of practice on braking at the many spotlights, not to mention the sluggish pace along that piece of road. She stopped on red before answering. "Do you need me to stay with Ella again? My dad wants me to go to the game and sit with the team, but I'd be glad for an excuse to get out of it. I don't want to be their crippled mascot."

"You'd be a beautiful mascot, but no. Ella connived to get invited to the ranch for the weekend. My parents aren't flying out to see the Sinners beat the Raiders. They'll have a few friends over to watch the game. She'll get to stay in Lorena's room like she wanted. My mom said I looked like I needed a break from Ella, so she'd take her for a few days. If the baby comes, they have Nurse Shammy on hand and can drive her to the hospital. I mean, I'll be free most of Saturday and Sunday if you'd like to come over and hang out with me." Relieved when the light turned and Jessie paid attention to the car in front of them, Teddy knew he had a blush coming on as he bungled his way through the invitation.

"Or you could come and watch the game with my dad on Sunday."

"Not exactly what I had in mind. I thought we could go out to lunch some place nice, maybe Don's Seafood. Do whatever in the afternoon, then drive over to Cajun Field for the game."

"Oh, like a date." She kept her eyes straight ahead. "Maybe a date with sex."

"Well, it could be that or just going to the game and getting a hot dog before it starts. Really, forget about it. You should go with your dad and sit with the players. You're used to being in the heart of the action. I'll bet you could help out, raise team spirit."

"Right. I might do my old cheers—without the cartwheels and splits of course. Mostly, me and the chair would be in their way." Bitterness crept into her voice like salt water encroaching on a fresh pond.

Not what he wanted at all. Why was this so difficult? He'd asked girls out before, been rejected by some, accepted by others, and had sex with the more adventurous and open-minded. In the last case, he made sure he didn't disappoint. Caring about Jessie too much wiped out any suave he might have possessed. He tried again.

"Okay. We could get takeout and watch some other team in the afternoon. Go to the UL game while I work. You can stay with your dad, hide in the tunnel, whatever you want, go home with him or come back here with me."

"You left out the best part."

"Dinner out?"

"No, idiot! The sex, the really good sex."

"That could be arranged before or after the game, maybe both. Up to you." He took a turn at studying the traffic pattern.

"It's a date, then."

Jessie executed a left across two lanes and into one of the nice old subdivisions running along the Vermilion River where her parents had found the single-story brick home with mature trees and shrubbery plus the amenities left behind by an elderly couple who built a bathroom for the handicapped before they'd succumbed to assisted living. As usual, her dad trotted out as if he led a team to victory. He retrieved her wheelchair from the rear and let Jessie slide into it herself.

"Want to stay and have some lunch, Teddy? Right after I have to get over to the college to teach my PE class and run the pre-game practice."

"No, thanks. I have to get back to my place and feed Ella. I'm bringing Jessie to the game tomorrow night."

"Great! I wanted her to come, but wasn't having much luck." Coach Mo gave him a wink so broad that Teddy sincerely hoped Jessie missed it.

"I bribed her." He neglected to say exactly with what. "I'm taking her out to dine Saturday."

"Whatever it takes, son." Maybe Coach Mo did suspect. They shook hands while Jessie fumed.

"Anyone care if I have some say in this? Pick me up at eleven, Teddy. I'll be ready to go."

"See you then." Whistling a happy tune like a

cartoon dwarf setting off to work, he took the wheel, made a stop to empty his post office box, and returned to his apartment in a thoroughly great mood.

The first thing he noticed upon arrival was a cigarette butt on his ramp and the smell of smoke in the apartment. Ella lay sprawled on the couch as usual. "What's for lunch?" she asked, also as usual.

"We have leftovers from the ranch barbeque—unless you've eaten it all."

Ella studied her painted nails resting on her big belly. "That's mostly gone."

"Then, toasted cheese sandwiches and soup. There's always fruit if you need something right away. Has someone been smoking in here?"

"Maybe the cleaning lady. I went out for a walk when she came."

"No, she doesn't."

"Oh, I met that couple from the childbirth class, the guy with the tats and the woman with the nose ring. They came to visit for a while. I guess he did have a cigarette. I give 'em some of the leftovers. I mean I didn't eat it all myself."

Not the friendliest couple in the group, but Teddy accepted her excuse. He certainly hoped the culprit hadn't been Ella.

Teddy sorted through a week's worth of mail, slinging most of it into a trash bin. A handful of bills remained and a couple of checks for past work. He'd do a deposit and pay online after he fed the elephant in the room. Putting tomato soup into bowls for nuking in the microwave and placing the assembled sandwiches in a large frying pan to brown, he opened the bills and sorted out the chaff of advertisements and special offers until he had only the chits to be paid. His pale brows rocketed toward the ceiling when he saw the total on the cell phone bill. Sure, he used it a lot for business, but this sum exceeded the past six months. One number recurred over and over again, calls lasting over an hour, all to a phone registered in Tennessee.

"Ella, just because I leave my phone on the counter, doesn't mean you can use it without asking. This bill is going to eat those two checks I just received and then some."

She shrugged as if it weren't her problem. "I thought you wanted me to make up with my daddy."

So she hadn't been talking to her baby those evenings he'd passed by her room. No, she'd been wasting his money on the repulsive Newton Smalls, trying to crawl back into his good graces, as if he had any! He considered checking the number to see if she'd told the truth, but the very thought of any contact with Newt made his skin crawl as if covered with small live snakes.

"I think the sandwiches are burning," Ella prompted.

Right, the sandwiches and his usually placid temper. Teddy flipped the bread to the other side. They'd eat them slightly charred because he wasn't making them over for his careless sister, not with the price of cheese. Screw it! He'd take Jessie out to dinner even if he shouldn't charge anything right now. They ate in silence. Ella cleared the dishes and cleaned up without being asked while Teddy opened his laptop and calculated the damages she'd done to his bank balance.

"You kinda mad at me?" She turned wet blue eyes away from getting the scorch marks off the frying pan toward Teddy.

"Yes. I'm trying to live on my own, not live off my parents. You put a big hole in my safety net with your phone calls. I still have your medical bills to pay."

"You gonna beat me with one of your crutches?" She offered him a wobbly smile as if knowing him incapable of doing violence.

"Don't think I couldn't, but I will never be like Newton Smalls. I need to get over my mad. I'm taking you to the ranch this afternoon instead of tomorrow morning."

"Why that ain't a punishment. It's a reward."

"It's cooling off time. Go pack for the weekend."

As soon as she left, he called Lorena Ranch, lucky to find his ever-busy mom at home. "Hey, do you mind if I bring Ella over right now instead of tomorrow morning?"

"To be honest, it is inconvenient. On Labor Day, she said she had nothing for the baby, so we're planning a surprise shower for her. Your sisters are coming, Mintay Bullock, Marvelle and some others from the clinic, Mawmaw Nadine, whoever I could get at short notice. Corazon is working on the food, and we've ordered a cake. We have a nice crib and a changing table left over from Edie she can have."

"I've been meaning to take care of those things."

"Well, time is nigh, Teddy. She could go into labor any minute."

"I know, I know. It's just that Ella burned a big hole in my bank account making long distance calls back home. I'm kind of p.o.'d with her right now." A good son simply didn't use foul language with Mama Nell, and he went for the initials.

"You should know we'll help you cover whatever you need. She really is your sister by the way. We used her blood sample at the clinic and sent it off to see if it matched your DNA from the test we had done to determine if Joe really was your father when you first came to us."

"Ella agreed to that?"

"You know how it is with medical forms. They shove a stack of papers in front of you with a bunch of x's telling you where to sign, and you do. Since I married Joe Dean Billodeaux, I take nothing for granted. You never know what will happen in this family. Best to make sure we aren't being conned." People always underestimated Mama Nell because of her small size, assuming she'd be a pushover. If anything, she was more logical and hardheaded than her genial husband—except when pregnant he'd probably add.

"I never doubted she belonged to the Wilkes family, her eyes, her accent, the things she knew about my mother, but thanks for looking out for me."

"Always. Give me an hour before you leave. We'll hide everything. Tomorrow, we'll get your dad to distract her. He and the other husbands plan to watch football in the theater away from the baby stuff, he said. Maybe he can play a movie for her while we set up the party."

"You are the world's best mother."

"You are my beloved son. Never forget it. We'll survive Hurricane Ella Sue together."

As they disconnected, Ella dragged her old suitcase into the living room. "I'm ready to go!"

"Mom has to get your room ready, so we'll have to

wait a while."

"That room looked fine to me on Monday, better'n any place I ever stayed."

"Fresh sheets, soaps and lotions for the bathroom, you know."

"Just like a hotel."

"Just like. Come on, I'll take you for some soft serve after I clean up from the gym."

Ice cream, a cheap luxury on a now tight budget, but Ella lapped it up like a cat does a bowl of milk. As they ate their cones, Teddy considered what he wanted more than dessert—Jessie Minvielle tonight in his bed. He checked his watch, repeatedly. At last, they hit the road driving somewhat over the speed limit in a mobility van. The sad state of the backroads made him slow down, but he had Ella at the gates where she was once refused entrance in record time. Ella Sue, thrilled to be there, took no notice of his quick departure with nothing more than a peck on the cheek for his mother.

As soon as he passed the first bend in the road, Teddy turned into a farm lane bordered by tall sugarcane awaiting harvest and whipped out his much-abused phone. He called Jessie's number and waited somewhat breathless. She answered.

"Jess, would you like to move our date to tonight— dinner at Don's? I took Ella to the ranch early. Did you know my mom is planning a baby shower for her tomorrow?" His rush of words seemed to amuse her.

"I was invited to the shower, but told them I had other plans. You are my other plan. I'll get her a gift when I see what else she received. Yes, to moving up our date to tonight. Not sure about going to a restaurant. I hate being gawked at by kindly strangers, or worse, friends. Let's get takeout."

"I don't think so. You need this experience, and believe me, it is all in the planning. Sticks and stones may break my bones, but gawkers never hurt me. Wear something nice."

"Teddy, no!"

"Pick you up at seven." He disconnected before he got further protests, found the number for the restaurant, made reservations, a couple of special requests, and gave some thought to how to spent the rest of the evening. Yes, it was all in the planning.

The rumbling noise of a high-rise tractor heading his way on giant tires interrupted those thoughts. Teddy backed out of its way and onto the crumbling tarmac. Plenty of time to dispose of the cigarette butt, air out the apartment, and put condoms in the night table drawer.

Chapter Fourteen

Dale Minvielle knocked on her daughter's bedroom door. "You need any help, honey?"

"No, I'm fine." Jessie wanted to add, "Leave me alone," but spared her mother for a change.

She sat naked in her chair rummaging in a dresser drawer that held her underwear. There it was under a pile of athletic bras, the one of black lace with a front clasp and matching panties. Where were those panties? Crumpled in a corner behind the cotton bikini briefs she wore to PT. Putting them on would have been easier with her mom's assistance, but who wanted their mother to see their sexy underwear? She bent and worked them over her feet, drew the lace up laboriously shaved and lotioned legs, and raised her hips, tugging to get the panties into place. The bra wasn't half the trouble.

Finding the dress, the classic little black one she'd worn to more formal university events, proved harder. It had worked its way to the back of a line of gym clothes and the khakis and knit shirts she wore as a trainer. Jessie made a gap in the hangers and burrowed in after it, pulling it off the hangar and revealing another dress far more magnificent sealed in a plastic bag—her wedding gown. She shoved the rest of her wardrobe back into place, obscuring it again. Having no zipper, the simple black dress slid easily over her head.

She raised up and smoothed it beneath her. Sitting, an inch or two draped her knees. The bra gave her some lift and cleavage.

Jessie brushed her hair again, stroking it into place, arranging a few locks over her shoulders. She strung a fine chain around her neck bearing a gold fleur-de-lis pendant and affixed small matching earrings. Only the problem of the shoes remained to be overcome. The pair she wanted sat in a stack of boxes behind pairs of athletic shoes. One by one, she opened the boxes of footwear she did not use anymore, came across the crystal-studded white satin that matched the wedding gown, and slammed the lid shut. The next yielded the red high heels she wanted, not stilettos, but they did have some kick to them. Cross one leg over the other, put them on, set her feet into place.

The doorbell rang. She made one last check of her makeup and touched up her red lipstick. Whatever else, Jessica Minvielle intended to be the best turned out cripple at Don's Seafood. She opened her door and wheeled out to meet Teddy garbed in a suit and tie and leaning on his sticks as he talked to her parents like a nervous prom date. "I'm ready to go."

"I see you are. Great shoes," Teddy said.

Her mother's thin face developed a crease between the eyes as she stared at the shoes and the stuffed backpack on the rear of her chair. "How late will you be?"

"I don't know. I expect to be back sometime Sunday." There, she'd laid it on the line. She intended to spend the weekend with Teddy Billodeaux. In the past, neither parent would have thought twice about her doing the same with Troy. Jessie swore the last time she'd seen that expression on her mom's face, she'd been leaving for her first sleepover at age six.

"Take good care of my girl," Coach Mo said.

"I will, sir." By now, Teddy had developed a flush. "If you could get the wheelchair down the stairs out front I can take it from there."

"Usually, they haul me in and out through the garage like the trashcans," Jessie snarked.

Coach Mo ignored the comment. "No problem." They went out the front door. He tipped the chair back, bumping it down two brick steps.

His wife followed, still anxious. "Call if you need a ride or anything."

"I'll make sure she gets home. Please, don't worry. I have lots of firsthand experience dealing with people in wheelchairs," Teddy said, trying to lighten the moment. He helped Jessie into the front seat and let her dad load the chair to save time. No doubt, he wanted to be gone, and so did Jessie.

As they drove to the old downtown area of Lafayette with its once premier department store now turned into a museum, and its small shops mostly converted to bars and cafés, Jessie confided, "I wish they'd stop babying me. You don't seem to have any trouble with that in your family."

"Because I've always been this way. You're all still adjusting. Go easy on them."

He turned into the lot of the venerable restaurant and swung the van into one of the handicapped spaces. Immediately, an eager bus boy, young and nervous, ran to their vehicle, unloaded the chair, and held it for Jessie. She slid into the seat. "You want me to push you?"

"No, thanks."

He ran ahead to open the heavy wooden door at the end of a walkway lined in wrought iron and tropical plants. Up a short ramp, and they were inside being escorted to a table for two in the rear. Jessie noticed she wasn't the only one in a wheelchair. An elderly couple, dressed for a big occasion, sipped champagne. Both were disabled by the many afflictions of age, but they smiled into each other's eyes. Neither stared as she passed. A small wave of envy passed over her at the depth of their love.

In the raw bar, the more casually dressed sucked oysters from the shell and chased them down with beer, too busy to gawk. Their bus boy yanked away the chair Jessie did not need and felt compelled to hold the other out for Teddy who leaned his crutches against the wall and sat down. He tipped the help generously.

A waitress hurried over, took their drink orders, two white wines, and coaxed them into having the alligator tidbits as an appetizer. Both ordered creamy crab au gratin topped with bubbly cheese, salad, green beans, and a stuffed potato to share. Teddy smiled over the wine and speared a cube of fried gator to dip into a sauce. "We think alike."

"We are alike, only you are better at it."

The meal went well. They spoke of Ella, the upcoming UL game, things they might like to do at the ranch, all the while thinking of things they might want to do back at the apartment. They dawdled over blueberry cheesecake and coffee, and finally prepared to leave. As they waited for the bill, a couple approached their table. The hearty male half of the duo slapped Teddy on the back. "How you doing, Sticks?"

"Still calling the games for UL and the Sinners, Barkley," he answered mildly, despite wincing. "You going tomorrow night?"

"You bet, got season tickets. May not have made it to the NFL, but I still enjoy the game. Now, I'm in sporting goods. This is Dodie, my date. Looks like you're doing all right in that department, too. Coach's daughter, right?"

"Yes, Jessica Minvielle."

"Guess you are made for each other now."

His date, more sensitive despite her bright red hair and bimbo boobs, tugged on his arm. "We should go. Nice meeting you."

"Not 'til I give my old buddy the Barkley bark. Ruff, ruff—ruff, ruff, ruff. Don't do anything I wouldn't do, pal. That gives you lots of leeway."

Eyes turned to stare, not at Jessie, but at the loud ass in the room who barked like a dog. Dodie tried again. "Speaking of leaving, we should." But Barkley spotted another friend and staggered off in that direction.

"Sorry," Dodie said. "He's been drinking. Don't worry, I have the car keys." She stalked after her date on black stilettos.

"Sticks?" Jessie questioned.

"Yeah, that's what they called me in college. Not too many guys lurching around the campus with armband crutches. Better to accept it than let it get under your skin. Just letting you know in case they start calling you Wheels. About what Barkley said. You could totally get an able-bodied guy."

"Maybe I don't want one." There, she'd drawn a smile from his concerned face. On to better things—at the apartment. She suspected Teddy had much more to offer than good advice on being handicapped.

Chapter Fifteen

Teddy ran through a checklist in his head on the way to his place. He'd pushed the cigarette butt into the bushes with the tip of his crutch and aired the apartment. A bottle of wine, purchased after he disposed of Ella at the ranch, chilled in the refrigerator. On the coffee table lay a selection of DVDs—romantic comedy, chick flick, suspense, action. He'd considered some soft porn, but no. He'd stocked his night table with all the accessories. No need to raid Mack's room this time. Planning counted.

They smoothly transitioned to his apartment. "Want to watch a movie, or we could catch a late show at the Grand?"

Jessie fixed her hazel eyes on his. The gold flecks caught the light from a couple of spicy cinnamon scented candles he'd lit to provide atmosphere in his rather plain space. "I'd like to sit on the sofa and make out."

"Hey! You've pre-empted all my smooth moves to get you snuggled against me." He took that as a good sign, a very good sign.

Smiling, she moved to the sofa and moved on him, taking off his tie, unbuttoning his shirt, running her hands over the smooth muscles of his chest, her fingers stirring the light hairs that covered it and making him shiver. He shrugged out of his jacket to free his arms, which went around her, pulling her close, her lips so soft and full, like the bosom pressed against his naked pecs. Teddy removed the dress that came off so easily, not a zipper or button in the way. A bra of black lace with her nipples straining at its seams opened in the front, spilling her breasts into his hands like precious gifts. His fingers stroked, fondled, worshiped them. He wasn't the only one who'd planned ahead.

His hand moved down to that little scrap of provocative panties and worked inside, thumb on her clit, one finger inside. Jessie wouldn't need lube this time around. She slicked his hand. His tongue kept busy in her mouth. When she came, she almost bit him. Quick withdrawal. With her shuddering in his embrace, Teddy brought both arms up, holding her tight to his thudding chest. His own need pressed hard against the fly of his trousers, but he waited to see what she desired.

Jessie's head raised, and he realized the light in her eyes did not come from the candles. "What's next?" she asked.

He had anticipated this question. "The wheelchair straddle, the wedge, you on top, me on bottom or vice versa in the bedroom."

"Let's try the first one."

Teddy removed the armrests from her chair and the suggestive panties from her hips before seating her there. "What about my shoes?" she said.

"Let's leave them. There is something so sexy about a woman naked except for a pair of red heels. Don't go anywhere." He shoved up on his crutches and headed for the bedroom.

She threw back her head and laughed. "Sure, I'm

going to roll out of here completely bare."

"That would give the campus cops a treat. Way better than chasing drunken male flashers."

Teddy hobbled to his night table where the penis ring laid waiting. He should have placed it in his pocket. Stripping off the rest of his clothes, he positioned it, glad the cuddle time and the banter had given him a break to deflate a little. He put on his black velour robe, palmed a condom, and went back to Jessie. She laughed again at the erection poking out of the front.

"What? This is my seduction attire. Note the chic black ostomy cummerbund matches."

"You look like a handicapped Hugh Hefner."

"Exactly what I was going for." He handed over the condom. "Would you do the honors?"

"With pleasure."

"No, the pleasure is all mine." Her hands smoothing the rubber on his shaft got him ready to go in no time at all. He removed the little tube of lube from the pocket of his Hefner robe. "To make sure you are ready."

"I am, but the tingle is nice. I'm anxious to see how this works."

"Simple." He drew her forward to the edge of her chair, spread her legs wide, settled on her thighs, and drew back to enter her hot, wet orifice. It closed tight around him, a perfect fit. He moved slowly. Jessie closed her luminous eyes. Teddy gauged her excitement by the rapid rise and fall of her breasts, the soft panting noises emanating from her lips. He held back until she convulsed around him, the best feeling known to man, especially when an explosive ejaculation follows. He laid his head against her shoulder, and she stroked his fine blond hair.

When they'd both settled down, he said, "We should adjourn to the bedroom. I'm guessing we need rest." Teddy backed onto the couch, taking his weight off of her.

"We can do that, but tomorrow I want to try the wedge." Jessie placed her feet in his lap, and he removed the red shoes.

She wanted bathroom time and wheeled off. He'd prepared before the date and would take care of himself again in the morning. For now, he required some downtime. In the bedroom, he disposed of the condom, put the ring back in the drawer, removed his braces, and retired under the fresh, clean sheets. With his hands clasped behind his head on the pillow, he wondered how he compared to Troy Gilbert in the sack. Couldn't help it. The girls he'd attracted previously tended to be artistic types not given to worshipping athletes, but Jessie had been engaged to one.

She got into the bed on her own, rolled close to him, put her head on his chest. He inhaled the scent of the shampoo she used, light and floral. "I know what you're thinking."

"You read minds, do you? Even Xochi can't do that."

"I believe all men wonder how they compare to others. Troy wasn't giving. We had sex when he wanted sex. If he finished first, too bad for me. He didn't plan or try to make the act something beautiful for me. You do, and you are good at it."

He smiled into the darkness. Yes! "There is more to come, lots more, Jessie."

## Chapter Sixteen

Jessie woke to find Teddy gone and the shower running to give away his location. Waiting her turn, she thought about last night. They'd awakened around three a.m., not really up for vigorous sex, but craving some more. Teddy went down on her under the covers, diving in, working her with a talented tongue good for something else other than sports announcing. With Troy, this sexual act only went in one direction—his. She'd never experienced it before. That laving of her cleft—the best, so good she wished she could have wrapped her legs around his shoulders to keep him there, but he stayed plenty long enough to bring her to her peak.

Wanting to reciprocate, she'd taken him in hand. He asked for a condom to avoid soiling the sheets. She groped in his night table drawer and laid her hand down on something cold and hard. "What's this? A gun, Teddy. Do you feel unsafe?"

He settled back against his pillow with a sigh, the moment ruined by forgetting which drawer he'd stored the condoms. "Not exactly. The Billodeauxs are sort of famous. Knox Polk, our ranger manager, but really our bodyguard, insisted all the children learn to shoot, including me. The first time we had target practice, the kick from the weapon he put in my hand pushed my chair backward three feet. 'You need a lighter weapon,' he said. We settled on a .22 double-action Smith and Wesson revolver for personal protection, but honestly, I usually leave it in that drawer. No children around to mess with it. I'll have to lock it up once I become an uncle to Ella's child."

Another new thing to try. Jessie tried to keep the excitement out of her voice. "Do you think I could learn to shoot?"

"Sure. We both have great hand strength. You do have to cock it, but after that it chambers the next round. When we go to the ranch to pick up Ella, I'll have Knox give you a lesson. We can plink at some targets."

"Speaking of great hand strength, let me show you exactly how good mine is." She made the interruption up to him in short order. Whole new worlds were opening for Jessica Minvielle. She'd gone back to sleep wondering what door would open next.

Draped in the silly black velour robe, Teddy rolled into the room. Ridiculous maybe, but the fabric felt warm, inviting, and furry beneath her fingertips last night, much like Teddy himself. As he neared the side of the bed, she turned in his direction, gripped the lapels, and gave him a lingering kiss of thanks. "You make me feel like a woman again."

He nodded solemnly. "Yep, all the girls tell me that."

"You want to see hand strength?" She bopped him on his bicep and doubted it hurt him one bit.

"Instead of hitting on me, why don't you take your turn in the bathroom?"

"I think I will." Jessie rummaged in the backpack on the rear of her chair and dropped a large T-shirt over her head.

"Shucks, I thought you'd stay naked."

"I can always get that way again."

She made use of the shower and commode. Carefully repairing her makeup, Jessie returned to the bedroom to find the night table holding a small tray with warm biscuits, butter, jam, cranberry juice, and coffee, served by a grinning Teddy.

"Not quite breakfast in bed, but very nice."

"I only warmed some of Ella's biscuits. Had mine earlier. We can get something more substantial later."

"This will be fine."

"What would you like to do today? We could watch some of those movies or stroll around campus and let people stare at the wheelchair convoy."

"No, thanks on that last suggestion. A movie, lunch, then that wedge you were talking about."

"In other words, stay in bed most of the day?"

"Exactly."

"I can run the movies on my computer back here." He plumped pillows to put behind her back and removed a chair in the way of the screen directly across from the bed.

Jessie tested his patience with the chick flick, then the rom-com. If Troy had been sitting between them, he would have insisted on the blow-'em-up video first and then the suspense.

"If you think you can scare me off with chick films, you forget I have five sisters and two sisters-in-law. I will neither retreat nor upchuck," Teddy informed her.

Between shows, they ordered takeout Chinese and ate directly from the little white boxes, dribbling sauce and losing grains of rice on her T-shirt and his robe. No need to get dressed, Jessie figured. As they cracked open their brittle fortune cookies while the second movie ran, her thoughts stayed on the wedge, whatever it was. Her fortune read, Explore new adventures. She added in bed, a word game she used to play with the other cheerleaders. No matter how stuffy the phrase on the little slip of paper, putting in bed on the end always livened it up.

They ate the candied apple slices and exchanged sticky kisses.

As another couple got their fictional happy ending, and the credits rolled, Jessie announced, "I am ready for the wedge."

"Stay right where you are." Teddy worked his way out of bed. He opened his closet. "Now, where did I put it?" He moved a spare wheelchair collapsed against the wall. "Always have an extra. They do break down." Shoving a tangle of athletic shoes out of the way with the end of his sticks, he at last found what he wanted in a dark corner. "The wedge." He drew out a triangular piece of foam.

"Kind of disappointing," Jessie teased. "I thought it would be some contraption right out of Fifty Shades."

"I don't do S&M. Now, take off that T-shirt and roll over on your belly."

"You sure you don't?" Feeling a little uneasy, she obeyed his instructions.

But this was Teddy, not Troy. Still, who would have thought a girl could open a drawer in his bedroom searching for condoms and find a revolver? Teddy Billodeaux surprised more often than anyone might have imagined. He positioned the wedge under her hips, raising them into the air, draping her legs down the other side, parting them wide. She felt compelled to say what she didn't want. "I don't do anal."

"Neither do I." Teddy readied himself, climbed on the bed and settled between her legs on his knees. He reached over and prepared her with lubrication.

"This is kind of an awkward position, Ted."

"You'll forget all about it once we get started."

She did. The new angle put pressure on all her pleasure points. With nothing to do on her part, Jessie found herself lost in sensation, his hands running down her torso, tickling along the sides of her breasts, clinging to her shoulders for better purchase. She became aware of every drop of sweat from his forehead as it splashed on her back, felt each deep thrust of his hips as he moved her toward completion. The pillow beneath her head smothered her cries of excitement and soaked up a small amount of drool she'd be embarrassed to admit later. When she finished and after he followed, Teddy left her body limp and satiated. When he removed the wedge, Jessie's sole desire was to turn her head to one side and sleep. She drifted off with Teddy massaging her back and shoulders and startled awake when he shook them gently.

"We need to clean up and get ready to go to the stadium."

"Not going. I'll stay right here in this bed. See you later."

"I'll let you sleep until I'm finished, then it's your turn. Jess, you must try other new stuff and facing the crowd at the game is on the list."

"Your list, not mine."

"I face my handicap every time I go there to call a

game. After a while, people simply stop noticing. Give it a try."

"But you'll be up in the booth, and I'll be down on the field."

"So much action on the field, they'll forget all about you." Another thing about Teddy: hard to win an argument with him.

She succumbed. He'd probably never wedge her again if she refused because she wouldn't deserve the pleasure. "I'll go just this once."

Maybe Jessie knew she'd concede because she'd packed her red trainer's polo and running shoes, but not the khakis. They'd have to settle for her in jeans like any other fan because she no longer had a reason to be down on the field, no longer had a meaningful job. Her unpaid sick leave time, all that she'd earned along with any vacation she'd had coming, expired with this game. Going on disability payments loomed ahead, dark and ugly, but at least she wouldn't be a complete burden to her parents with some money coming in. Might as well get it over with, her last appearance on Cajun Field, because she wasn't coming back!

## Chapter Seventeen

They entered the vast parking area crammed with tailgaters in campers and SUVs, rear hatches open, grills unloaded, tarps up to ward off sun and rain. A faint smell of charcoal and sizzling meat permeated the van. Some fans spotted Teddy's van and waved. A couple of times Jessie thought she heard her name called, but she stared ahead. Predictably, her father waited by Teddy's reserved parking place ready to grab her wheelchair and help her into it. Teddy left his behind, relying on his sticks and an elevator to get him to the press box, best view in the stadium.

"See you after the game," he said, lurching away as fast as possible to join his counterpart, an older man named Leo Klein who did the play-by-play, up in the box.

That should have given her warning. Her father walked by her side as she steered toward the team entrance. Coach Mo cleared his throat. "Jess, the team would like you to lead them out onto the field. I'll push."

"I'd rather come out afterward. Maybe once they kick off."

"That would disappoint an awful lot of people, Jessie. Don't let them down. They want to do something nice for you."

"Kind, you mean. No, thanks."

Oh, but Teddy had timed it well. The team, completely kitted out in their red uniforms, gave her a rousing cheer as she entered the locker room area. A banner above the door leading to the field read Welcome Back, Jessie! There would be another one, she knew, waiting for her to burst through as she led the team. The cheerleaders in their crimson halter-tops and black, navel-exposing spandex leggings lined up on either side and rustled their pom-poms. One of them thrust a pair into Jessie's unwilling hands. "Lead us to victory, Jessica!" she demanded. From where she sat, Jess figured she could probably land a blow in the girl's solar plexus and knock the wind right out of her. Though her fist balled, Jessie held back. They paid cheerleaders for this kind of crap—sign making, pom-pom shaking, relentless cheerfulness, win or lose. She'd been one of them once and couldn't fault her.

Forcing a bright smile perfected at high school and college games, she said, "Let's roll!" And get over this. Coach Mo went into action, and sure enough, they crashed through a large paper banner and onto the field with the Ragin' Cajuns thundering behind. The crowd went into a chant. "Give 'em hell, UL! Give 'em hell, UL!" Over the roar, Teddy's mellow announcer's voice said, "Welcome back to everyone's favorite trainer, Jessica Minvielle. This game is dedicated to you." The chant stopped for an enormous round of applause.

Finding herself in the middle of the field, she kept that shining smile in place and waved those pom-poms high for the duration of clapping hands. At last, her father pushed her to the sidelines and parked her at one end of the bench, deserted as the players warmed up. She let the smile drift from her face and the pom-poms drop to the ground.

One of her fellow trainers thrust bottles filled with a sport drink into her hands. "Keep 'em hydrated, Jessie." Of course, he went off to assist those with minor injuries in doing their stretches. She'd been demoted to water bottle spritzer, an honor usually given to eager students, many of them female, who really, really wanted to be down on the field with the players hygienically delivering mouthfuls of liquid through the bars of their facemasks. So humiliating.

Trying to disappear, she slumped in her chair and waited for the ordeal to end, but they gave her no peace. She suspected a conspiracy to keep her busy as player after player squatted low enough to get a drink from her bottles. On the field, the game progressed against a Sunbelt Conference rival, not one of the large universities who paid to practice against a weaker team. The Cajuns did seem motivated, whether by her presence or simply because the team was always motivated for the first game of the year. Knowing how superstitious athletes could be, she did not want to become their good luck charm, forced to attend every game, and almost hoped they'd lose. How petty of her.

A player went down after a long sprint toward the goal. As a medic and a couple of the trainers jogged onto the field, Teddy's voice filled the gap in the action. "That's number 51, X-avier Hopkins being helped off the field. A native of New Iberia and a graduate of Westgate High School, X-avier is a tight end JUCO transfer who just moved the chains forty yards for UL. Let's give him some encouragement." Light applause rose from the audience. More were interested in the resumption of the game that might give the Cajuns their first score.

"Jessie, leg cramp. Massage it out," her father barked.

The two male trainers big enough to help a two-hundred-pound, six-foot-one tight end to the table laid X-avier out stomach down. "He's all yours, Jess."

"Shit, this hurts," the player said, as she positioned herself and dug her fingers into his knotted calf muscle, forcing it to relax. "You got strong hands for a girl. Hey, that pinches."

"My bad. I have to trim my nails." She continued massaging until the caramel-colored leg smoothed beneath her fingers. "You can sit up now."

X-avier swung his legs over the side of the table. Jessie shoved a cup of Gatorade into his hands of impressive size. "Drink, then get some more. Don't let yourself go dry in this heat."

"You're strict like my mama. I like that." X-avier treated her to a flirtatious grin, but a roar went up from the UL fans and it faded. "Damn, that shoulda been my touchdown," X-avier moped.

Teddy's voice gave last season's statistics on the kicker trotting out for the extra point. "And it's good!"

"You'll get another chance. This is only the first game." Her chances of being around for the second, not so high.

"You give one good massage, my lady. I'm gonna ask for you every time I got a cramp."

"Thanks. Not sure I'll be around after tonight."

"Don't see why not. Like you said, it's only the first game. Say, you want to go out sometime?"

Jessie started to point out her wheelchair-bound situation, but stopped when she considered that X-avier, a splendid figure of a young black man with a cross and "Praise the Lord" tattooed on one bicep and "Mom" encircled with thorny roses on the other, probably had twenty-twenty vision and did not need to have the obvious pointed out. Besides, he'd witnessed that well-meant greeting in the locker room. Her next defense might have been their age difference, but she didn't go there either.

As the UL defense took the field, Teddy came on the air again. "Looks like trainer Jessica Minvielle has X-avier Hopkins up and ready to run again."

"I appreciate the offer, but I'm in a relationship." It might not last beyond tonight if Teddy didn't desist in dropping her name all over the crowd like Mardi Gras beads, but a good enough excuse for now.

"Him?" X-avier jerked a head with a moderate fro matted down by sweat and his helmet toward the booth. "I know Teddy. Seen both of you working out at the rehab place. Pretty impressive what you can do."

"Again, thank you." Jessie tried her best to hold in a smile, but it burst forth, lighting her face.

"Great smile and great hands. If you and Teddy break up, you let me know."

"The ball is loose!" Leo Klein declared high above them. The players formed a scrum, trying to squeeze the ball from the guy on the bottom of the pile. The refs blew their whistles and began to unravel the heap, tapping each participant on the shoulder, telling them to get up. Two walked away limping. "UL's ball!"

"You're in, Hopkins. Jessie, check that ankle coming off the field." Coach Mo turned his attention to the game and the play clock.

Their cornerback, who had retrieved the fumble,

hobbled to the table and sat down. She removed his cleats and probed the ankle. Only a slight sprain. Jessie wrapped the ankle and applied cold packs. "Lie down. Keep it elevated." She shoved a rolled towel under his foot.

"Think I can play again, Jessie?" He looked so mournful, a person would think she'd suggested amputation.

She knew this guy from the past two years, a man headed toward the pros regardless of the fact that he played for a small college because he had determination and a will to do his best. "If it doesn't hurt when you stand on it—and don't lie to me when you get up. Otherwise, you'll be out a week or two. Not a big deal."

"Thanks for fixing me up, Jess."

After that, she dealt with a string of minor injuries, taping thumbs and toes, more cramps, issuing temporary braces of various kinds, advising players to get on the bicycle to keep their muscles warm as the sun went down, not that it cooled off all that much. She sat in on the pep talk at halftime.

"Yes, we're ahead by two scores. We still have to play the second half with all we've got. No one gives up or expects the other guy to do their job. Understood?"

"Yes, Coach Mo!" rumbled the team as if they were a squad of Marine recruits.

Once or twice, her dad glanced her way as if his words also applied to his daughter. No one on his team gives up. They do their job. She did the one she'd trained for the rest of the game.

After a twenty-eight to seventeen victory in their favor, the players insisted she lead them off the field again. She kept on rolling out to the sidewalk and Teddy's van after giving a cheery wave and the best smile she could muster. He father would be a while dealing with the local media. She had no idea what Teddy's shutdown routine was, or how long it took.

Under the glaring lights of the parking area and the gridlock as drivers jockeyed for a chance to escape to an exit, night settled over her like a velvet blanket far too hot for the temperature. Her high ponytail threaded through a red UL cap felt lank against her neck, and boy, did she need a shower. The heat and humidity had taken a toll on her as well as the players. She paid for her exertions now, but she experienced the good exhaustion of doing a job well done again. Cars honked at her incessantly. She dragged her smile from some deep sweaty pocket of her personality and waved like a beauty queen.

Teddy approached. She recognized the sound of his crutches hitting the concrete despite the hum of traffic. He came on slowly, carefully. Maybe he felt fatigued too, or maybe anticipated her reaction.

She greeted him with, "You set me up."

His pale face pinked beneath the streetlight. Guilty. "Not exactly. Your dad wanted me to persuade you to come to the game. I thought it would be good for you to face the whole enchilada and get it down in one bite. I suggested he see if you could still do your old job, be of use to the team. You were, big time."

"Yeah, I'm exhausted, and I need a shower. I'm going home with my dad."

"Jessie, don't be this way. I have a perfectly good shower, and we haven't used it for sex yet."

"What's this about showers?" Coach Mo boomed

as he neared.

"Ah, nothing. The one at my place is handicapped accessible."

"Got one of those at our house. Ready to go, Jess?"

"Very."

"I thought we could go to the ranch tomorrow and do target practice. Ella will want to show you all her loot from the baby shower before I bring her back to my place."

Jessie cocked her head. "Right now, learning to shoot a gun seems very appealing, and I wouldn't want to disappoint Ella."

"Okay, get a good night's sleep. I'll pick you up around eleven. We can catch the clan for Sunday dinner after they get back from church."

"Fine." She turned her chair briskly and moved away, not sure if she was punishing herself or Teddy more.

Chapter Eighteen

The silent treatment lasted most of the way to the ranch, though Jessie gave her anxious parents a happy goodbye wave as if she were going to cheerleading camp and glad to be on her way. "Did you bring the gun?" she asked as they turned off the highway for the backroad.

"In the glove compartment. Knox will have plenty of ammunition. He always does."

"Good," Jessie answered a little ominously.

As they approached the gate, Teddy said, "Give me a break. We wanted to show you still had a job if you wanted it. Get all the fuss about your accident out of the way and get on with your life."

"I'll bet you're the kind of person who thinks ripping a bandage off fast is better than doing it in stages. That's great if you don't take any skin along with it."

Teddy opened the gate. Okay, she seemed determined to be difficult. He tried a compliment. "You did really well working on X-avier."

"He asked me out."

"What! I mean, that's great. I knew you could get an able-bodied if you wanted. Are you going?" Target practice hadn't started yet, and he'd already shot himself in the foot.

"Of course not. He's too young, and I'd only be a

165

novelty for a while. X-avier is very appealing though, great bod, nice smile, and he loves his mama."

"I didn't mind being a novelty if it got me some—and I love my mother, too."

"You shouldn't mention both in the same sentence. But yes, Miss Nell is wonderful. Same for the rest of your family."

"You don't know Mack, but Mom is convinced the right woman will come along and straighten him out like she did with Dad."

"So a good woman is all it takes?"

"Or the right man, I mean if you are a woman. Which you are." They arrived at the mansion so often called the ranch house before he could experiment with putting his foot in his mouth again.

As usual, fairly easy to tell who had come to watch the opening Sinners' game by the vehicles parked near the door. Xochi drove her husband's husky SUV. His twin sisters' small sub-compacts, as petite as they were, sat next to it. Jude and Annie had probably stayed over after the shower. Brainy Trinity always showed up for Sunday dinner driving his electric Tesla, an environmental statement for him. Judging by the car seats in the back, Stacy had carted the grandchildren from New Orleans. Only family then, though more people might show up later. Mack played with the Cowboys at noon. Dean, Junior, Tom, and his wife were slated for a three o'clock start with the Sinners on the west coast, a good afternoon of football ahead.

Teddy got Jessie set up in her wheelchair before claiming his own. As they pushed through the kitchen door, Corazon raised a crispy stuffed pork roast from the oven. The herbs of the seasoning, bay leaf and garlic among others, filled the room. She followed that with a huge pan of rice dressing.

"Teddy, good, you are here. You slice the French bread for me. Miss Jessie, can you set the table in the dining room? The dishes are already in place." She turned over a bread knife to one and a silverware caddy to the other.

"No one else back from church yet?" Teddy inquired.

"Any minute now, they all come and want to eat fast, fast to watch the game. Jude and Annie, they don't go. They sit with Ella by the pool." Corazon moved the pork roast to a platter and worked the drippings into a rich gravy. "My husband take the rest in the van. I been to the early service already."

In the complicated religious life of the Billodeauxs, that meant Joe, Trin, T-Rex, and Xochi, probably accompanied by Mawmaw Nadine, went to the Catholic Mass while Nell, Stacy and the grandkids went to the Episcopal service since the twins had evaded a dose of sanctity. Mama Nell wouldn't push Ella to attend, though she could most likely use a pinch of godliness. Knox generally read the Sunday paper somewhere in the shade while waiting to pick them up again.

Corazon checked a large pot of simmering green beans boiled with bits of ham, and added a dash of Cajun seasoning, completed her gravy and poured it into two serving boats. Jessie returned with the empty caddy and reported, "No bread pudding on the sideboard, but we have four pecan pies."

The housekeeper sniffed. "Mawmaw Nadine made those pies. Mine are not good enough, she thinks. But I make better cakes." Corazon spread the sliced bread out like a deck of cards into an oblong basket. She popped the heels of the loaf inside a plastic bag and set it by a tower of refrigerator containers, one of them already filled with greens. Plunking the basket into Jessie's lap, she said, "You take to the table, por favor. Teddy, get the salad, bottom shelf. I hear the van."

Putting a layer of rice dressing into the bottom of a container, Corazon forked two pieces of the roast on top and baptized them with gravy. The rest of the sliced pork roast ringed a large platter. She filled another with green beans before pouring the vegetables into a serving dish. "All ready," Corazon announced and began packing Sunday dinner for herself and her husband into a shopping bag.

Teddy returned. "You know, you and Knox are family, especially since Xochi married Junior. You could eat with us. No one would care."

"I care. I like my quiet Sunday afternoon off in our cottage. We watch the same games, but with not so much noise."

"I kind of hate to ask, but would Knox set up some targets for us and show Jessie how to shoot my revolver, maybe at halftime?"

Immediately, Corazon's brown forehead creased. "Why? You got troubles?"

"No, no, just something new for Jessie to learn."

"He do it. I tell him."

That statement seemed to settle the matter as the clan left the van and flowed into the kitchen. One grabbed the platter of meat, another the bowl of vegetables, a third the pan of rice dressing, and a fourth the iced tea from the fridge. Out by the barbecue pavilion, the clang of an iron triangle summoned the people from the pool. Corazon edged toward the kitchen door with her bag. Jessie backed her chair into a corner out of the way of the traffic.

Mawmaw Nadine bullied her way through the throng, calling, "Wait, Corazon, one of my pies is for you." The sturdy old woman fetched it herself and placed it into Knox Polk's hands as he held the door for the girls trooping in from the pool and mingling their scent of sinful Sunday cocoa butter and chlorine with the aftershave and perfume of the family members dressed for church. In a flowing flowered muumuu, Ella trundled to the dining table.

Joe Billodeaux relieved Knox of doorman duty and sent him and Corazon on their way. "Enjoy your peace and quiet. Quick, quick! Game starts in fifteen minutes."

Nell scooted under his arm. "We will not gobble our food. You know they only blather about the game for a while, have to do the National Anthem, coin toss, and all that before beginning. Everyone take a seat. Nice to see you again, Jessie. Why don't you sit next to Teddy?"

Having restored order, Nell Billodeaux took her place at one end of the table and offered a sincere but very brief grace. As the butler and his wife also had the day off, the family passed the various dishes, helping themselves to as much or little as they pleased. Nell granted permission to everyone to cut a piece of pie, top it with whipped cream, and adjourn to the den with their desserts in-hand. She started coffee for those who wanted it, and joined them slightly after the Cowboys kicked off.

Mack scored a dramatic touchdown in the first half

to the cheers of his family, but drew a fifteen-yard penalty on kickoff for excessive celebration as he danced and dabbed in the end zone. His Cajun frustration showing as the game progressed, Joe muttered, "I've told him, me, over and over not to do dat."

At halftime with the Cowboys ahead by seven, Knox Polk summoned Ted and Jessie to handgun practice. He had the paper targets set up in a glade used for the purpose far from grazing livestock and rumbustious children. "Set your break," Teddy cautioned Jessie.

"Yep, I do remember Teddy's first try with a gun." Knox allowed one very swift, thin-lipped smile, so rarely seen, to cross his lean face. "You won't have any trouble, Miss Jessie. You right-handed?"

"Yes."

"Put your right hand high on the grip. That helps with recoil. Left hand around the grip under the trigger guard. Fit your hands together. Extend your arms. Aim with your dominant eye, lining up the sights. Cock your gun and squeeze, don't pull, the trigger. Let it surprise you when it goes off."

Bam! Jessie hit the lower end of the target.

"Got him in the groin, which I guess would do the job, but being in a chair, you might want to aim higher," Knox said, absolutely deadpan.

"Maybe that's where I aimed," Jessie answered.

Again, a flicker of a smile lifted Knox Polk's lips. "Be careful of this gal, Ted. But not bad for a first shot. You have strong hands and arms. Did better than Teddy his first time."

"Hey, I was a skinny twelve-year-old!" Teddy

knew his face burned.

"What counts is that you improved, but you don't come out here and practice enough. Stay as long as you like. I'm leaving plenty of ammo. All casings get picked up before you leave. Teddy, make sure she learns how to clean her weapon when you're through. I've got the end of the game to catch." Knox loped off in long strides.

Jessie emptied the revolver, moving farther toward the center of the target each time. Teddy reloaded and executed a fair cluster in the center of his. "I'm not that bad."

"Sometimes, I wish you were. Look, I appreciate all you are teaching me. Just don't push me before I'm ready."

"I understand. So are you going to call X-avier for a date now?"

"Hardly. My dad wants me to ride on the team bus to Lake Charles this coming weekend. See what you started?"

"Something good, I hope. The Sinners play at home. I'll have to be in New Orleans on Sunday. Ella will be home all week. There goes our opportunity for some more hanky-panky." He punctuated that statement with a regretful smile.

"Yes. I feel like I wasted a night pouting."

"You did."

Jessie swung the unloaded gun his way. Teddy pushed it aside. "Knox would say, never point a gun in anyone's direction unless you intend to use it. Never know when a forgotten bullet might be in the chamber."

"I still have a lot to learn."

"You know I'll help every step of the way."

They resumed practice until they expended the bullets, policed the area, and headed back to the house for the Sinners' game after a Cowboys' victory despite Mack drawing a couple more penalties for taunting. Leftovers for dinner, then back to Lafayette with the red van crammed full of baby furniture and gifts Ella couldn't wait to show Jessie. Teddy hoped he'd given another gift of independence today.

Chapter Nineteen

Awkward, trying to set up a crib when sitting in a wheelchair, but Teddy managed with help from Jessie and Ella. The changing table went easier. The women stretched the soft cotton sheets covered with pink and blue bunnies over the mattress, washed and dried the little onesies in mild detergent, and put them in a drawer. Being nurses, the twins had gifted Ella with practical items: king-sized sacks of disposable diapers, packages of wet wipes, and a warmer to make them more acceptable to a baby's behind. Teddy had no idea such things existed. A baby carrier sat in one corner of the now-cramped bedroom, and out in the living room, a carriage the size of a small yacht lay folded in on itself awaiting the arrival. A large but stylish diaper bag sat next to it. Bottles and nipples awaiting sterilization cluttered the kitchen counter. Who knew babies required so much equipment? Women, he guessed.

Ella mounted a mobile of colorful butterflies on one end of the crib and folded a hand-crocheted blanket of multicolored yarn over the side. "Ain't it pretty? Xochi's friend, Miss Rosemarie, give it to me. Her granny made it long ago, but it's just like new. Maybe this furniture is used stuff to the Billodeauxs, but it's better'n anything I could afford to buy."

Teddy and Jessie exchanged glances. He shrugged, remembering the blanket the old seer made for him long before he arrived at the ranch. Multicolored—who knew what that meant? Teddy eyed Ella's belly. Not twins, he hoped, but she certainly seemed big enough.

"Have you picked out any names for the baby?" Jessie asked.

"Wyatt Wilkes Smalls for a boy. I want something classy for a girl, so I thought Elizabeth Jane after those two ladies in the movie we watched."

"I like them both." Each noticed the touch of wistfulness in Jessie's voice.

"I shouldn't have asked you to help me set up on account of maybe you can't have babies. I'm real sorry about that," Ella said with more sensitivity than anyone would have credited to her.

Jessie's bright smile broke through. "But I can, or so the doctor told me. I wasn't paying much attention at the time."

Ella stared at the wheelchair. "How you gonna manage that?"

"The same way you are. Taking care of a baby might be more of a challenge for me, but thanks to Teddy, I know I can do it."

"Teddy knocked you up?"

At his appalled expression, both women burst into laughter. "No, not yet," Jessie said, giving a hint to their recent relationship.

"I hope if he does, he treats you better'n my boyfriend did me." Ella's mirth evaporated like fog in a mountain pass.

"I know I could count on Teddy. I'd like to help you take care of yours to get some practice."

"Oh, I'd love that. I really don't know what I'm doing, even with all those classes my brother dragged me to."

"Between the three of us, we'll manage. You aren't alone."

"No, no, I'm not." As an afterthought, Ella added, "I appreciate that."

"If we're done here, Jessie and I should get in some gym time."

"All this setting up wasn't enough exercise?" Jessie questioned.

"Slacker. Get your things. We'll only be gone a couple of hours, but I'm leaving my phone in case you need me, Ella. No long-distance calls, okay? The number for the gym is in the contacts list."

"Sure. I'll behave. Gonna lie down for a while. Have a good workout, you two." Ella studied the top of her belly, not looking her brother in the eye, a bad sign, Teddy believed.

"I mean it, Ella. I'm having trouble paying these big bills you ran up."

"Said I'd be good."

"Right. Let's go, Jessie."

They put in two hours of sweat time and went to relax in the juice bar before heading back to the apartment. One of the women from the front desk found them there splitting a banana pineapple smoothie. "Phone call for you, Teddy. She says it's an emergency."

The word hello had barely left his lips when Ella sobbed out her situation. "I got up to pee and now it's coming down my legs. I can't stop it."

"That's not pee. Didn't you pay any attention in the Signs of Labor class? Your water broke. Just go sit on the pot until we get there. We have to take you to the hospital asap!"

"What if the baby falls out in the toilet water?"

"Doubt that will happen, but if it does, just fish it out really quick. We're on our way." Teddy sent a desperate glance to Jessie. "It's show time."

"So I gathered. I'd like to go with you. Birth can take hours. I could spell you with Ella."

"That would be great."

They found a tearful Ella in her nightie squatting on the commode. "Now there's pains too."

"We're only minutes from the hospital. Don't panic," Teddy said, though he directed the last words at himself. "Where's your hospital bag?"

"In my bedroom by the crib."

Not taking the time to transfer to his wheelchair, he swung his crutches in that direction. Ella's bedding lay tossed on the floor. He trod in a wet spot as he moved toward the crib. Teddy crinkled his nose, that stench of smoke again, its source coming from the bottom of a Burger King coffee cup on the night table where a cigarette butt swam in the dregs. The odor thinly disguised another scent he had no time to analyze. Couldn't chew her out now. He grabbed the bag and called to Jessie. "I got it. Put a towel between her legs and a light blanket over her shoulders, and let's go."

With the multicolored afghan from the crib thrown over her thin shoulders, Ella walked like a bow-legged cowboy to the van. Jessie followed with more towels in her lap and laid them out on the front seat to make a thick wad for the leaking girl. Ella seated herself and buckled up before Teddy told her to do it for a change. Instead, he faced another quandary.

"Jess, I really want you to come, but just don't

have time to fool with the ramp. You stay here and get cleaned up. As soon as I get my sister settled, I'll come back for a shower and pick you up."

He waited for anger or disappointment, but got a nod of understanding tinged with a little sadness that jumping into a van to go anywhere quickly was no longer a part of her life. Jessie shut the door and rolled back to give the van room. She watched them out of sight. He made the left onto Johnston Street, passed the Agricultural Center and the old Colosseum, right onto Bertrand, and straight to the emergency entrance of University Medical Center, cursing the snarl of traffic and the impediment of red lights all the way. Ella unsnapped her seatbelt and yanked at the door handle.

"No, stay here. I'll get a wheelchair." One thing Teddy felt sure of—a frantic man on armband crutches always got attention. People waiting with feverish children or blood-soaked rags wrapped around minor injuries sure to require stitches stared. He swung toward the reception desk, not bothering with the careful placement of his feet as he usually did, and almost stumbled into the face of the woman shuffling paperwork. "I have a woman in labor in my van, the red one. Her water broke."

Though she looked up, the woman with gray eyes who'd seen a thousand emergencies merely nodded. "Are you the father?"

"No, her brother, her birth-buddy. She's my sister."

"Yes, I understand that. Are you preregistered?"

"Yes, we are. Ella Sue Smalls is the patient. I'm Teddy Billodeaux, responsible for the bills. She's in the van. She needs a wheelchair."

"Do you also require a wheelchair?"

"No, I have my own."

She tapped at a keyboard with practiced efficiency. "Here you are." A printer spit out wrist tags and other necessary papers. In some magical way, she'd also summoned an orderly. "Woman in the red van needs a ride to the maternity ward. Mr. Billodeaux, go along and please move your vehicle to a parking space."

"Sure, right." He followed the wheelchair pusher to the van. Sweat dripped off of him from the exertion and anxiety. His clothes remained damp from the gym. His hair, lank and stringy, hung in his eyes. Ella Sue, golden hair recently washed and bed-tossed, makeup applied even if her pink lipstick had smeared a little, nails polished the way Jessie showed her but with one broken off, looked considerably better than he did if the image in the side view mirror didn't lie. Only their wide, frantic blue eyes matched. The attendant eased his sister into the wheelchair and jogged away with her.

By the time Teddy parked the van and returned, an aide already worked at mopping up the trail of dribbled birth fluids that led to the closed box of the steel elevator. He pressed the Up button three or four times. "Mr. Billodeaux, your paperwork," the registrar called. She kindly reminded him of the floor of the maternity ward as well. Exiting the lift, he humped to the nurses' station. "Ella Sue Smalls?"

They issued the number of the labor room and sent him on his way. Teddy absorbed the sounds of various television programs as he passed, and startled at the scream of a woman loud and anguished enough to raise the hairs on his arms, all overlaying the pings of medical monitors. At first, he'd tried to convince Ella to try a birthing room, so nicely decorated in soothing colors, complete with a rocking chair, and less costly because a natural birth did not require anesthetic or a delivery room. Midwives charged less too. Now, he rejoiced that he hadn't gone cheap.

"There he is," a nurse remarked cheerfully as he burst in the door. "We'll need those papers and especially the wristband. See, Ella, one for you and a matching one for your baby. No mix-ups." She applied the band to Ella's arm.

Already garbed in a hospital gown and modestly covered, his sister sat swinging her pale legs like a restive child on the gurney. "About time you got here. I'm in pain, and they won't give me nothing."

"She's only three centimeters. We can't do the epidural until she reaches five." He could tell the nurse had said this many times before.

"Yeah, I know. I told her the breathing exercises were necessary. Ella, deep cleansing breath, then hee-hee-hoo, hee-hee-hoo. Remember?"

"Well, now the pain went away."

"Get ready for next time."

A gentle inquiry and a mild reassurance issued forth. "Are you the daddy? Ella admitted trying to bring on labor, but no harm done. Nothing to worry about. The baby is quite ripe and ready to come into the world."

"No, I'm her brother. Did she try to harm herself?" He knew his sister hated being pregnant, but surely she wouldn't try to break her own water?

The nurse and the LPN in the room exchanged an amused glance. "Perhaps the father had to leave for work earlier this morning. As I said, not unnatural this late in the game."

"There is no father. I'm her birthing partner."

The nurse administered a deft change of subject. "Then you know what comes next. We need to shave her and administer the enema. You should step outside until we finish. Here." The nurse offered a large plastic bag. "Why don't you take her personal items to the car?"

"That's my best nightgown, Teddy. Needs handwashing, and you take care of the afghan, too, because it belongs to the baby," Ella Sue ordered.

His mind still held an image of his sister on the toilet with a thin cotton nightie hiked up around her hips. So sheer he could see her pregnancy-darkened nipples, the neckline possessed a merry circle of brightly embroidered flowers—another gift from Xochi, no doubt. "Sure, I'll take care of it. I might go home and clean up. I'll bring Jessie back with me. We won't be long."

"Good. I'd like to have another woman around since Mama can't be here."

"Yeah, I wish she could be here too. Sorry I didn't have a chance to see her again." And tell her he understood his abandonment now and thank her for the good life she'd given him. He'd see this baby had a great beginning and an existence full of opportunities to repay her sacrifice. As he headed down the corridor toting the plastic sack, the woman enduring natural birth screamed again. He moved a little faster to the parking lot.

Back at the apartment, Jessie didn't hear him enter over the blast of a hairdryer. He stood in the bathroom entry watching her honey-brown hair float around her head on the waves of warm air. Low of him to want to spend some time in bed with her when his sister labored in the hospital. Jessie wore fresh clothes and new makeup. He wanted nothing more than to sneak in and kiss the nape of her neck, but she glimpsed him in the mirror. Teddy hoped his naked desire didn't show in his face.

"How's Ella doing?"

"We got her checked in. Right now, she's in a labor room jonesing for the epidural. I need to get a quick shower and do the rest of my routine in case it's a long haul."

"I'll get out of your way. I can finish drying my hair in the bedroom." She swung around, and he homed in for a kiss on her lush lips so perfectly painted like Ella's. He left a smear behind and wiped at it with his thumb.

"Sorry."

"Worth the redo." Her cheeks flushed slightly, and he credited himself with causing the blush. But no. "I think Ella might have been doing the same with a man while we were gone. I striped her bed and used the soiled sheets to mop up the puddle and the dribble to the bathroom. They reeked of sex, Teddy."

He shared in her embarrassment. "I think that's what the nurse tried to imply about her, an attempt to get labor started."

"It's possible. I have married friends who've told me they tried the same at the end of their pregnancy to bring on labor—the fun way, they said. Sometimes it works."

"But who would do that for her? One of the food delivery guys? She's gotten to know them really well and tips high with my money."

Jessie tossed her half-dry tresses. "I think someone who smokes and drinks Burger King coffee like the guy I caught her with when she got ahead of me. I don't know how, but I believe she hooked up with him."

Teddy shook his head in disbelief. "That would be dangerous for her and the baby. What if he carries some disease?"

"I don't think consequences rank high on her list. They'd fall to the bottom buried under the lives of the rich and famous and the latest hairstyles. She wants what she wants immediately, no waiting. I hate to say this about your sister, but she's fairly shallow in the gene pool."

"Oh, I think she's sharp enough, just ignorant. It's pretty obvious she didn't make her boyfriend use a condom, but a total stranger? I didn't see a used one laying around."

"No sign of it, unless the guy flushed it, but the sheets had that semen smell."

"This explains why she prettied up only to take a nap and put on a nice nightgown—which she wants hand-washed by the way, along with the baby's afghan."

Jessie gave him an eye roll worthy of a disgusted teen. "I'll take care of that for you. All the baby things should be washed in a mild detergent."

"You seem to know a lot about this."

"Tons of babysitting and a dozen baby showers, though I haven't been to any lately. I wish people wouldn't assume I can't reproduce simply because I can't walk."

Teddy wanted to wipe that sudden sadness off her face. "Hey, lots of people think I must be impotent, which is way worse. I had to prove them wrong."

Her lips formed a slight crescent of a smile. "Want me to write you a testimonial?"

"Actually, that would be great. I could frame it and hang it over the bed."

He loomed close enough to her to receive a light blow to his bicep. "For other women to read, no way!"

"We need to get ready for the hospital. Jess, I'm glad you're here." He settled for a light kiss and a slight shove of her wheelchair toward the door. "I won't take long."

By the time, he finished, Jessie had the nightgown soaking in a basin and the sullied sheets washing in the stacked washer and dryer unit stowed in one of the small closets. "My cleaning lady usually does the sheets, but thanks."

"I doubt they'll keep Ella more than overnight once the baby arrives. We'll have to make up her bed again before she comes home if these are your only sheets."

"Oh, I have plenty of clean sheets thanks to my mom and Corazon. When I left for college they made sure I came fully equipped."

"Shouldn't we call them?"

"No, the whole family will come running. This is my responsibility, but I appreciate your being here. So you ready to help bring a baby into the world?"

"Nothing I'd like to do more."

Chapter Twenty

They found a much happier Ella hooked up to an IV and a fetal monitor, and by the smile on her face, an epidural. "I've never seen a primipara get to five centimeters so fast," her nurse said.

"Willpower," Ella claimed. "Glad you came along, Jessie. Now I have someone to talk to." She clutched the television remote. "About time for Price Is Right. Mama and me used to watch it every day. I know the price of everything."

Teddy would bet she did.

"Oh, we'd sit together, and she'd say how you lived on a ranch with a pool and a gym and horses to ride and servants to wait on you hand and foot just like some of these western spa trips they give away. She wished she could get that for me too. No, you dummy, six-thousand-eight hundred for a resort in Arizona! It ain't Paris," his sister shouted at an inept contestant. "This would be great if only I had a co-cola right now. My soaps are on after this."

"No soft drinks. You'll only throw them up like they said in class. I can get her ice chips, right?" Teddy asked the nurse.

"Yes, I'll show you where. Looks like Ella is in good hands. I'll check her progress from time to time, but now it's mostly a waiting game."

Ella took her eyes off the ring being offered to

contestants on the screen. "Five-thousand-ninety-nine. Those are biddy diamonds, not like Stacy's big rock. How long?"

"No one knows. Don't do any pushing until we tell you. I'll be watching." The nurse wagged a motherly finger at her and led Teddy off in search of ice chips.

By the time he returned, Jessie had her manicure kit out trimming the broken nail and repairing chips in Ella's polish. Ella put out her free hand for the cup of ice, took a mouthful, and crunched it. "I think you're supposed to suck on that slowly."

"You're just a big, ol' party pooper, Teddy. If I didn't have so many things stuck in me, this would be like a trip to the spa. That enema was no pleasure, though, and only done because the doctors don't want me to shit on their hands."

"Lots of stars do deep cleansing. Look at it that way," Jessie said.

"Then, they must be nuts. Wish I had some corn nuts right now. Didn't eat much for breakfast, only that biscuit and jelly. Felt a little off. Should have known this was coming on."

Teddy debated about asking her if she'd had a visitor, but delayed. She'd only lie. He and Jessie took turns going for breaks, having that cola Ella wanted out of sight, and getting some dinner in the hospital cafeteria. By the time the evening news came on, their patient had lost her bounce. She perked up a bit when Wheel of Fortune played, but faded again when sitcoms and dramas aired.

After the nurse arrived to check her monitors and the progress under the sheets, Teddy gave in and called the ranch. This birthing business took a very long time.

Besides, his mom would want to know.

"Do you need some company? Xo and I could come," Nell said.

"No, Jessie is here with me."

"That's good. This shouldn't all be on you, brother or not."

"I'll let you know when the baby is here. Maybe you could bring flowers or balloons or something since she has no family but me."

"Will you call her father?"

"Hell, no. He threw her out. She can contact him if she wants. I'll be in touch."

He returned to the room to get the news. "Eight centimeters. We have a little way to go yet, but before midnight, I'd say."

"What the hell! I been here near all damn day seems like."

"Since noon. Seven hours would be quite a short labor for a first baby. A couple more should do it." The nurse moved on to her other patients.

"A couple more fuckin' hours! I'm thirsty and starving."

"Entering transition," Teddy murmured to Jess. "She doesn't mean it."

"Yes, I sure damn do!"

"Want me to rub your belly with lotion?" her brother offered.

"Shit, no. My own brother rubbing my belly— that's too Uncle Merv the Perv for me. But Jessie can do it."

Jessie's brows shot up at the odd reference, but she accepted the tube of lotion from the birthing bag. Teddy stepped out to get more ice chips. At this point, he knew nothing would please his sister. Truth to tell, he loitered a little and had some coffee to sustain him through the night. Then feeling like a coward, he returned to give Jessie a break. To have her here helping him meant all the world to him.

The labor room smelled of roses from the lotion. "Couldn't feel that, but the scent surely is nice." Ella took a deep inhale and accepted the ice chips. Afterward, she appeared to doze.

"Her belly is rock hard when she has a contraction. You can see how long they last on the monitor. I don't believe it will be two hours," Jessie confided.

"The sooner the better. I don't know why any woman would want to do this."

"I would, gladly."

"I'll bet you wouldn't complain as much either."

"I can't promise that."

Teddy took Jessie's hands and raised them to his lips. They were soft and sweet smelling from the lotion. "I am truly grateful you are here. I thought I could go through this alone. I know my mom would have helped, but I wanted to flaunt my independence again. Sometimes that's just dumb. Anyhow, glad we are sharing this."

Jessie reclaimed her hand and used it to brush the fine, blond hair from his forehead. She placed a kiss on his brow. "Anytime you need me, just ask."

Ella's blue eyes popped open. "Well, if you two are done cooing like a pair of mourning doves, one of you could call that nurse. I swear I want to push. She needs to get her ass in here."

Teddy tangled in his crutches in his haste to get up, straightened out, and moved as fast as he could to the nurse's station. A page went out for their nurse. By the time he traversed the long hallway again, she'd arrived, checked the vital signs and the mystery under the sheets again.

"We have crowning. Well done, Ella, only eight hours. We'll have the doctor here in a moment. Mr. Billodeaux, if you are going to witness the birth, wash your hands and put on the gown and booties in the bathroom. I'm sorry, miss, but only one person can attend."

"That's all right. I'll go to the waiting room." Jessie smiled as Teddy took his own deep, cleansing breath. She made way for the doctor, an Indian woman in the expected white lab coat.

After doing her own inspection, the doctor declared, "Yes, we are ready for the delivery room."

Teddy moved along behind the gurney, his feet slipping in the booties, paper gown flapping around him, his hair confined under a cap. They stationed him at Ella's shoulder. When asked if she wanted to watch the birth in a mirror, she said, "Hellll, no!" Privately, he was a little disappointed and yet a little relieved. His only task seemed to be encouragement and lifting Ella's shoulders to help her push. The pushing lasted longer than he anticipated.

"This is a big baby, coming slowly. We will do the episiotomy and use the forceps to help the birth along. Nothing to worry about," their doctor reassured them.

"Teddy, Teddy, they gonna cut me open?" Ella turned desperate eyes on him. "I don't want no big scar up my belly."

"No, Ella. The episiotomy is a cut to keep your vagina from tearing. They'll sew you right up. It's no big deal."

Teddy noticed the doctor's dark eyes crinkle at the corners, an indication of a smile behind the mask. "Someone has done their homework. What a good daddy he will be."

"Uncle. I'm the uncle."

"Also good." All the while, the doctor's hands worked under the drape, inserting what appeared to be a huge set of forceps to grasp the baby's head. Teddy's nephew or niece entered the world with a sucking sound as it popped loose and slithered into the world, purple and covered with blood and cheesy vernix.

"Something's wrong with it!" Ella shouted.

"No, no, your daughter is a big, healthy girl. Her color will improve once she breathes on her own." The doctor continued to do her work, calling for a pan to receive the afterbirth. She gave Teddy another of her eye smiles. "Would you like to cut the cord?"

"I guess so." He moved to the far end of the table where his niece lay on the clean white sheet. The cord, thicker than he'd imagined and far more rubbery, had stopped its eerie pulsing. He positioned the medical instrument between the two clamps as instructed and freed his niece from her mother. She cried loud and assertive.

"Did I hurt her?"

"No, excellent job. I think she simply woke up in a new world. The crying is good. It clears the lungs, but we will do a suction to make sure. You may go back to the head of the table and help your sister push out the placenta now—unless you want to watch."

"No, ma'am, I mean doctor." As it was he caught a glimpse of the afterbirth, big as a good-sized beefsteak laying in the pan after Ella gave a few more pushes. Birth, not for the squeamish.

"Eight pounds, fourteen ounces," the delivery room nurse announced as she cleaned and weighed the baby, placing a considerably more presentable swaddled child in Ella's arms.

Ella frowned at the round, little face. "She shouldn't be so brown."

Teddy bent over the infant who squinted at him through bright, blue eyes. "She has our eye color, like Mama's, too."

Ella refused to be consoled. "Don't you recall their eyes can turn dark after a while? Even I know that."

"She'll still be a beauty," the new uncle said with conviction. "Like Xochi, maybe."

"She's not what I bargained for. She shoulda been blonde like me, not have all those dark curls pressed against her head."

The nurse, a diplomat, said, "Would you like to carry the baby to the nursery, Uncle, while we clean up Mama and get her to her room?"

"I want to, but I'm afraid I'll drop her."

"We'll get a wheelchair for the both of you. What name did you pick?" she asked Ella who still glared at her bundle of joy. Ella turned her head and declined to answer.

"Elizabeth Jane," Teddy replied.

"Classic, very nice. We get so many odd ones these days."

The wheelchair arrived. Teddy seated himself, turned his crutches over to the nurse, and settled Elizabeth Jane on his lap. Ella's voice cried out as he approached the door from the delivery room. "You better remind them I want that shot in my behind to stop my milk. Don't want no saggy, leaking breasts."

"It is in your records, marked very clearly," the doctor said. "Take the baby to the nursery, Uncle. Roll the patient on her side for the injection."

As Teddy rode down the hall, he thought Elizabeth studied his face through the blue slits of her eyes, though he knew newborns didn't focus all that well. More likely she watched the overhead lights flash by on their journey to the bassinet. Maybe she would recognize his voice. "Hi, I'm your Uncle Teddy. I'll take good care of you. Want to shake on that?"

He offered the baby a finger. She latched on with a remarkably strong grasp. Sure, all babies did that, a reflex to cling to their mothers, but somehow he felt they'd made a pact. In the nursery, he immediately missed the warm bundle transferred to a rolling cart with a small container on top.

A nurse checked the baby's wristband and filled out a card declaring her Baby Smalls. She covered her curls with a tiny knit cap sporting a pink bow. "She'll sleep now. When she wakes, we'll bring her to her mother to be fed." Teddy nodded, reclaimed his sticks, but didn't move. "Really, she's in good hands. Get some rest."

He headed to the waiting room, but Jessie met him halfway. "A nurse told me it's a girl. Let's go see her."

Teddy reversed his steps. Right now, Jessie's chair looked mighty comfortable. Maybe she'd give him a ride if he asked, but held that request in until their noses pressed against the glass to view Elizabeth Jane, bigger than any of the other babies and sleeping calmly.

"I'm afraid Ella is rejecting her." He voiced his

fear in Jessie's ear. "Says she's too brown."

"I imagine the father was brown, too. What did she expect?"

"That the baby would look exactly like her."

"We'll deal with it—together." Jessie wrapped a hand around his. "We can bring her around if we mention the Kardashian offspring. Several of them are brown."

"You think?"

"I know."

"I'm going out to find some flowers. Albertson's isn't too far away."

"Teddy, you are beat, and you don't get any of those good hormones that are supposed to rush into the mother's system and make her want to nurture."

"It won't take long. Once Ella is settled, we'll go home and get some sleep. I think I'll tell Mom and Xo not to come this late. If all is well, Ella and the baby will be back at the apartment around noon. They can come and fuss over them then."

"Okay. I'll keep Ella company."

Not that the new mother was good company. "I swear my legs feel like two logs o' pine. Can't move nothing."

"It's the epidural. It will wear off," Jessie said—unlike her own paralysis.

A tray arrived with a choice of fluids and a light meal. "Drink the Gatorade the way my athletes do," Jessie prompted. She put the cup into Ella's hand.

"Funny, I felt just fine after they got the kid out of me. Could have eaten a cow, but now I kind of lost my appetite."

"Try some broth." Jessie raised the plastic lid over

the plate. "We have eggs, toast, some applesauce. Eat as much as you can."

"How come you're here? Teddy run out on me too?"

"No, he'll be back shortly." Jessie seethed, thinking of a dead tired Teddy seeking out flowers for his ungrateful bitch of a sister.

He appeared in the doorway as soon as the thought entered her mind. He'd switched to his wheelchair and held a simple arrangement of pink rosebuds, baby's breath, and ferns in a green glass vase between his knees. Jessie took them and placed them on Ella's bedside table. She shot the girl a look that demanded, "Be grateful."

But Teddy apologized. "Sorry, you can't get much this late at night."

"Thoughtful of you to get them." Jessie sent Ella another pointed glance.

"Yeah, they're real pretty."

Another visitor arrived, a very cheerful nurse wheeling the basinet. "This big girl is already hungry. I have the bottle all ready for her first feeding. Now, crook your arm, and I'll hand her over." A small, tight fist waved in the air as Elizabeth Jane fussed.

"Can't you see I'm eating?" Ella snarled.

The nurse covered her initial shock very well and remained pleasant. "I'll take her back to the nursery and one of the aides will give her a bottle."

"Don't do that! I'd like to feed her." Jessie held out her arms. The nurse draped a clean cloth over Jessie and settled the baby into the right position. She delivered the bottle with minimal instruction to keep the nipple full and stepped back to observe. Elizabeth Jane made short work of three ounces of formula before she closed her eyes again. Automatically, Jessie transferred her to a shoulder and patted out a burp.

"Someone is a natural at this," the nurse complimented as Ella forked up eggs.

"Next time, I get a turn," Teddy said, his earnest blue eyes alight at the sight of Jessie holding the baby.

"You can have as many turns as you want." Ella bit into her toast with a savage crunch.

"I'll take her back to the nursery for the night. We'll feed her there, and let the mother get some rest since she isn't nursing. See you in the morning." That ended Elizabeth's first visit with her mother.

As soon as the nurse cleared the door, Ella spoke up. "She ain't my baby. Can't be."

Teddy sought Jessie's eyes and nodded. "Sure, she is. I saw them put the wristband on her in the delivery room. No mistake. She has our eyes."

"Don't mean nothing."

"I think she looks like Kanye and Kim's babies, but prettier. If she keeps those blue eyes, she'll be so striking."

"Her daddy ain't black. He's one of those Melungeons I told you about. They got white blood and Cherokee, too. Some folks think they came from Turkey, and the Turks ain't black."

"Elizabeth certainly has an interesting background," Teddy observed mildly. "We're going now, but will be back in the morning. Get some sleep. You'll need it." Very aware of Jessie's hands clenched on the wheelchair, her knuckles turning white, he nodded Jess toward the door and got her moving down the hallway before the outburst occurred.

"I know your sister had a hard life and is as ignorant as a person can be, but to deny your own child! She doesn't deserve to be a mother."

"Probably didn't want to be one as far as I can tell. I won't let her neglect Elizabeth."

"I know, I know." Jessie pressed the elevator button as they sat side by side.

"My mother didn't reject me at birth even with part of my spinal cord exposed. She loved me when she should have hated me because her uncle was my father. She left me safe with the Billodeauxs when her boyfriend would have killed me." Maybe that truth shouldn't have come out just now, but it slipped from his exhausted lips. "Ella will come around."

"Oh, Teddy, I doubt it, but we'll make sure the baby is loved."

Jessie seemed to have missed his stunning confession. "You don't think less of me because of how I came into the world?"

"It's not the child's fault who its parents are."

They escaped into the private box of the elevator away from the nurses silently padding around, and the occasional squall of a newborn. "Jessie, would you stay the night with me, just sleep next to me? I'm too beat for the wedge or anything else."

"That is exactly where I planned to be."

## Chapter Twenty-One

Teddy woke the way he'd like to awaken for the rest of his life—with Jessie spooned against him and one of his hands resting lightly on her breast. Something had brought him out of a deep sleep. Oh, yes, the doorbell. It rang again, followed by a knock, then the sound of a key in the lock. Voices, female, sounded in his living room.

"Teddy must have gone to the hospital already. Let's decorate. We can go visit when we're done." His mom.

Thank heaven he'd shut his bedroom door last night. Much as Mama Nell tried to respect her children's privacy, she always asked for a spare key to have in case of emergencies. In all the years he'd been in college and working in Lafayette, she hadn't used it once.

"His door is closed. He might still be sleeping. I'll check." Xochi, the rhythm of her gait slightly altered by her pregnancy, approached. "Teddy, you in there? Are you okay?" How often had she said that when her bedroom lay directly across the hall from his at the ranch?

Actually, he felt better than okay. Slowly, he removed his hand from Jessie's warmth. "You woke me up!" Ted eyed his alarm clock. "Jesus, nine o'clock. I should be at the hospital. Give me a minute."

Jessie roused, rolled over, and snuggled against his chest. His nether parts reacted. Not now! He shook her shoulder gently. "Jess, my mom and sister are out there."

She opened one of her gold-flecked eyes. "Better that than my parents. Your family is cool about us."

"Yours isn't?" he said because he needed more to worry about. "I thought your dad liked me."

"He does, but I'm still his little girl. He wonders about your intentions."

"Honorable, totally honorable."

Xo rapped again as she'd often done when he wanted to stay in and she thought he should go riding with her before it got too hot. "Well, rise and shine—or are you talking in your sleep?"

"No, ah, I've got company. Jessie is here."

His sister bathed them in her hot chocolate laughter, warm and throaty. "Okay, backing off. Clearing the bathroom. We'll be in the living room decorating."

He reached an arm down to the floor to retrieve his underwear, not clean but handy. Transferring to his chair, he tossed Jessie his robe lying at the foot of the bed. He still marveled at the beauty of her body, most of the damage around the back, as she covered herself. Took all he could manage to say, "We'd better get our morning routines done. You take the shower. I'll wash at the sink and um, change my pouch." He prayed that wouldn't get messy as it sometimes did.

"I'm right behind you." She got into her chair and followed him out. Only giggles from the living room as a balloon popped suddenly.

Teddy waited for the shower to steam up before he

changed his appliance. By the time Jessie finished, he'd
sponged off, brushed his teeth, and scrounged up clean
clothes. Bare-chested, he wanted to get in a quick
shave. Jessie, wrapped in a towel, joined him at the
sink. "Pretty sexy watching a man shave."

"Troy didn't shave in front of you?"

"No, he preferred the perpetual scruff."

"When I grow a scruff, my beard comes in so light
no one notices."

"Then stay clean-shaven." As he wiped off the
shaving cream, she ran her fingers down his smooth
cheek. "I'm glad you aren't like Troy. But I need to get
my makeup on."

"You don't really need it."

"Your opinion, not mine."

Teddy shrugged into a white UL T-shirt. "The
mirror is all yours. Got to get my braces on. I'll see
about putting some breakfast together."

No need for that. His mom had the coffee on and
eggs in the pan. The microwave pinged. Xochi removed
a pan of Ella's reheated biscuits. "These are great. I've
already had two, one for me and one for the baby."

"Better not do that. I just witnessed the birth of a
large baby. Considering Junior's size at birth, you
might want to watch your weight."

"Spoilsport."

"Suit yourself."

His mom buttered a biscuit and added a dollop of
jelly. "These are wonderful."

"I think she makes them with butter."

Nell shook her head. "No, lard. You have a block
of it in your refrigerator buried under the real bacon.
The turkey bacon has gone bad. What has your sister

done to you?"

"We take turns cooking. I work mine off at the gym."

Xochi seized a third biscuit and squeezed honey on it. "Let him enjoy. He survived a hard night."

Jessie arrived looking fine as a sunrise, all gold streaked and pink-cheeked. "The living room looks so nice. Ella will love the extra attention. It might be just the boost she needs. Already showing signs of baby blues."

Teddy had barely noticed the decorations as he followed his nose to breakfast. Two balloon bouquets sat on either side of his TV. A silver arc of letters spelling out "Welcome Baby Girl" spanned his drapery rod. On the coffee table, a grand arrangement of pink and white flowers studded with plastic storks made his small bouquet appear pretty shabby. Little cakes, each topped with a frosting rosebud, sat on either side of it. The women of his family had hauled the rocking chair into the room and placed the baby carrier right next to it. They'd gone all out for a girl they barely knew. Bless them.

He scraped up the last of his eggs and ate the lard-laden biscuit anyhow because delicious is delicious. "We'd better get over to the hospital. Ella and the baby will probably be released around noon once the doctor makes rounds. You ready, Jess?"

"I am."

"Why don't we all go? We can see the baby and help carry all the stuff they give you," Xochi suggested.

Nell agreed, packing the dirty dishes swiftly in the washer. She and Xo went in her car, Teddy and Jessie in his van, a small caravan of support for a new mother.

They found Ella already dressed, sitting gingerly on the edge of her bed, remote in hand, watching morning talk shows. No sign of the baby.

"We've come to see Elizabeth," Nell said, ramping up the cheery in her voice.

"I told 'em to keep her in the nursery until we're ready to go. My bottom hurts bad, but you only get Tylenol in this place. You're a psychologist. Can you write a prescription for something stronger?"

"Couldn't and wouldn't. We'll get you a donut cushion. That should help along with some Tucks. I think Xo and I will go see the baby." Mama Nell had changed to her no-nonsense voice.

As soon as they'd made their exit, Ella said, "Guess she's pissed at me now."

"You haven't seen my mom pissed yet. Don't try to con her, Ella. She's been nice to you, and you aren't her responsibility."

She rolled her eyes at Teddy and sighed. "Look at me, just look at me. I still got a big gut. I thought it would go away once I squeezed the baby out. I planned to belt this maternity dress around my waist, but I don't got none any more."

"They told you what to expect in class. You should have listened."

"In a few months, you'll be back to normal," Jessie consoled. "You can come to the gym with us as soon as you get the all clear from the doctor."

"Yeah, that will be great. As if." The bedside phone rang, and Ella picked it up. "Elizabeth Jane," she said. "I decided on that and guess I'll stick with it, but she doesn't look it. What do you mean, spell it? Like it's always spelled."

Hastily, Jessie wrote out Elizabeth on a notepad and handed it over just in case. Ella spelled it out, didn't need help on Jane. "Elizabeth Jane Smalls, ain't no daddy in the picture." She slapped down the receiver.

"You can't be too careful about the spelling," Jessie said. "I knew a girl in high school who wanted to name her baby Felicia, but spelled it out as Felassa. That's the kid's name forevermore." If she meant to bring a smile to Ella's face, she failed to do so.

After the call about the birth certificate, they aimlessly watched a game show. Nell and Xochi were slow in returning, but when they did, they had the donut cushion and a large container of Tucks. Ella went into the bathroom to soothe her behind and settled on the cushion afterward. The doctor arrived with her release. The nurse loaded them up with instructions and starter kits. She inquired about a car seat.

"I had one installed in my van, but I admit I took it over to the firehouse to get help."

"Good, then it was done right. Be sure to secure all the straps."

With that, the nurse delivered the baby into Ella's arms and placed both of them into a wheelchair for the ride out. Teddy rolled ahead to get the van. As their small group waited, Elizabeth began to fret.

"Probably pooped herself already, and I can't change her here," Ella said as sour as the smell coming from the diaper.

"Here, let me soothe her." Xochi reached out and within a minute had the infant sleeping against her chest. "Maybe just a little gas. Sleep, Lizzy Jane, you'll soon be home."

"Suits her better than Elizabeth. Shoulda named her that. Guess y'all noticed she looks black."

"Brown and beautiful," Xochi said. "I hope mine will be this pretty." When the van came around, she settled the baby into the car seat as if she'd been practicing this skill at home. Ella took the seat in the rear next to her child, and Nell stowed Jessie's wheelchair to help things along since Lizzy began to cry as soon as she left Xo's warm breast. She emitted a pitiful wail all the way to the apartment. Ella was the first one out.

The flowers, balloons, and cakes did please the new mother, as did the willingness of all four of her helpers to change the diaper and give a bottle. Ella sat enthroned on her cushion with a plate of petit fours resting on the remains of her belly and a co-cola by her side. The baby rested in the carrier on the floor. About the time that Nell and Xochi left, she declared herself ready for a nap too. "You'll see to the kid, huh?" she asked Teddy and Jess.

Of course, they would, but once she'd gone into the bedroom and shut the door, they conferred. "Still not showing much interest in the baby. I'm worried," Teddy admitted.

"I'll stay over tonight and help you get through it."

"That would be taking advantage. We need to get our routine established, they said in prenatal classes. You can't be here all the time."

"If that's how you want it. I'll stay until Ella gets up."

That wasn't how he wanted it, and he suspected by the tone of her answer he'd hurt her feelings. He'd like to have Jessie at his side all time, but right now that seemed impossible. Ella took a long, long nap. They changed and fed Lizzy Jane again, marveled over her blue eyes opening and trying to fix on their faces as they did so.

"Why can't she see this child is wonderful?" Jessie questioned.

"Because she's still a child herself, craving attention and wanting to be spoiled."

Before she left, Jessie repeated his words to Nell. "Don't let her con you, Teddy."

"I won't."

But when Ella complained she couldn't get any rest with the baby making noises in her room, they moved the crib to Teddy's bedside where he managed a midnight change on a plastic sheet over his spread and offered Lizzy Jane a bottle from a small cooler on his nightstand. It wasn't warm like breast milk, but the baby didn't seem to care. He repeated the process at three and six a.m. When Ella emerged around seven, she did bring him breakfast in bed and plonked Lizzy into her carrier to keep her company in front of the television. Too tired to protest that the baby shouldn't be exposed to TV, he slept three hours until she wailed again.

## Chapter Twenty-Two

Teddy's phone rang. He barely heard its tone over the crying of the child. Delving among the wipes, a short stack of newborn diapers, two empty baby bottles, and the spit cloth he'd put on his shoulder when burping Lizzy, he finally found it flashing Jessie's number.

"Hi, give me a second. Ella, would you get the baby? Ella!" The siren sounds from the living room drowned out the female voices of The View, but he got no response from his sister.

"Teddy, are you okay? You usually to take me to the gym by now."

"I was sleeping. Had the baby in with me since her noises bothered Ella."

"She's taking advantage of you."

"Most women have a mother to help out when a baby is born. Ella only has me. Ella!" he shouted again.

A door slammed. "Yeah, yeah, I got her. Can't even get a breath of fresh air." The baby failed to quiet in Ella's arms.

"Look, Jessie. I have to get out there. We should skip PT today." He hoped she didn't detect the frantic in his voice.

"Hey, you're the one who said no excuses on exercising. I'd come over there, but both my parents are at work."

"Maybe I'll pick you up later. Let me get this under control. Call you back."

Teddy pulled on yesterday's jeans draped over the arm of his wheelchair and shrugged into a T-shirt with baby spit on the shoulder acquired before he unearthed the pads meant for the purpose. He swung into his chair and wheeled toward the howls. Ella stood ineffectively jostling the baby in her arms. "She's been asleep 'til now and won't shut up."

"Get a bottle. Maybe run it under warm water a little to take the chill off. I'll change her."

Teddy took Lizzy on his lap and gave her a ride to his impromptu changing station in the bedroom. Despite the kicking feet and flailing tiny fists, he managed to get her out of a soaked onesie and into a dry diaper. He practiced his skill at hoops, lobbing the dirty one into his wastebasket by the desk where the two others from the night before resided. On the way back, he stopped by Ella's room and took one of the garments they called a baby sack from a drawer. Soft and blue, its color complemented Lizzy's eyes—if they weren't still squinched shut in fury. Anyhow, easier to get on than something with legs as well as arms. He pulled the drawstring at the bottom and covered her drumming heels.

"All dry. Soon you'll feel better." He carried Lizzy to the living room where Ella stood holding a bottle. "Well, sit in the rocker and feed her."

"Can't. Got a terrible cramp." She handed over the bottle and walked doubled over to the bathroom.

"It's you and me, babe." Teddy touched the side of the infant's mouth with the nipple and let her turn her head in the right direction and find her nourishment, a trick they'd mentioned in the prenatal class. Lizzy latched on and sucked hard. In the calm that followed, he took a deep breath—detected a taint of cigarette smoke in the air, though no butts littered the debris of Ella's breakfast and junk food snacks on the coffee table.

She returned pale and shaken from the bathroom. "I just passed a clot the size of a hen's egg. You better get me back to the hospital."

Teddy shook his head. "The nurse said you'd had a big baby and that might happen."

Ella positioned herself on the donut cushion and sank her face in her hands. "Yeah, I remember now. She said this lochia shit is gonna come out of me for like a month, the world's longest period. Gross. Everything about childbirth is gross. My breasts are still leaking. I'm ruining this nice top Xo give me. You sure they did that shot to dry me up?"

"The baby isn't gross. There are nipple pads in the bag the nurse gave you." Teddy smiled down at the head of little scalloped curls. Ella had dressed in her maternity jeans and one of the less full tops, done her hair and makeup. Maybe a good sign. Didn't depressed people neglect their appearance?

"She likes you. Not me. She didn't calm down when I picked her up."

"Hungry and wet. Change, feed, burp, rock to sleep, and repeat at this age. Easy."

"How come you know so much about babies?"

"First, I listened in class, but I was old enough when Edie and T-Rex were born to help out when the women needed a break. We all did, the advantage of a large family. When you have a second child, it will come easier."

"Won't be no second child if it's up to me!" Ella leaned back and took a swig of Coke.

"Carbonated beverages aren't going to help those cramps. Try tea instead."

"Know-it-all." But she rose and went into the kitchen to put a kettle on.

"Ella, you haven't been smoking, have you?" He raised his voice and the baby startled but didn't give up the nipple.

"I done told you, I got nothing to do with cancer sticks. It's the smell I let in from the Burger King when I opened the door."

"Okay." He accepted her excuse because he had no alternative. "Smoke would be bad for the baby."

"I know that!"

Teddy raised Lizzy to his shoulder, not bothering with a pad because the T-shirt already sported her spit-up. She gave him a satisfying belch and relaxed against his neck. He discovered he enjoyed the feeling of his niece all warm and snuggled against him. Reluctantly, he lowered her into the baby carrier, rolled forward and turned down the TV. "She should sleep for a few hours now. If you want a nap, now is the time to take one. I certainly could use more rest."

"Nah, I want some time to myself."

"Will you be all right if I go to the gym with Jessie?"

"Sure, why not?"

Teddy didn't answer that. He went into the bathroom, took care of his needs, and found a clean workout shirt. Skipped a shower and shave. He called Jessie from the van and told her he'd be there in fifteen minutes. Teddy didn't plan to linger in the juice bar today, not with a new baby in Ella's hands.

They worked out for an hour. He felt fatigue coming on faster than usual, but pushed on for another thirty minutes before admitting to Jessie that he couldn't keep up with her today. She ran a sympathetic hand down the side of his face and felt the roughness of his beard.

"Oh, we have tough Teddy here today."

"Yeah, you can feel it even if you can't see it. Look, I'm going to shower at home. Sorry about that, but Ella isn't taking to the baby yet. I don't want to leave them alone. I'm not sure what I'll do this weekend. UL has a home game Saturday afternoon and the Sinners play at three the next day. I can leave early Sunday to get down to New Orleans, but won't be home until nine in the evening at best. The trouble is my family will all go to the Sinners game, or I'd ask one of them to stay with Ella. I can't ask you; your dad needs you on the field."

"Not really. He has plenty of trainers. I feel like I'm more a mascot now."

"You aren't. I can see you working on the players from the booth. You contribute. You do the job you were trained for."

"Sort of. I can't really go out on the field and help. I've been thinking of retraining to counsel people like you and me, plan their rehab, and teach them all the things they can still do like you did for me."

"Great idea! You should go for it. But we have to leave."

On the way, Jessie suggested, "Maybe Xo would stay with Ella while we are at the UL game. It's only a few hours. She'd be free to go to New Orleans after we get back."

"My sister likes to be there on Saturday so she can drag Junior to early Mass Sunday morning when the Sinners have a home game, but this time of year we still have plenty of daylight—and she has a soft heart. I'll ask."

"Then, I'll come stay with Ella on Sunday early. I'm sorry I can't spend the night. My dad wants me home. Says he has something special planned for my birthday."

"You didn't tell me!"

"You have enough on your mind without stressing about my birthday on Saturday. Think of a new sexual position if you want to give me a gift later."

"I will! But don't expect much right now. Being up and down all night with a baby has sort of sapped my energy."

"Actually, that's kind of charming in a man. Ella and Lizzy are lucky to have you."

"I am lucky to have you stand by me."

Jessie's father waited curbside to receive his daughter. "Lunch is on the table. You want to come in, Teddy?"

"No, have to get back to Ella and the baby."

"You sound like an old married man, but I understand. When you have time, I've got something to show you."

As Teddy drove away, he thought he detected some barely suppressed glee on Coach Mo's face and hoped it meant something wonderful ahead for Jessie whether he could be a part of it or not.

## Chapter Twenty-Three

Saturday went off as planned with Xochi arriving promptly to spell Teddy, bringing along some movies she thought Ella might like and a few more baby outfits she couldn't resist buying. When Teddy returned from calling the game, unfortunately a UL loss, he came bearing pizza, too tired to cook. Xo had the baby, rocking her in the chair, while Ella slept sprawled on the sofa. No surprise there. She'd been complaining that even with the child in another room the nocturnal crying kept her awake.

Xo slipped Lizzy into her baby seat. "She's really such a good baby. Goes right back to sleep after her feeding."

"Stay for dinner such as it is?"

"No, thanks. Pizza gives me heartburn in my condition. I'll be on my way to New Orleans from here since I'm a half hour closer to Junior this way. Lots of places in Baton Rouge to get a quick bite." Xochi gathered her things, her eagerness to see her husband still fresh and wonderful on her pretty brown face. Teddy suffered a pang of envy along with the pangs of hunger.

Ella roused, sniffed the air. "Pizza! You are the best brother on earth."

"He certainly is one of them," Xochi agreed. "Have a quiet evening."

After her departure, they polished off the pie and a salad Teddy insisted on throwing together. "There's ice cream if you want dessert. I'm going to shower and take a nap before you go to bed, get ready for my night duty."

Teddy failed to sleep as well as he'd hoped. He missed Jessie and hated having to pass on the small birthday party in her honor. Bad enough he couldn't get out to search for a gift and had ordered a necklace online that didn't seem as special as he wanted, though it was pretty enough for Ella to covet when it showed up express delivery.

"You know, some husbands get their wives a nice piece of jewelry after they have a baby for them. Royalty does that." Ella held up the necklace above her still-swollen breasts. Asymmetrical, three small pearls spaced apart led to a swirl of gold wire, then a drop of three more pearls. A tiny diamond nestled in the wire.

"Not royalty and not your husband," Teddy answered, thinking of all he'd done for her already: free room and board, payment of her medical bills, and now night duty with Lizzy, not to mention that phone bill. He guessed in Ella's mind only material things counted.

"Well, I'll be a good sister and wrap it for you while you rest."

"Thanks." When Teddy finally settled, he slept like the dead—or a worn-out father who had worked all afternoon.

After he woke, he found Lizzy in her crib by his side, the little cooler restocked with formula, and plenty of diapers piled on the night table. Jessie's wrapped gift gleamed in silver paper he later recognized as aluminum foil on his computer table. Ella had topped it with a pink bow from one of her shower gifts. No one could say his sister wasn't both resourceful and frugal when she wanted to be.

Realizing the baby's red-faced grunts had pulled him out of sleep, he prepared to change a poopy one by elbowing up against his pillow and waiting for her to finish her business. Teddy picked her up before she began to cry, cleaned her bottom, lofted the diaper into the wastepaper basket, and dragged out a bottle. He'd completed the whole process with barely a whimper from Lizzy. Ella should be well rested by tomorrow, but he thought he heard her talking to someone in her room. A quick search among the baby items confirmed she'd palmed his phone again. Not wanting to holler at her and wake Lizzy, he let it go and sank back into slumber, forgot about it at the three a.m. feeding, and recalled it once more when the wakeup alarm he'd set for seven didn't go off. Lizzy Jane did, but she'd put in a solid four hours first. Good kid.

Though he picked up the infant and offered her the comfort of his heartbeat, Teddy did call to Ella. "Get in here! Your turn."

"Yeah, yeah, coming. I thought she'd be up at six for you to feed, and I'd have more time." His sister slumped into the room, all prettied up for this early, and a spit pad draped over her shoulder to protect another of Xochi's maternity tees.

"Time for what? Making long-distance calls on my phone again?"

"Just calling my daddy. I kept it short. Here." She slapped the phone on the night table and removed Lizzy from his arms. "Hey, I have coffee on and biscuits in the oven. Get dressed while I make up the eggs. You earned them."

"Look, Ella. I need my phone by me at all times for any emergencies and because I had my alarm set. I must leave by nine while traffic is light. You never know on these highways what might hold you up, and I can't afford a reputation of showing up at the last minute. We have sound checks to do and information to go over."

"Well, the baby woke you in plenty of time. Wish I could make a livin' by just talking."

"Not as easy as it sounds. Go on, let me put myself together."

Ella sauntered out with Lizzy fretting and rooting for food on her shoulder. Teddy hoped she changed the diaper before offering a bottle, or they might have a rash to deal with later. He'd double check before he left.

Breakfast was great as usual, full of lard-laden biscuits with a side of bacon, plenty of coffee, and eggs made the way he liked them. When Ella set up her own place, he'd miss the food and probably lower his cholesterol. Teddy watched the clock and waited for Jessie's arrival. He hoped to give her the gift before he took off for the city. Not like her to be late.

His phone rang around ten. Jessie's voice came through full of apology tinged with excitement. "Sorry, complications. I can't get there until eleven most likely, noon at the latest."

"That's cutting it close for me." Teddy threw a troubled look in Ella's direction as she cleaned up the kitchen.

"For Gawd's sake, I can take care of the kid alone for an hour. Get the hell out of here."

He almost told her not to swear in front of the baby, but settled for making sure Lizzy had a dry diaper before he left. "Jessie should be here in an hour or two. Lizzy might sleep that long. You should rest, too."

"That's my plan. Nothin' on the TV but religion and those egghead talk shows on a Sunday morning. We'll be watching the game later and doing our nails." His sister made shooing gestures as if he were a pesky fly hovering over the congealed eggs.

"Good." Teddy gathered all he'd need for the day including his laptop and phone, gave Lizzy a kiss on the forehead, and Ella a wave as he headed out to make a living.

**** 

Jessie pulled up in front of the apartment all by her lonesome in the best birthday gift ever. Her dad had outfitted her old car with hand controls, giving her a new independence. Sure, getting her chair folded and into it presented a challenge, as did getting it out again, but she'd rejected help earlier and so caused more of a delay. Too bad her father hadn't remembered to check the battery and air in the tires on a vehicle just sitting around for months. First, a delay for jumping the battery, then a stop to get the mushy tires inflated. After dropping her beaming father at home and waving goodbye to her worried mother, who thought the idea of Jessie being on the road alone a bad one, she headed to Teddy's place only to get caught in church traffic. Finally turning into his street, Jessie saw immediately that some clod had parked in the handicapped space, not that it belonged to Teddy alone, but the battered pickup truck bore no handicapped plates or special tags. Maybe someone was moving in as a small television swathed in a blanket and a blue suitcase so old it didn't have wheels sat in the back, the tailgate hanging down like a broken wing.

Jessie parked next to it. The lack of extra space made the struggle to erect her wheelchair more difficult, but she managed. She checked her watch. Damn, noon already. Teddy would be gone, and she'd wanted to surprise him by driving herself to his place. Oh well, she had the key he'd given her and let herself in quietly without disturbing Ella or the baby if they napped. Initially, she heard voices coming from Teddy's bedroom and thought he'd remained until her arrival, which would make him late for the Sinners game. Jessie started to call out, telling him to get on the road right away, but no, the red van was gone, the old truck hogging its space. Nor was the voice his. This one had a harsher twang roughened by cigarettes. A smoky aroma hung in the air. Not something Teddy would allow. Jess wheeled silently down the hall, stopped halfway to listen.

"She-it, this guy got nothin'. I have a better TV in my trailer. Who uses a desktop anymore? I guess we can take it and see what it brings. Jesus, I thought he was your rich brother, Ella Sue."

"His folks are rich, not Teddy. Leave the computer. He needs it for his job, and like you say, it won't bring much."

"The plan was for you to stay out at that fancy ranch and get what you could from them. Then, we take the baby and sell her to some desperate people who really want a kid, a blue-eyed blond kid. You really screwed this up, Ella Sue. Babies like this end up in foster homes. Nobody pays for a brown child."

"Teddy says her eyes will stay blue and she'll grow up pretty."

"Ain't he Mr. Sunshine? Well, he's welcome to raise her because I won't."

"I figured that would be your feeling. I wrote a letter telling him I want Elizabeth Jane to stay with him. Teddy might not be rich, but he's decent, real decent."

"You sayin' I'm not, Ella Sue?" The male voice took on a dangerous edge. Jessie moved closer, ready to ram into him if she must to save Ella and the baby.

"No, Wyatt, no. And I'm Ella now, just Ella. Let's go before she wakes. I'll put the letter in her crib where Teddy will find it. Jessie is going to be here any minute. We need to move."

Jessie centered herself in the doorway. She took in the scene. Lizzy swaddled in her crib. Ella standing between the crib and a dark man, tall, lean, wiry, with black curls resting on his shoulders, the guy from the backside of Burger King. "Ella, don't do this. Tell the guy to leave. Teddy and I will help you raise Lizzy."

The man swung in her direction, his features too sharp to belong to a black man, burnished skin, lots of Cherokee blood maybe, and white, also, eyes dark and threatening as a thundercloud about to send out a bolt of lightning. Handsome in a very bad boy sort of way, the kind of guy who would attract a girl like Ella Sue.

"This is her father, so he's got a say. Never wanted no baby in the first place, and Daddy would have found the money to abort Wyatt's kid. He hates him. True enough he threw me out when I caught a baby by a Melungeon. Old Newt is a racist bastard. But Wyatt convinced me we could get a good stake to move elsewhere and live large on money some people would pay for a pretty, white baby. Didn't reckon on the kid to look so much like him."

"You didn't tell me the best friend you babbled about was a cripple like your brother, Ella. But she is beautiful enough to tempt a man who can't have sex with his woman for another five weeks—unless you're lyin'." His black eyes bored into Ella's frightened blue ones.

"I can take care of you, Wyatt. Right now if you need it so bad." Ella Sue turned paler than pale as she offered herself.

"She can't! You could tear out her stitches or give her an infection." Jessie regretted her words at once.

"So you volunteerin', pretty lady?"

Jess reversed, but Wyatt made a quick grab, dislodging her by her shoulders, making her fall forward toward the floor, hit on her numb knees, and nearly do a faceplant before catching herself on her arms. Ella's boyfriend rough-handled her onto Teddy's bed, the place of so much pleasure turning into a place of horror and fear. If only she could kick out. Beating on the man with her fists seemed to do no good, and when she forked her fingers to poke his eyes, he simply grasped both wrists and held them over her head.

"Come on, Ella Sue. Help me with her clothes. Get her zipper down. I been livin' poor waiting for this kid to be born. Couldn't even afford a cheap whore all these weeks while you lived mighty well."

"No! Let her be. We got to go. These walls ain't that thick. Someone will hear if she screams."

Given a cue, Jessie hollered as loud as she could but knew by now most in the building would be gearing up for the Sinners game, TVs turned on, or off in a sports bar doing the same. Wyatt released one of her wrists to backhand her across the face.

Ella leaped on his back, tugging at his narrow shoulders. "No, no, I'm your woman, not her. Take me." He elbowed her off into a heap on the floor with one savage blow.

Jessie took advantage of the distraction. Her free hand worked its way toward the night table drawer and groped for the grip of the revolver. She rolled off its safety and drew Wyatt's attention.

"You searchin' for a condom, honey? I'm clean, but maybe I'll make another baby prettier than this 'un."

Lizzy began to scream and flail her tiny hands loose from her wrapping. "Shut the brat up, Ella Sue, or I'll bash its brains out against the wall. Then, you get over here and help me get this done, you hear?"

Ella started to rise, holding out a hand, begging his help. Wyatt yanked her upright—and Jessie squeezed the trigger, once, twice because she knew Teddy always kept it on an empty chamber. With her elbow sunken into the mattress and her other arm still in Wyatt's control, the shot went lower than she intended as the gun bucked back in her hand. She wished it had gone into his groin, but angled as he was, he took the bullet in the hip. His hand flew up, and she secured the revolver with both of hers, preparing to pull the trigger again.

"Christ, she tried to kill me! Bitch, I got my own gun in the glove compartment, an automatic, and I'm coming back here to waste you and that kid."

"Try it." Jessie stilled any shake in her grip and drew a bead on his heart.

"Wyatt, we got to leave. You're bleeding all over. DNA, you ever think of that? If they can't match it to your record, my daddy will give the cops a good idea who was here." Again, Ella tugged on his arm. "Jessie, please don't shoot us in the back. We're going now, ain't we, Wyatt? Far away. Won't be any trouble no more. You and Teddy take care of my little girl." Wrapping an arm around her lover, Ella tried to support him on a shoulder, but he slumped, too heavy for her to carry.

"Put me in her chair. She can't follow and don't have the guts to shoot again."

"Oh, but I do." Jessie stared him down.

Ella shoved her wheelchair beneath Wyatt's hips, pressed him into it, and turned the chair quickly to put herself between Jessie and her lover. She pushed him hard down the hall and out the door. It shut behind them. All the while, Lizzy shrieked, a tiny siren wailing.

Jessie stayed as she was, holding the weapon two-handed, waiting for their return, but over the baby's cries, she heard only the gunning of a truck with a bad muffler taking off down the street. The gun grew heavy in her hands, and her urge to calm the baby surged. Finally, Jess laid the weapon on the night table and told Lizzy how things would go down.

"I'll give you a bottle, but first I must get mobile again. My phone was in the pouch on my wheelchair. I need to call for help." The baby listened intently and quieted to a whimper.

"Might have to drag my body the length of the hall and try to hike myself high enough to hit that panic button. My chair is going to be curbside, and I'd rather not pull myself over cement. I don't feel injuries below the waist and have to be careful about that." Lizzy found a thumb to suck on while Jessie explained, using the baby to organize her thoughts that wanted to skitter away screaming for help.

Jess positioned herself on the edge of the bed, preparing to let herself drop to the floor when she remembered Teddy's search for the wedge in the closet. What had he said? Always have a second wheelchair handy. You never know when one will break down. The closet loomed way closer than the front door. Softening the drop by putting a hand on the night table, she lowered herself, rolled on her stomach, and inched along the floor until she could shove open the accordion door with her fingertips. The wheelchair sat right in front. A pushup into sitting position, and she was able to spread the seat of the chair, lever herself into it, and maneuver it into the bedroom. Thank you, Teddy for all those trips to the gym.

First stop, the crib. She glided through a puddle of Wyatt's blood, placed the baby on her lap, and moved toward the front of the apartment. A second thought had her reversing to pick up the gun and put it in the side pouch with the safety on. Lizzy, having dislodged her thumb in the transfer, began to fuss again. Tracking skid marks of blood behind her, she made it to the door and hit the emergency button. "Won't be long now, kiddo. Hang on."

Chapter Twenty-Four

Not knowing who would respond or when on a Sunday afternoon with the Sinners playing, Jessie took care of the baby next, backtracking to the bedroom to get a bottle from the cooler and a clean diaper from the stack. She completed the change, careful to avoid the splotch of darkening red on the spread, and stopped Lizzy's insistent cries with the bottle. Just as the baby settled, the doorbell rang with urgency, someone laying on the button, followed by loud knocking as if she were the recipient of the world's most important delivery.

"Sorry, Lizzy. I have to take care of this." Down the hall again, she opened the door just as a passkey jiggled in the lock.

"Campus police, Officer Dooley here. What's the emergency? Do you need an ambulance?" The light eyes of the officer tracked the smears of blood on the floor leading to and from the bedroom. Young enough to be a student or a dropout from the police academy, his face bore a trace of acne and a pitiful attempt to grow a mustache. He seemed rattled by the signs of carnage. His hand went to his holster.

"No, but someone does. I'm Jessica Minvielle. I shot a man who tried to assault me back there. Threatened the baby too. He's gone now. You won't need your weapon." Jessie jerked her head toward the rear.

"Domestic dispute?"

"No. His girlfriend, Ella Sue Smalls, is the baby's mother. His name is Wyatt. I don't know the last name. They decided to take off without the child, but not before the guy had some fun with me. Actually, Ella tried to stop him. I managed to get the gun from a drawer while he was distracted. I wounded him in the hip, and Ella used my wheelchair to haul him away. They took off in an old beater of a Ford truck."

"Color? License?" His hands shaking a trifle, the officer frantically jotted her words in a notebook.

"Rust, I'd say. Lots of dents, a broken tailgate. Sorry, I didn't get the license though he was parked in the handicapped spot. I meant to write it down and report him to your office, but never had the chance."

"I think this is a little out of our jurisdiction. Have to call the city police." The relief of passing on the case was obvious in his voice, going high, then low as he cleared his throat.

"Fine, I'll just sit over here and finish feeding Lizzy. Maybe if I turn on the TV she'll recognize her uncle's voice and calm down."

"Her uncle?"

"Teddy Billodeaux. This is his place. He's calling a game in New Orleans this afternoon." She checked her watch: only one. How could that be? Seemed like hours had passed. "I guess the game hasn't started yet. I'm not sure when he left or if he has arrived at the Dome. All his contact numbers were in my phone. It should be in the pouch on the wheelchair outside."

"Didn't see one, ma'am."

"Add theft to the charges—of a wheelchair, a cell phone, and..." Her eyes roved the living room and noticed for the first time the absence of the television and DVD player. The cables draped over the stand like severed arteries. "Add in a TV."

"Will do. I'm stepping out to get backup."

She had to keep busy or else the whole situation would collapse with only her will currently holding up that shaky structure. Jessie poured her attention on Lizzy, transferring them to the rocker to complete the feeding. Moving the chair by shifting her torso back and forth, she made up new words to the old folk song, Little Liza Jane.

*I've got a guy and you've got none, li'l Lizzy Jane.*
*I've got a guy who calls me "hun", li'l Lizzy Jane.*
*Oh, my Lizzy, li'l Lizzy Jane.*
*Lizzy Jane has come to me.*
*We're as happy as we can be.*
*Oh, my Lizzy, li'l Lizzy Jane.*
*Come my love and live with me.*
*I will take good care of thee.*
*Oh, my Lizzy, li'l Lizzy Jane.*

The song evoked evenings spent around bonfires when she went away to camp as a child and loved every moment, unlike more timid children who feared the spiders in the cabins, the occasional snakes in the woods, the slimy bottom of the lake, and the ghost stories told in the dead of night. Jessie wondered what type of child this baby might become, one full of confidence and courage, or a sly liar like her mother. She doubted Lizzy would be shy. Even as the baby nursed, her blue eyes focused on Jessie's face, intense and searching, perhaps for Teddy who most often cared for her.

The screech of a siren announced the arrival of a

squad car and startled Lizzy so the formula dribbled from the side of her mouth as it opened wide. Jessie transferred her to a comforting shoulder before she began to squall or choke. Judging by the amount of equipment on their utility belts, solid physiques, and eyes undisturbed by the blood on the floor, the real cops had arrived. They flashed their badges and identified themselves, Officer Nelson, the elder, and Officer Paton, somewhat younger, one white, one black. "Thank you for coming," she said with rather feeble formality. Wasn't this their job?

"I filled them in outside," Officer Dooley reported as if he'd done her a great favor. "I didn't want to go back to the bedroom and disturb the crime scene."

"You did the right thing, son. Now you can run along. We'll handle it from here."

More accustomed to dealing with men exposing themselves to coeds, drunken football fans, fraternity pranks, and booting illegally parked cars, Dooley took off jackrabbit fast and left them to it. Despite his good intentions, Jessie had to repeat all she'd told him. They did examine the bedroom, called in a crime scene team to verify the evidence, and asked for the gun in question. Not wanting to wake the baby, Jessie nodded to the pouch on the wheelchair. They bagged the weapon.

"Look, this Wyatt said he had a gun in his glove compartment. Be sure to note he is armed and dangerous. He also has a police record of some kind. And please try to keep Ella safe. She did try to help me in her own way."

"We'll do our best. You're Coach Mo's daughter, right? Why were you here again?"

224

"To help Ella with the baby while Teddy is away. She's very young and inexperienced. I guess I should tell you she intended to desert the child and left a note that she wanted him to take care of Lizzy."

"We found it, but didn't open it. More evidence. Since you aren't any relation to the baby, we'll have to call Child Welfare to take her until Mr. Billodeaux returns."

Jessie saw their steely eyes glance at the wheelchair. "I assure you I can care for her until Teddy gets home."

"Sorry, Miss Minvielle. That's not how it works. We have to make sure this child is safe and in good hands."

Jessie stiffened in the rocking chair. "My hands work perfectly well."

"I'm sure that's true, but this is procedure." Officer Nelson asked his partner to contact someone to take the child away. He stayed put as if Jessie might suddenly vault into her wheelchair and take off with the infant. "You could pack a bag for the kid, save some time."

Jessie eased Lizzy into her baby seat and herself back into the wheelchair. "Sure."

She rolled to Ella's bedroom and filled the huge empty diaper bag with the sweet little clothes, diapers, and light blankets. Best to put in some bottles and formula, too, but she couldn't seem to make herself leave the momentary privacy of the room. Without Lizzy to keep her courage up, the horrible moment of being flung to the bed, her legs leaden weights holding her down, having only her hands to put up a fight, returned like a tidal wave. If Ella hadn't thrown herself on Wyatt's back, what might have happened? Jessie began to tremble. Tears came. She dried them with a newborn diaper before forcing herself back to the living room and over to the refrigerator to pack the bottles. She'd hold Lizzy until another woman came for her.

Officer Nelson made no remark about her swollen eyes. She probably had makeup smeared under them to rival the mask of a raccoon. So much for wanting people to notice her face, not her dead legs. They'd certainly stare now. "Would you like us to call someone to take you home?" he asked, not unkindly.

"No, I can drive myself." At least, she'd shoved her car keys into a pocket and not into the pouch on her chair. The thieves had gotten her driver's license. Not that she'd tell the cop that. She needed a new one anyhow listing her disability.

The joy she'd felt that morning at her new independence was as deflated as the balloon bouquets that celebrated the baby's birth and lay close to the floor like wilted flowers. She'd failed Teddy and Lizzy. The police had his gun and his niece and the letter confirming the mother's wishes. How long it would take to untangle, she did not know.

When the Child Welfare social worker arrived, Jessie had no choice but to turn the child over to her, bag and baggage. She pressed a kiss into Lizzy's soft, fuzzy hair before letting her go. The woman possessed a grandmotherly air, a broad soft bosom, and careful arms that held Lizzy safely. "Don't worry. We'll take good care of her. I have a secure car seat, but if you'd bring the baby seat and the diaper bag that would be a big help."

Unable to respond without sobbing, Jessie nodded. She loaded her lap with the requested items and followed the woman to the curb. At least the social worker didn't find her totally useless. Once she watched the car holding Lizzy out of sight, she had nothing more to do than drive herself home as she'd said she would.

Chapter Twenty-Five

Home by two-thirty where her dad had the Sinners preshow airing on the TV, a beer in his hand, and a bowl of peanuts to shell by his side. Jessie rolled through the kitchen and took a place by his side.

"Didn't think you'd be back so soon. Grab a beer and join me. Teddy and the other guy are trying to make this match sound like it won't be a blowout, but I mean they are playing the Browns. The Sinners could start with their second team and the backup quarterback and still win."

Jessie studied Teddy on the screen. He didn't know yet. Running through the injured list, who had returned to play, who stayed out, he appeared cheerful and upbeat. She heard her mom come in from the yard where she'd been watering plants as September appeared to be mimicking a scorching August only with less rain.

"Hey, what kind of gunk did you drag in, Jessie? You've make marks all over the floor."

"Blood," she said, flat and without explanation. That brought her mother running to her side.

"Did you hurt yourself trying to get your chair in and out of the car? I knew you needed help. Is that why you're home so early? Where's your backpack. Why didn't you call?"

"I'm only bruised as far as I know. This is Teddy's

spare chair. Ella and her boyfriend made off with mine, including my phone and the backpack. I'm sure she'll love owning my makeup. I hope they enjoy using those catheters. I know I'd like to shove one way up Wyatt's…"

"Jessie, who is Wyatt?"

"Ella's rotten boyfriend. He manhandled me and would have done worse if she hadn't stopped him. I shot him with Teddy's gun."

To give her father credit at the mention of the word gun, he turned off the TV. Then, she had to tell the whole story over again, ending with losing Lizzy to the social worker.

"That's as it should be. You can't be expected to take care of the child for hours on end. Come into your bedroom. I need to check your legs." Her mother used her no-nonsense coach's voice almost as deep and stern as her father's when he was on the field.

"I can do that myself."

"And not tell me if you need to see a doctor."

"All right. I submit."

Jessie went to her room and hiked herself onto the bed. She allowed her mother to lower her jeans and examine her legs. The knees were bruised and slightly swollen, the skin not broken. Her wrists bore a ring of black and blue where Wyatt had circled them in a vicious grip, but she demonstrated to Dale that she could still move them just fine, nothing broken. "I'm okay, Mom. I need to cath myself. Why don't you go out and watch the game? There's nothing you can do."

"Leave your jeans off. You need ice on those knees. In fact, put on a robe. You aren't going out again today." Dale shook her short-cropped head. "Here I believed Teddy Billodeaux was good for you. Your dad certainly thought so, getting you out and about, but now I don't know. The Billodeaux family attracts crazies like those kidnappers who took Xochi, always some drama about them in the tabloids."

Jessie indulged in the eyeroll she'd perfected as a teen. "They can't help being celebrities."

"Well, I don't want you involved with them anymore."

"You have no say."

"As long as you are dependent on us you will…"

"Obey our rules. Simply because I'm crippled doesn't mean I'm in my second childhood. If you want me gone, I'll find my own place like Teddy did. I can manage."

For a woman who seldom backed off from calling out an official at her basketball games, Dale stopped ranting and clamped her mouth shut. "I'll get something to ice your knees."

At this moment, nothing appealed to Jessie more than cleaning up and putting on a robe. After taking care of her most urgent needs, she studied her face in the mirror. Not as bad as she'd feared, more like she'd put on heavy smoky eyes for a hot date. She washed away all of her makeup, shook out her ponytail, brushed her hair, and got into the robe. Raising one leg after the other, Jessie put on a pair of fuzzy slippers she'd once favored. Her feet still got cold even if she didn't feel it.

In the living room, Teddy's voice beckoned as the game began. By its ease and friendly banter, he still had no idea she'd been attacked and lost Lizzy to Child Welfare. Forcing herself to join the family, Jessie waited for a sign. It came just before halftime when his delivery turned stiff, and he lost track of the game after a commercial break. One of the female sportscasters usually found on the field sat in his seat after the next ad. With a blinding and somewhat smug smile, she announced that Teddy Billodeaux had been summoned home to deal with a personal situation. As soon as they knew more, they'd certainly share the information. "Wishing you the best of luck, Teddy," she chirped before ripping into commentary on a bungled pass by the Browns like a woman whose time had come.

What if this personal situation cost him his job? Could she have handled it better by hitting that panic button sooner and not confronting Wyatt and Ella? But she had no way of knowing who Ella talked to in that back room before she approached. Or she might have simply returned to her car and let them leave? Lizzy would still be in her crib, no bloodshed, no violence brought into her small world or Teddy's life. Jessie just didn't know.

****

The Browns lost miserably, a game not worth watching, Coach Mo declared before turning the channel to a better match. Jessie helped her mother make a salad to go with the grilled salmon for dinner. Time moved so glacially it might as well have been winter rather than a long, hot September day. Jessie waited for some word from Teddy, any word. He did not call. But then, she'd lost her phone to Ella, too, so much stuffed into the pouch and backpack on her chair. Still, her parents hung on to a landline, and he had the number.

At seven, he drove up in his van, and selecting his

chair over his sticks, approached the house by way of the garage. Jessie let him in and spoke before he could say a word.

"I'm so sorry I made a mess of everything. Oh, Teddy, Child Welfare took Lizzy, and Ella meant for you to have her."

"Not your fault. You defended yourself and Lizzy. I'm proud of you and glad you were there to be with her. Are you hurt? The cops said her boyfriend assaulted you." The deep concern that troubled his eyes and erased his smile nearly broke her.

Jessie showed off her knees still draped by bags of frozen peas. "Sexy, huh?" she said, trying to make light of her injuries, of the whole assault scenario. "I'm fine. Ella pulled him off of me. I hate to think how she'll pay for that. Will you be able to get Lizzy back?"

"Not tonight. I had a chance to read the letter. Ella left very clear instructions about Lizzy. It certainly explains why she didn't want to become attached to her child. She knew she was going to give her up one way or the other. This Wyatt sure has a mercenary heart—or none at all."

"Any chance the police will find them?"

"It occurred to me while the officers filled me in that I had the number Ella called over and over again in my contacts list. Not her father after all. We phoned to see who might answer and if we could determine their direction. Ella picked up. She said she was taking Wyatt for medical help since you nearly killed him, but wouldn't say where, not to chase them since they were never coming back. Right after that the phone went dead. Sounded like a semi ran over it so they were on one of the major highways, I-10 or 95."

"We can still track them. My phone is in the pouch on my wheelchair. They stole that along with your TV. They might not even hear the ring tone if it's in the back of their truck. If I could kick myself, I would, for not thinking of that sooner."

"Doubt if I'd have thought of that with all that went on. We'll call and tell the police."

Coach Mo stuck his head around the corner. "You going to keep that young man sitting in the hall all night, Jessie? Let him in. Did you have dinner, son? I'll bet not."

"No, sir, I didn't. After I got word, I hightailed it back to Lafayette. I'm not looking forward to returning to the apartment. My spread and sheets are considered evidence. They took them away. All that mess is still on the floor, and well, no Lizzy and no TV to take my mind off of this situation. When I think I put Jessie in danger…"

"You couldn't know, and Jess, she handled herself very well." Coach made his hand into a gun and pulled the trigger. "Ka-pow! Wish she'd hit him in the nuts. That'd be the last baby the guy who tried to rape my daughter ever made."

Dale Minvielle added to the crowd in the hall. "For heaven's sake, Mo, this afternoon was dreadful. Do we have to relive it again?" She jerked her head in Teddy's direction. "You probably have lots of paperwork do. Thanks for stopping by to check on Jessie. She'll be fine."

Jessie figured if her mom could have gotten by the two wheelchairs to slam the door in Teddy's face, she would have.

"Dale, the boy needs a place to stay tonight until he

can get his apartment straightened out. You could stay in our son's room, and Jess has that special shower. She dragged some of the blood in here, too, but my wife cleaned it up like it never existed and wiped down your wheelchair, too. We'll have to borrow it until we can get our daughter a new one. I'll bet Dale could get you some supper, too. We had plenty of salmon left over. It's not my favorite."

Dale nodded as her neck were stiff. "No, you'd rather have fried catfish. Certainly, I can put a meal together for you, Teddy, but wouldn't you rather stay at the ranch until this is straightened out?"

"Usually my family remains in New Orleans after the Sinners play, goes out for dinner, and hangs around watching the night game together. Even Knox Polk and Corazon sometimes go along now that they are family, though Knox hates leaving the ranch out of his care. I sent them a text saying there had been a problem with the baby, and I had to return home sooner than I expected, not to worry."

Jessie's mom nailed him with her stern coach's eyes. "You lied to them."

Teddy shook his head vehemently. His fine blond hair drifted across his blue eyes, making him seem like a guilty child. "No, ma'am. There was nothing they could do to help right now, and I didn't want to spoil their day. Tomorrow, I'll start right on it and see if my folks can do something about getting Lizzy back. I hate to think of her in a foster home even for a night. I'm all she has."

Despite the distress on Teddy's face, Dale hadn't finished with him. She dressed him down like one of her players who had seriously screwed up. "Do you really think they will give that child back to an unmarried handicapped man with a job that takes him away from home?"

"Mom, stop!" Jessie put in her plea. Her stomach knotted at her mother's attack. She could taste the oily salmon in her mouth.

"Yeah, Dale, leave the guy alone. Go rustle up some grub. I'll bet he's starving. He's staying the night with us. It's all settled," Coach Mo, one of the few people who could handle Dale Minvielle, ordered.

"Make sure you stay in your own room tonight," Dale said, before making an almost military turn and stalking off to the kitchen. A dish slammed down on a table. The refrigerator door shut with a vengeance.

"Why don't we go into the living room until the food is ready," Coach Mo suggested, his voice affable enough, but his broad features set like a bulldog.

"I need to put on some clothes. Teddy, keep my dad company, would you?"

When Jessie returned dressed in comfortable sweats to accommodate her swollen knees, they pretended to watch the game until Dale stuck her head into the room and asked as if it were a great bother, "Beer or iced tea?"

"I really could use a beer right now," Teddy answered, swinging his chair in her direction to be polite.

Determined to find fault, Dale countered, "Do you drink a lot of beer?"

"Not all that much, Mrs. Minvielle. Thank you for the meal."

Coach Mo took his eyes off the screen and turned to his wife. "If everything is ready, why don't you come put your feet up with me? Let Jessie sit with him while he eats."

"It's my kitchen, and I can stay in it if I want."

Mo shook his head. "She's hard to get along with when she gets this way."

Jessie, her cheeks red with fury, spoke up. "Forget about the food. We'll go out for something."

"And waste the salmon?"

"Throw it in the garbage for all I care. Teddy, I'm driving."

"Huh?"

"Dad installed hand controls in my old car for my birthday. We had some complications. That's why I was late. If I'd been even later, I'd have missed Wyatt and Ella altogether. Wish I had."

"Sometimes, it's all in the timing," Teddy said.

"Damn right, in football and in life. Go on, get a pizza or something on me." Coach Mo fished out a twenty and thrust it at Jessie. "Get going. Your room will be ready when you return."

Neither of them argued with Jessie's dad. They headed out but had to pass the kitchen first where Dale scraped salmon and rice into the garbage disposal and declined to look at them. As they opened the door and went down the ramp, they heard Coach Mo shouting at his wife, "You see what you're doing here, Dale, driving our daughter away."

Though they had some difficulty getting two chairs in the backseat, Teddy got Jessie set behind the wheel first, then folded his as he sat in the passenger seat and managed to cram it behind the headrest. Jess concentrated on the driving, trying hard not to seem like a person with road rage. She got them to Buffalo Wild

Wings where they could snack on sticky chicken and pretend to watch the game on the multiple screens. Neither had any interest in it.

Once they finished ordering, Teddy said, "I can go to a motel or drive to the ranch even if no one is around. That would be better than making your mom madder at me. I understand she's upset by the danger I put you in however accidentally."

"Teddy, Ella said it, you are too good. If this keeps up, I'm moving out. She can't mother hen me for the rest of my life, and she'll try if I stay in her house. Help me find a place I can handle."

"Mine," he offered so quickly she knew it had been in the back of his mind. "You can have Ella's room if you don't want to sleep with me."

Jessie's hand found the side of his face, cupped it, and she gave him a kiss despite some hoots from neighboring tables filled with college guys. "I want to sleep with you again and again. For tonight, let's get a hotel room. I'm not going home."

"I really don't want to come between you and your mother."

"She started this. She'll come around, but it is time I went out on my own."

"If you're sure."

"I am."

Teddy dug in his pocket. For a split second, she thought the small box might be a ring—but most jewelers didn't use tin foil for wrapping paper.

"I got this for your birthday. It's not much." He shoved the box in her direction.

Smiling, Jessie ripped off the cheap wrapping and opened the box—empty. Her smile didn't drop, though

Teddy's did. "Ella strikes again. I got a gold and pearl necklace she admired and gave it to her to wrap."

"Let her keep it. I have what I really want. You." She followed that statement with another kiss, longer and deeper. Let the whole world hoot if it wanted.

## Chapter Twenty-Six

In the end, they decided to go to the ranch. They executed a stealthy switch of vehicles to Teddy's more accessible van, which probably fooled no one inside the Minvielle home, but no doors opened or blinds raised as they completed the complicated procedure of getting two wheelchairs stowed and both people buckled into the front seat. That maneuver completed, the couple headed out of town.

"We'll have the place to ourselves since the family usually stays over in New Orleans after a game. We can share my bed if you don't mind sleeping under a teddy bear afghan—or sleep in Lorena's adjoining room if you want. But I'd really like you to be by my side when I have to explain myself to the clan tomorrow. My parents won't let me off easy when they find out I tried to brush them off. Call your mother and let her know where you're going." Teddy activated his phone and offered it to her.

"Why should I after the way she treated you?"

"Because my own mom would want to know no matter how angry she got. She's trying to protect you."

"Make that overprotect." Yet Jessie conceded by leaving a text and immediately turning off his cell.

Teddy's phone had been off for hours, partly because he wanted no interruptions while dealing with the police, and partly because he wished to avoid being bombarded by calls from his family on his long and frantic drive to the apartment. The message from the authorities transferred to the booth requested his immediate presence in Lafayette because an act of violence had taken place in his residence. An Officer Nelson added that the baby and Miss Minvielle were safe and well. He withheld information on Ella, saying that would be best handled in person. Undoubtedly, he'd used a lure to gain Teddy's immediate compliance, and had gotten it. The drive from New Orleans to Lafayette never stretched out longer. Thank God, no cop felt like pulling over a van with a handicapped license plate doing seventy-five most of the way.

Teddy opened the gate of Lorena Ranch and took his red van down the winding road to the mansion by the bayou. As they passed each live oak lining the drive, motion sensors in their boughs activated the security lights turning the leaves to silver and the Spanish moss into ropes of gold. Beautiful, but the ranch had gone into full surveillance mode. "Uh-oh. Looks like Knox Polk stayed home."

Rounding the last turn to the house, they couldn't help but notice the chandelier in the foyer glittered through the sidelights of the front door the family seldom used strewing the lawn with a pattern of diamonds. All of the lights downstairs appeared to be on as well as some of the ones in the bedrooms.

"Oh, no," Teddy muttered. "Judging by the cars, the family has gathered already. Don't be fooled by the number of vehicles. They probably doubled up. Brace yourself. You are in for the full Billodeaux again, and this time it's not a party."

Greeted only by the family dogs, they took their

time arranging their wheelchair entrance through the kitchen. Only Corazon occupied the usually homey space. She arranged quartered quesadillas around a bowl of dipping sauce. Her welcome less warm than usual, she said, "Team meeting in the den. You the last to arrive." She hefted the large tray for transport to possibly hungry people.

"Are you going too?" Teddy questioned.

"Si, I am family now."

"I guess it's okay if I bring Jessie."

"You ask."

They followed Corazon's broad behind into the lion's den where the pride lounged waiting to pounce. Most sat on the floor. Junior held Xochi in the nest made by his muscular crossed legs. His large hands rested protectively on her baby bump. The perpetual honeymooners, Tom and Alix lay stretched out, long limbs intertwined as usual, near Dean and Stacy on the brown leather sofa. His twin nurse sisters perched on the edge of their seats like small doves of mercy waiting to descend and do their part. Intellectual, bespectacled Trin had a look on his face that said, "You've done it now," but spared him a nod of support for all the years they'd worked together producing the camp's newsletter.

Teddy caught a break with Lorena still being in Australia and Mack out on the west coast getting ready to play a Monday night game with the Cowboys. Lori would have been on his side, but Mack definitely tended to enjoy seeing someone else in trouble other than himself. They'd get the whole story before the night ended from the Billodeaux hot line no matter where in the world they were. At least, the grandchildren were nestled in the nursery, which explained the upstairs lights shining, so a little less noise and chaos than usual.

The ever-hungry T-Rex, his youngest brother, reached for a quesadilla and had his hand slapped away by Mama Nell. "After we talk."

"Yeah, after we talk," his tiny and rarely ravenous twin, Edie repeated. Being tucked in beside Daddy Joe made her appear even more petite than usual. The hand that predicted her brother would grow into a very big man retreated.

Nell turned her wounded brown eyes on Teddy who had never given her any trouble outside of medical emergencies since the day he'd been caught spying on a pair of lovers in the palm grove. At times like this, Teddy became all too aware that only he had no blood connection to the Billodeauxs. Though he'd long ago gotten over his fear of being kicked out of the family for any kind of misbehavior, being the always-good kid seemed ingrained in his nature by now. In trying to spare them another crisis after the ordeal with Xochi and handling this himself, he'd disappointed.

Teddy rolled to the center of the room. Jessie followed, parked by his side, and took his hand. He started by announcing, "Jess stays. She's part of this." No one objected. He tried to waylay some of the scolding without much luck by saying, "The baby is fine."

As with many emotional issues, Nell took the lead away from her husband. "Did you really think we'd just sit there and watch the rest of the game after we got your note about the baby and you went off the air? We were only a half hour behind you once we got everyone in a vehicle. Annie phoned into the neonatal nursery asking for a sub for the night shift. She's more current on caring for endangered infants than any of us. And then to have your phone turned off! Do you know how worried we all were?"

"Yeah, we headed for Chapelle as soon as we got out of the showers. Our wives had the cars ready to go, my kids packed into the back of one of them. We've been here an hour. Where were you?" Dean asked, seriously irritated.

"I figured you'd be tired after the game and only want a good meal and your own bed." No way would he confess he'd been eating chicken wings with Jessie.

"Coach put in my backup for the second half the score ran so high. He took Junior out too. Tom and Alix had to stand by because you never know when the team will need a kicker, so we couldn't leave. They drove up with Junior and Xochi."

Tom nudged Dean's foot with his own. "Thanks for acknowledging kickers are indispensable, but we were concerned too. Junior wouldn't let me drive because of Xo's condition, or we'd have been here sooner than Dean."

Teddy hung his head, let his blond hair fall over his eyes, a way of hiding he'd perfected long ago. "I apologize to all of you. I should have given more information. Nothing happened to the baby and Jessie is okay. She walked in on Ella and her boyfriend planning to desert Lizzy after stripping my apartment of anything they thought they could sell."

Annie's usually kind brown eyes narrowed. "For the sake of your television set, I'm going to owe someone a double shift."

"Sorry, I appreciate your sacrifice, I really do, but there is more. Ella's man attacked Jessie. She got to my gun and shot him in the hip."

Knox Polk, usually a silent presence, stood behind the recliner where his wife had plopped down and put her feet up. He spoke. "Good for you, honey. A little more to the left and you'd have got him in the crotch."

T-Rex snickered. A few other smiles blossomed, easing the tension in the room. Teddy took advantage of that by racing on with the rest of the story.

"They took her wheelchair and escaped, but she found my old one and summoned help." He gave Jessie a "proud of you" glance and noticed Knox had done the same. "When I got home, I had to deal with the police, lots of questions, and a walk through the apartment to see if they'd taken anything more than the TV and Jessie's chair. Then, I went to see Jess to make sure she was okay."

Mama Nell nodded her approval, but asked, "Where is Lizzy?"

Jessie broke in to take her share of the heat. "I said I'd care for her until Teddy arrived, but the police called Child Welfare to take her away. I suppose they didn't think I was able enough for the job. I'm the one who lost her." Her grip on Teddy's hand tightened until her knuckles turned white.

Nell shook her head. "No, it is procedure." Her eyes turned to Teddy. "If only you had called us before you left New Orleans. We're still licensed for foster care—have been since Xochi joined the family. You of all my children should know that as we got to keep you with us until the adoption went through. Lizzy could be with us right now if only you'd asked for our help."

"We're a team, son. No one wins the game alone, and you have all of us." Joe Billodeaux spread out his famous hands and gestured to the room full of family.

"What he means is we admire your desire to be independent, but you shouldn't be ashamed to ask for a little aid if you need it," Nell said, interpreting the football metaphor.

Teddy's head came up. Jessie reached over and brushed the fair hair from his eyes. "Can we get Lizzy over here tonight?"

"I'd like to say yes, but I think it would be best to try in the morning. She's probably settled in for the evening, and Wynn and her baby brother are sleeping in the nursery tonight. We'll set the wheels in motion first thing tomorrow until you get legal custody. Lizzy can stay here until everything is straightened out. You may too. I imagine your apartment is a mess right now."

"It is. Might Jessie stay over tonight?"

"Certainly. She can have Lorena's room next to your bathroom to make things easier for her."

If his mother suspected they'd be sleeping together, she didn't let on. Instead, she stayed T-Rex's stealthy hand making for the quesadillas again, and said, "Are we finished here?"

Knox Polk cleared his throat and weighed in again. "About this man you shot, Jessie, did you give the police a good description, get a name or license plate, anything to help?"

"Yes, I did. First name, Wyatt, long curly black hair, dark eyes and complexion, lean build. He has a record and planned to sell Lizzy to some couple desperate for children, but said she'd turned out too black for that. No one would want her."

Compassionate Xochi sucked in a breath. "She can always have a home with me and Junior. We'd love her like our own." Junior nodded his big head and kissed his wife's dark, wavy hair.

"We'd have plenty of room for her too," Dean offered.

"We raised twelve. One more would be fine," Daddy Joe countered.

"Thanks to all of you, but Lizzy is my only connection to my dead mother now that Ella is gone. I want to raise her, give her a safe place and a good home, the same as Maydell did for me." The worry that creased Nell's face wasn't lost on him. She didn't believe he could do it but wouldn't say.

Jessie homed in on that look as well. "I'll help all I can."

"As will each and every one of us," Nell responded.

"Glad that's settled. Now about the culprit. I think I might have a picture of him from the gate security camera. Any idea what kind of vehicle he drives?" said the supremely unsentimental Knox Polk.

"I wasn't quick enough to get a license number, but it's a beat up old Ford truck with more rust than paint," Jessie answered.

"I figured no taxi dropped her off all the way out here no matter what she said. Sounds like the truck that brought Ella to our gate in the first place. I thought she'd been hitchhiking and didn't want a lecture. I have his face and probably the license plate stored on the computer in case I needed it later. He got down to haul her suitcase from the back of the truck."

"The Lafayette police will have his last name by

now. I told them to contact Newt Smalls about him," Teddy added.

"Good. I'm going out to the security building to send them the information right away." Knox turned to leave, but Corazon grabbed his arm. "You eat something first. You probably don't eat the whole time I am gone."

"I had a beer and a sandwich while I watched the game, but it's been a while. Nothing as good as your cooking. Wonder I don't weigh as much as Junior by now." Knox scooped up two quesadillas on his way out.

Taking her eyes off her retreating husband, Corazon turned them toward Teddy. "You know I babysit anytime for Lizzy."

"She'll probably have to fight off half the family and our Nurse Shammy for the privilege. She's been yearning for more babies to take care of, and DJ is too far away in New Orleans. See, you don't even have to ask for help, Teddy," Nell added.

"I know, I know. Let T-Rex eat. He seems to be starving."

Edie's little hand got to the quesadillas before her twin. "He's always starving. You have to be fast to get anything when he's around."

The family polished off the snacks before Xo and her husband departed for their house in Chapelle. As Junior helped her up from the floor, she said, "I recognized Ella as a liar from the start. I wish I had been able to see the future as well to spare you all of this, Teddy."

"Not your fault. You warned me. Some good might result from all this. You never know."

"You are an eternal optimist, but I hope so." With

her husband's big arm sheltering her shoulders, Xo and Junior left by the kitchen door after giving Corazon a kiss on the cheek.

Tom and Alix reclaimed Tom's old bedroom and left the quarterback and his wife to sleep amid Stacy's frilly princess décor since Mack had long ago claimed Dean's former space. Neither of the kickers appreciated a welter of lace. The twins automatically returned to their mutual bedroom.

Teddy hung back. "Go ahead, Jessie, since you know the way. You get to use the bathroom first. I want to talk to Mom and Dad for a minute."

"What?" Nell asked as soon as Jessie cleared the room.

"Dale Minvielle believes I put her daughter in danger. She doesn't want me hanging around Jessie anymore. They had a big falling out, and well, I invited Jessie to come live with me."

"I thought something was up when she came here without her backpack," Joe observed.

"Ella made off with it when she stole the wheelchair to get her wounded boyfriend out of the apartment. Jess stormed out with me and didn't take anything with her. We'll go back tomorrow when her parents are out and collect her car and clothes. I did make Jessie leave a message saying where she'd be tonight."

Nell gave her approval. "That was the right thing to do no matter what your feelings at the moment."

"I'm not as upset as Jessie. Coach Mo is on our side, and that counts for a lot. So you see I won't be alone if I get Lizzy back. The two of us can handle it."

"You should have the chance to try," she agreed.

"Hell, yes, any son of mine will make a great father." He squeezed Teddy's shoulder in a man-to-man kind of way.

"Well, maybe not Mack right now, but he'll get better," his wife said a bit sadly.

"He'll grow up just like I did when I found the right woman. I think Teddy has discovered his."

"You two are always great. Thanks for raising me to do the right thing. One other item. Jessie might need some catheters since she left without any."

"I'm sure we have some in the Camp Love Letter medical supplies. I'll leave them in the bathroom along with a new toothbrush."

Teddy gave his mom a kiss, his dad a firm handshake, and wheeled off to join Jessie. He doubted sex waited at the end of this long and turbulent day, but his greatest desire amounted to wanting to curl his body around Jessie and keep her as safe as he was able.

## Chapter Twenty-Seven

Teddy, like a gentleman, let Jess have first use of the bathroom in the morning after they'd uncurled from each other and decided on quiet sex around sunrise. Across the hall, Dean showered for an early departure to New Orleans, and the team meeting before claiming some time off prior to the endless training sessions beginning again. Likewise, the other Sinners moved around the second floor trying not to wake anyone else, especially Dean's children. When the baby, DJ, started howling for his first meal of the day, and Wynn shouted, "Mommy, Deej hungry," so loudly any coital noises Jessie and Ted made got lost in the uproar.

"Do you think I should rumple the other bed?"

"If it makes you feel better, but I already told my parents you're moving in with me. I doubt they'll be either fooled or upset."

"Okay. So would you like to shower with me?" Jessie closed the bathroom door.

"Start the water, climb on the bench. I'll be right there!"

As they explored what could be done with lots of gel and a handheld sprayer, the other inhabitants made their way down to breakfast without knocking on Teddy's door to say goodbye. He strongly suspected they knew what was going on as well.

Dried and dressed in yesterday's clothes since they

brought no other, Teddy shaved his light beard with an electric razor while Jess fretted over having no makeup. "I keep telling you that you don't need it, but if you must, Lorena might have left some of her gunk in the drawers on the right-hand side."

Jessie sorted through the offerings, most not quite right for her skin tones, but she used a light application of blush, some mascara and liner, drawing the line at painting on someone else's lipstick. They took the elevator downstairs to find Nell, Joe, and Corazon drinking coffee around a mostly depleted platter of turkey sausage patties and buckwheat pancakes.

"I make more if is not enough," Corazon offered, starting to rise.

"Plenty for us. We're not athletes. We'll get our own coffee and juice." Teddy checked his watch. "When we finish here, we're going over to Jessie's house to pack her things. Might take us a while since her parents will be at work."

Nell put down her coffee mug in a rather decisive way. "Corazon and I will clean up your apartment while you do that. I don't have any appointments until two."

"Me and Knox will go along to the Minvielle's and help you haul," Joe announced. "Dean, Tom, and Junior said they'd drive back after the meeting if you need them, but positively no lifting for Xochi. That's Junior's condition."

"Not necessary. We can manage by ourselves." Jessie's hand alit on his forearm, staying any more words. He'd observed the gesture often when Nell wanted to calm her often-excitable husband. Had he and Jess come that far already?

"Who gave me the lecture about accepting help

graciously? Sure, we could manage ourselves, make dozens of trips to the van with a couple of boxes or bags on our laps or wait for your cleaning lady to mop up the blood and put sheets on the bed. However, if we can do all that this morning with their help, we should accept."

Joe Billodeaux brought out his best grin. "I like this girl. She's bossy like your mother."

"Hey, I'm not bossy. I'm logical and sympathetic. You are hard-headed and emotional." Nell squeezed his arm in a way that said love you anyhow.

"That's why we're perfect together. Soon as you finish eating, we move out." Joe clapped his hands as if he'd just come from a huddle about an important play.

While they finished breakfast, Corazon and Nell assembled enough cleaning supplies in bags for a small hospital. Joe and Knox Polk lugged the stuff to the truck and seated their wives in the double cab. Teddy and Jessie lead the way in the van, first stopping to drop off the cleaning crew at the apartment and next pulling up to the Minvielle's equipped with boxes and bags thanks to the forethought of Knox.

Jessie emptied the contents of her dresser drawers and closet into the containers. The two tall, able-bodied men hauled. She cleared out her bathroom of makeup, a hair dryer, and her medical needs.

"You taking any of the furniture?" Knox asked.

"No, it's theirs. Just my laptop on the desk. Good thing I didn't take it with me yesterday or Ella's boyfriend would have taken that, too."

"Yeah, I had mine on the road. I wonder they didn't rip the desktop out," Teddy said, feeling a little irrelevant, a bit pushed aside.

"Ella convinced the guy no one would buy it. She did do that for you."

"Well, good for Ella." Teddy did a doublecheck of the closet. "Hey, you left something way in the back in a garment bag."

"Nothing I need." Jessie did a three-sixty survey of her bedroom. "Do you want me to take the TV on the dresser since yours is gone?"

"No, I'll buy another one. I wouldn't want your mother to accuse me of stealing it." Okay, so a little bitterness sneaked into his tone when he dropped his guard. No one thought he could take care of a baby or Jessie or even move her into his place without help, and it seeped through behind the wry smile.

His father, stacking four boxes under his chin, caught his mood like a well-delivered pass. He'd always been good at motivating his teammates. "Stop goofing off, Teddy." He dropped the lower two boxes into his son's lap. "Get those out to the truck and spare my back. Hand them to Knox. You know how he always has to arrange the cargo just so."

Two more trips, and they had the truck loaded. Jessie penciled a note to her parents and left it on the kitchen counter. Moving in with Teddy. I have to get a new phone since mine was stolen. Call his number if you need to get in contact. Short, blunt and to the point, the nicest thing about hard copy is that no one could argue with it.

Teddy glanced at the note. "You should add Love, Jessie no matter how angry you are right now. That's what Mama Nell says. Even when she thought the baby might be mine, she said, 'Love you no matter what.'"

Reluctantly, Jessie added the words. "You are too

much of a good influence, Teddy Wilkes Billodeaux. Hard to keep a good mad on when you're around."

"Glad I'm good for something."

"I can think of others." Jessie made sure both of the older men were out of earshot. "Because I don't plan on sleeping in the second bedroom."

That brought out the sunny smile missing all morning. It pretty much stayed on his face on the way to the apartment to unload as Jessie followed him in her reclaimed car. The blood and wilted balloons had vanished, but he found a television bigger than his own with a built-in DVD player waiting to be installed and his bed made up with hospital white sheets covered by his spread and the teddy bear afghan from the ranch. His smile turned upside down.

"I appreciate your efforts, but I planned to buy my own set and thought maybe Jessie would like to help me pick out the spread."

Mama Nell put her rubber-gloved hands on her hips. "The TV is from one of the Love Letter cottages. You can consider it a loaner. Suit yourselves on getting another spread, but I thought Lizzy would love that afghan just like you did when you weren't pretending to be too old for it. We were simply trying to get you back to normal as fast as we could."

Corazon, also rubber-gloved, loomed behind her. "We clean your bathroom too."

"Muchas gracias. Well, we'll just put all the bags and boxes into the second bedroom and let Jessie sort it out later."

Jessie quirked an eyebrow at him.

He added, "Because she's going to be living here with me, together, in my room." The dreaded blush heated his cheeks.

Daddy Joe laughed and dropped a stack of boxes to slap him on the back. Knox just nodded, assimilating the fact, but his wife pressed her hands to her broad, big-hearted chest, and said, "I am so happy for you."

"No need to be embarrassed, Teddy. If you want to pay for something, you can treat us to lunch once the unloading is done," Nell suggested.

Teddy took advantage of that suggestion to escape to the truck for a pile of bags. With so many hands, the job took little time. He suggested a Mexican restaurant for lunch, but Corazon vetoed that. "We eat Mexican all the time and mine is better. Greek, I would like some Greek food."

Over heaped platters of gyro meat, hummus, and stuffed grape leaves, Teddy's phone sounded. "Excuse me. I'd let it go to voicemail, but it might be about Lizzy. You did call Child Welfare this morning, didn't you, Mom?"

"As soon as they opened. I wouldn't forget something so important."

Automatically following the rules of his upbringing that dictated no phones or other devices at the dinner table, he took the call in the lobby and returned to share the news.

"Not Child Welfare. The police tracked Ella and Wyatt, last name Coffey, to an emergency clinic in Opelousas where he claimed he'd shot himself cleaning his gun. They treated him and gave him a tetanus shot and something for the pain. He paid with a credit card, but they were gone by the time lawmen showed up. Next hit came in Shreveport. Ella hocked the TV and the necklace I got for Jessie. They left the truck with the wheelchair and cell phone parked behind a cheap motel. The management picked up the call from the cops, but the two of them were long gone in a boosted car from the motel lot. Turns out that's what Wyatt did time for: stealing cars. Evidently, he has mechanical skills."

Nell took a long sip of her lemon and rosewater-flavored Lebanese iced tea. "Too bad he didn't apply those skills to an honest job and make a home for Ella and the baby."

"I don't think the idea ever entered his mind." Teddy seized a lozenge of grape leaves and dipped it in tzatziki sauce. He took a vicious bite out of the unoffending appetizer.

Knox Polk pondered the criminal mind for a minute. "From Shreveport, they could go in any direction: Texas, Arkansas, back across the state to Tennessee, or head south again. But I wouldn't mess with Texas or come back here. Arkansas and Tennessee have plenty of woods to hide in, and their accents won't make them stand out as much."

Before he could go on with his analysis, Nell's phone rang. "Child Welfare. I'll take it in the lobby."

She got a unanimous, "No, you won't."

"Forget about manners, Mom. Tell us what they have to say," Teddy insisted.

"All right." The way she smiled and nodded, said, "Yes, I understand" several times, and ended with "That will be fine. We'll be waiting for you," her audience knew the news must be good. She disconnected and picked up her fork again.

"Come on! Don't tease us," Teddy begged.

"The social worker will bring the baby to the ranch this afternoon. If I'm not there, Corazon and Nurse

Shammy will be standing by to receive her. It practically broke Shammy's heart when Stacy didn't want her to come help after DJ was born. Stacy has her own way of doing things and thought our family nurse might be getting too old for night feedings. I don't think Shammy got over that insult until camp started again to keep her occupied. She's said over and over that gardening and long walks don't take the place of meaningful work, and Clive agrees with her. Call them semi-retired, she always says. Call them whenever needed."

Ted explained the situation to Jessie, the only outsider at the table. "Nurse Shammy is married to our sometimes butler, Clive Brinsley. They found love late in life and have no children but us. When they won a big civil suit for personal injuries against the actress, Layla Devlin, they considered building a retirement house on the ranch since Dad offered them land, but decided to renovate the place that belonged to Dad's aunt near the front gate of the ranch."

"I've noticed it! White picket fence, a garden full of flowers in the front, and vegetables to the rear. Rockers on the porch. It's a beautiful old place."

"Yes, the gingerbread cottage appealed to them both. They don't need tons of room—but it is rumored they put in a Jacuzzi big enough for two."

"This is true. I have seen this with my own eyes," Corazon swore. "What do you think, mi esposo? Maybe we get one."

The light in her eyes gave away the fact that she jested, but Knox, being Knox, gave her statement grave consideration. "If you think it would be good for your sore back, I'd consider it." He appeared puzzled by the

Lynn Shurr

laughter that followed.

"Everyone, finish eating. We want to be there when Lizzy arrives." Teddy signaled the waitress for takeout boxes. "Maybe I can take her home with me."

"Not so fast, Ted. The social worker will do a walk-through to make sure nothing has changed at the ranch since the last time we hosted a child, and she'll check the nursery at our place. After that, she wants to interview you at the apartment and do the same. Lizzy has to stay with us until the case is settled. You must understand." Nell touched his hand a second before Jessie reached out to clasp the other.

"Yeah, I guess. So I have to go home and wait." Teddy dumped the generous remains of gyro meat and rice into a takeout box and asked for the check.

"Remember, I'll be there with you." Jessie blessed him with a smile that made most of the hurt go away.

Chapter Twenty-Eight

Waiting, waiting, waiting. The doorbell rang at three accompanied by the small flashing light a deaf person using the suite might need. They'd ruled out sex while waiting and instead put away Jessie's clothes and cosmetics. She claimed two of Teddy's dresser drawers for her underwear and T-shirts, but hung other items in Ella's closet in order not to crowd him out. They placed the boxes and bags out on the curb and made certain the nursery bedroom appeared clean and inviting. Teddy brewed coffee as if they needed to increase their jitters, and Jessie insisted on going to Albertson's bakery for fancy cookies to offer the social worker. After all, the trip killed time, and they needed to impress.

They let the social worker in and posed their chairs on either side of the coffee table set with a plate of cookies and decorated with a bouquet of supermarket flowers. After the scrubbing Nell and Corazon had done, the place smelled fresh, no taint of Wyatt's cigarette smoke or funk of a guy living alone, not that Teddy had been sloppy, but they wanted to make sure not even a dishtowel lay out of place on the counter.

This was a different woman from the one who had taken Lizzy away, younger, more gaunt and bony, a dishwater blonde, hair in a bun escaping in wisps around her face, a face possessing thin lips, and an unpierced ear with a very sharp pencil for taking notes stuck behind it. The social worker took a seat between them, opened her black briefcase, and got straight to the point.

"I'm Miss Simms, Elizabeth's case worker. While I've seen a copy of the letter left by the mother expressing her desire to leave the child with you, there are other considerations such as your ability to care for her physically." Her eyes, gray as rain clouds, swept over their wheelchairs.

"I've been taking care of her nights since Lizzy came into the world. I cut her umbilical cord." Teddy's normally pleasing voice came out more sharply than he intended at her implication.

Jessie rushed to soften the situation. "Could we offer you some coffee and cookies?"

Miss Simms answered in an I-cannot-be-bribed tone of voice. "No, thank you. Who are you?"

"I'm Jessica Minvielle. I'll help Teddy take care of the child."

"Coach Mo's daughter, paralyzed from the waist down, I've heard. How are you going to help Mr. Billodeaux exactly?"

Did everyone know her business? Jessie guessed she shared her father's local fame, and heaven knew she should be used to being crippled by now. She answered politely. "Both of us have been feeding and changing her. We put a pad on the bed so we can do it easily. We keep a small cooler of formula nearby in case either of us is out of our chairs when she cries. I've rocked her to sleep. Lizzy's mother didn't take much interest in her."

"That's fine for an infant, but what about when the child starts to walk? They are as fast as rabbits and into everything like puppies. This apartment is only a couple of blocks from one of the busiest streets in Lafayette, not to mention the constant student traffic along this road. If she got out one day, she could be run over as quick as a stray dog."

"Teddy can get around on crutches. We'd watch her constantly and keep her inside."

"There is no fenced yard, no yard at all, for fresh air and outdoor play."

"We'd take her to the park and my folks' place. You've been there. She'd have acres to roam and ponies to ride." The edge in Teddy's voice turned to desperation.

The social worker drew her sharpened pencil from her hair and wrote a note in the case file spread out next to the colorful macarons. "I understand you work some nights and in New Orleans on weekends during football season. Would this young lady be the caretaker when you're away?"

"I'd be willing to do that, but he has a large family that can offer help also." For now, Jessie kept her currently part-time job as a trainer quiet, but she'd give it up for Teddy and the baby if necessary. She'd already decided that. Unlike UL, they truly needed her—and Teddy had already given her tastes of freedom unimaginable only weeks ago.

"Yes, Martha Gilmore spoke very highly of the Billodeauxs and their values. She's the one who collected the baby after the terrible incident in which you were involved. I've seen the police report. Their home is certainly impressive and very secure," Miss Simms said as if nothing truly impressed her.

"Would you like to see the baby's room here? It's down the hall on the right." Teddy said, grabbing at anything positive.

"Of course, but don't get up. I mean, stay here while I inspect." The faux pas brought a little color to the woman's cheeks as she went off briskly to view the nursery. Over the sounds of closet doors opening and drawers being shut, Teddy whispered, "How do you think it's going?"

Jess had to admit, "Not well. She seems to have made up her mind before she came."

"We'll change it." His optimism shown on his face like sunshine.

Miss Simms returned from poking into their lives. "I assume you are cohabiting. How long have you been together?"

Teddy always seemed to choke on questions like this, so Jessie answered at once. "We've been together for a few months. I only moved in recently, but we've known each other since high school." Fine, she'd changed weeks to months and one day to recently. Would the supervisor take her word or dig deeper?

"Not very long then. Cohabitation is not commitment, you must realize. Relationships like this come and go and are not stable enough to provide a child with a good home."

"But I love Teddy and Lizzy. I am committed." Jessie knew she'd done it now, said the words that Teddy might not be able to reciprocate. She'd come a long way since he'd told her off at rehab, but had she come far enough to earn his love?

"Until you tire of caring for a baby that's not yours cooped up in this little place. Believe me, I've seen it before. This is how children end up in foster care to begin with. One partner moves out. The other can't cope."

"I do most of my work at home on the computer. Jessie would be free to go out, take more college courses, and get a second degree if she wanted." Teddy threw out all the possibilities he could think of. Obvious to Jessie, but she hoped the social worker didn't realize he grasped at straws that would not keep them afloat.

"I am sorry," Miss Simms said, but Jessie doubted she meant it. "Between your dual disabilities and lack of marriage plus the location of apartment, I can't in good conscience place the child here. She will remain with the elder Billodeauxs, who have a proven track record and might possibly adopt Elizabeth. You are welcome to visit as much as you want with unrestricted access since you are her uncle and a member of the family. Of course, you can contest my decision legally, but I doubt that you'd win."

Miss Simms tucked her pencil behind her ear again and closed the folder. Now that the decision had been made, she felt free to help herself to several cookies and wrap them in a paper napkin, as they no longer constituted a bribe. "Thank you for the treat. Really, I do wish both of you well. I'll get out by myself."

Speechless, Jessie and Teddy watched her bony backside, clad in gray gloomy like her eyes, retreat and disappear. Teddy muttered as the automatic door slowly closed, "Don't let it hit you in the ass on the way out."

Jessie picked up one of the delicate pastel macarons and squeezed it a little too hard. As the cookie crumbled, she said, "Sugar wouldn't melt in her mouth."

"I'll have to work harder, make more money, and get a better place with a yard in one of the suburbs. I need to…"

"Get married." There, Jessie said it for him. "I'd be willing."

"Do you mean that? You'd go through with one of those marriages they talk about in historical romance novels—what are they called?"

The disbelief in his baby blue eyes almost caused her physical pain. Why would he doubt her sincerity? She'd read her share of romance novels and supplied the answer.

"Marriages of convenience. Oh, they still happen. I knew a girl in college who married a foreign student to keep him in the country. But no, I'd want a real marriage, Teddy. One with sex and more children, and yes, that house with a yard when we could afford one. Weren't you listening when I said I loved you and Lizzy?"

"I thought you said that to impress the social worker. I mean I hoped if you lived with me for a while you might eventually feel that way, but I'm no X-avier Hopkins or one of the Sinners. You could aim way higher than me, Jess, way higher."

"Remember, I was engaged to a football player. If things had moved forward, I doubt Troy would have stayed with me one minute longer than he had to in order to look good—if he'd survived and I'd still been paralyzed. My October wedding might have been cancelled whether or not he lived."

"In a couple of weeks, you could have that October wedding—if you don't want anything fancy. In fact, we can get a license today, right now. Then, I want to take you to Chapelle to pick out your rings at LeClerc's. They know me and will extend credit. Get anything you want. After that, we'll visit Lizzy and tell my family."

Teddy radiated total happiness so unlike Troy who'd worn an expression of smug self-satisfaction when Jessie agreed to marry him and abide by his schedule for, well, everything from his career moves to having kids. The ring had been five carats, sold to pay some of her medical expenses uncovered by insurance. That seemed right since the bastard had left her broken. Do better than Teddy? She thought not. Still, Jessie waved a hand in front of his face to stop the flood of plans.

"One more place to go before we do all that. I left my wedding gown in the back of my closet at home. We need to swing by and pick it up. I think we'll need my birth certificate too."

Teddy's fingers flew across the keyboard of his always-nearby laptop as if not providing an immediate answer might cause her to reconsider. "Yes, we do. Picture ID, certified birth certificate, and social security number—twenty-four hour waiting period and a twenty-five-dollar fee in cash." He slapped the pocket containing his wallet. "Got that much on me and my birth certificate is in my desk. Let's go!"

Chapter Twenty-Nine

With the wedding dress secured in Teddy's van, Jessie dug through the fireproof box where her mother kept important papers. "Got it!" She waved the birth certificate in the air, but her elation lasted only a few seconds. A car pulled into the drive at the Minvielle home.

"Let it be Dad, please let it be Dad," she murmured. No way to tell by the sound of the engine since her parents drove identical SUVs in different team colors. Tucking the certificate into her spare backpack of supplies, Jess put the box into the desk drawer in her mother's small niche of a home office just off the kitchen.

Teddy waited in the hall for lack of room and bore the full brunt of Dale Minvielle's anger when she entered the house. "What are you doing here? Returning my daughter, I hope."

The hardness of her light eyes made him grateful he'd never be a referee at one of her games. He heard Jessie come up behind him. This time, he'd be the one to take the lead. No sense in lying about it being nice to see her, not when Dale already fumed like a bull in the middle of a narrow road.

"We stopped by to pick up a few more things. Jessie needs her birth certificate in order for us to get a marriage license."

"Marriage license. You are both crazy—unless you've gotten her pregnant. Is that it?"

"I'm too responsible to do that to Jessie." He didn't bring up Joe's perpetual advice about always wearing rubber raincoats, knowing it wouldn't draw a laugh from the enraged woman.

Jessie interrupted. "We've hardly had the time to know if that were the case. Don't be ridiculous."

"How am I supposed to be aware of what you did when you said he was taking you to the gym? For all we knew it was his euphemism for climbing in the sack, exactly like calling a bar The Library. Regardless, you haven't known each other long enough to marry. I forbid it! So will your father."

"Mom, we're both years past twenty-one, and I no longer live here. You can't stop us."

"You aren't competent to make this decision. Troy hasn't been dead six months yet. This—this Romeo on wheels has lured you into all sorts of dangerous activities, riding horses, carrying guns."

Teddy couldn't help himself. He smiled. How often had he wanted to be considered a little bit dangerous, a bad boy, not the guy in the chair who had a nice personality? "Riding is good core exercise and a gun saved Jessie from her attacker."

"You think the last part is funny?"

He packed that smile away. "No, ma'am."

Behind him, Jessie sighed so hard Teddy felt her warm breath on his neck. "Mother, could we get out of the hall and into the kitchen? I want to explain."

Dale gave a curt nod and led the way. She propped her slim length against a counter, folded her arms, and refused to sit down. "Talk. I can't imagine how you would justify such rash behavior."

Both turned their chairs to face her, but Jessie spoke first. "I love Teddy and the baby. The Child Welfare people won't let him have custody of Lizzy because of his disability and the lack of a wife. We can manage to give her a good home with just a little help from family."

"That's what this is all about, the little black bastard his white trash sister birthed and deserted."

Stunned for a moment by the harshness of her mother's words, Jessie fought back fast. "Most of your basketball players are black. I've never seen such prejudice in you before."

"Yes, they are, and I've lost a good many of them who went off chasing boys and having babies while in high school instead of working toward a scholarship. Jessie, what will people say when you show up holding a colored baby in your arms?"

"I don't know, Mom. Maybe that I've adopted a child who needs me. Or perhaps they'll think I got in trouble with one of Dad's players and Teddy loved me enough to marry me anyhow. Frankly, I don't care. Let people make up what they want. Besides, you haven't seen Lizzy. She has beautiful skin like café au lait and the most lovely blue eyes—like Teddy's."

Dale paced as if she stalked the sidelines in a championship game, scouting for any advantage. "Believe me, I know what it's like to fall in love with a baby. You're my only daughter, and I adored you at first sight, those big hazel eyes staring up at me. But it's not your baby, not my grandchild."

"She could be if you'd accept her," Teddy said in his most gentle manner. "Mawmaw Nadine struggled a little when Xochi came into our family, but now I believe she's her favorite grandchild. The only true Cat'lic among us, she says."

Dale didn't spare him even a slight smile. "That's your family, not ours. If you think for one minute I'm going to rush around trying to reschedule the church and reception hall, you've got another think coming, Jessica Claire Minvielle."

"I don't expect that. We'll have a small civil ceremony in the next few weeks. I don't know where or when yet, but I'll let you know." Jessie turned and started out of the room.

"Don't bother!" Dale shouted at her daughter's back.

Teddy remained behind for a minute. "Mrs. Minvielle, I hope you will attend. I'll leave a message with Coach Mo when it's all decided." Following Jessie, he thought he heard the sound of weeping from hard-as-nails Dale Minvielle.

****

Teddy found a parking space in front of LeClerc's Jewelry. The small bell brought old Mr. LeClerc from his glass-walled office, a loupe screwed in one eye as if he wore a monocle, or maybe been captured by the Borg and spied them from afar with this device. The overhead lights shone on his bald head and stooped shoulders.

"Ah, Teddy and Miss Jessie. Either one of you lose your class ring?" he said with so much hope in his voice they knew sales must be slow.

The couple moved toward the old fainting couch where parents learned the damages for class rings, often feeling the need to lie down, and past the antique hutch where Jessie's selections for silver and fine china once sat on display with a little white card proclaiming the Minvielle-Gilbert wedding. Teddy took a seat on the couch, and Mr. LeClerc perched on a large, studded, but cracked leather chair opposite with the class ring binders resting on a faux Chippendale table between them. With the tiniest of sighs suggesting he suspected a watch repair or battery replacement, the jeweler asked, "How may I help you?"

Teddy straightened his substantial shoulders, flicked the hair out of his eyes, and cleared his throat. "We'd like to look at engagement rings."

That brought old LeClerc bolt upright in his chair. The loupe dropped into his hand. He gestured toward a nearby case. "Take a look in there and see what you like. Might I wish you every happiness and thank you for not buying in Lafayette or New Orleans. LeClerc's Fine Jewelry always has the latest styles."

Well aware that his brothers and brother-in-law had done exactly that, purchased in the larger cities, Teddy said, "I wouldn't go anywhere else." Besides, he could hardly afford those ten-carat stones high-class jewelers kept in their vaults. He watched Jessie approach the case and wondered how big a diamond Troy shelled out for with his income as a football player. He'd never minded not being a professional athlete and having their income as much as he did right at this moment.

The rings were in the current style, many small diamonds running along the bands with a central stone in the middle, not a solitaire among them and no plain gold wedding rings in sight. He began to sweat as Jessie circled the case peering through the glass at the dazzling display.

"Oh, Teddy, look at this one. The diamonds on the band alternate with little sapphires, and another small blue stone is mounted beneath the larger one filling it with highlights. That's my birthstone, the sapphire."

Mr. LeClerc arrived with the key to the case and supplied the magic name in weddings. "That's a Vera Wang. Excellent choice. Let's try it on."

Teddy thought of the modest necklace he'd bought for Jessie's birthday, a few inexpensive pearls, no thoughtful sapphires. And no price tags exposed in the ring case. The ring fit a trifle loose. "We can size that for you, no extra charge," LeClerc offered. "How about that matching wedding band?"

Teddy gulped and wished Jessie hadn't heard him. Immediately, she twisted the ring from her finger and declared, "You know, we could just get gold wedding bands and forget about all this expensive stuff. I don't need it."

"You deserve these rings." He tried to say that with conviction. He bet Dale Minvielle knew to the penny how much Troy had spent to engage her daughter. "Mr. LeClerc, let's talk about this in your office." Teddy put on his most winning smile. Financing available if he asked for it. After years of trying to assert his independence, no way would he ask for a loan from his dad, though the jeweler couldn't know that.

The total came to a little over five thousand; a bit more with the not very wide gold band he chose for himself. He had that amount in his bank account now, flush with his seasonal earnings from calling the UL and Sinners home games, but in the leaner months after football ended, the sum amounted to several months of living expenses. And he'd taken on a wife and possibly a baby. Jessie would do her part, but Lizzy might sometimes require childcare if Jess wanted to take classes toward that psychology degree. His hands grew clammy as he wrote the check after wheedling a discount for a cash sale.

"Could you put the engagement ring in a box? We'll bring it back for sizing after we've told the family."

"Nothing I wouldn't do for the Billodeauxs—even if some of them choose to shop elsewhere." With a small sniff of disdain, LeClerc placed the ring in a white satin box with his gold logo on the top and handed it over.

As the newly engaged left the shop, Jessie reached up to put a hand on Teddy's forehead. "Are you okay? You're sweating. I know the old man scrimps on the air-conditioning a little, but it wasn't that hot in the store."

"I'm fine. I'll put down the windows on the van and let it cool off a little. Let's go sit in the shade on the green while we wait."

They crossed at one of the three stoplights in Chapelle and moved into the shadow of a giant live oak among the many dotting the green in front of Ste. Jeanne d'Arc Catholic Church. One mighty branch dipped so low it nearly touched the group.

"Can you get up on the branch?" Teddy asked.

"Sure, thanks to all my muscle building with you." Jessie flexed her biceps playfully and hiked herself onto the limb.

Teddy leaned his crutches against her wheelchair and lowered himself to his knees. He wouldn't be able to hold the pose long, but he wanted to do this right. He withdrew the ring box and flipped the lid to expose the diamonds and sapphires. "Jessica Claire Minvielle, will you marry me?"

"Hey, I asked you first, and you didn't know my middle name until this afternoon when my mother yelled at me. But yes, Teddy, I will marry you with all my heart and all my soul."

Teddy placed the ring on her finger, and she leaned way over to kiss him on the lips, lost her balance, and took both of them to the ground amid a clatter of fallen crutches.

For a moment, they lay there until cars began lining up at the red light and drivers stared at the two laughing lunatics cavorting in the oak duff. A few people rolled down their windows and offered, "You two need any help?" because this was after all Cajun Louisiana, not the big city.

"No, no, we're fine. Just got engaged!" Teddy shouted.

Horns honked at the good news. He grabbed his fallen crutches and pulled himself up. That earned a few cheers as the light changed, and traffic moved. He held the chair for Jessie to raise herself into the seat.

"What an engagement story we'll have to tell Lizzy and our other children," Jessie said, still laughing.

"We'd better get a move on telling my mom and the rest of the family. Nothing pisses off a Billodeaux more than not knowing family news first. That's why they hate the tabloids. We'll try the clinic since it's nearby, then the ranch."

They should have known any line of traffic that long signaled what amounted to the rush hour in Chapelle. Between the confrontation with Jessie's mother, getting the license, making the drive into town, and selecting the rings, they'd lost track of the hour.

At the clinic, Marvelle, closing up for the day, informed them that Nell had left, gone to Xochi's to pick up Corazon. "Who's watching the baby? Is she over there?" Teddy asked.

Marvelle bathed them in that warm smile she offered everyone. "The child is with Nurse Shammy at the ranch. Your mother said she practically ran off the rest to get her hands on Lizzy." Eyes that missed nothing spied the glitter of the ring. "I see congratulations might be in order."

"Might be, but don't tell anyone yet. Mom first."

"If none of the people driving along Main Street don't call her," Jessie added.

This time, Teddy phoned ahead and asked the women to stay put until they arrived. "I have Jessie with me. We'll meet you outside."

"Wait until you see, Teddy!" Xo exclaimed. "I had ramps built for my second favorite brother after Tom. I was saving it for a surprise when you visited, which you don't do nearly enough."

"You sound more like Mawmaw Nadine every day, my second favorite sister after Stacy. We'll be there in five minutes. Big news to share."

"Tell me, tell me!"

"Nope. See you soon."

The women stood lined up along the front porch railing when they arrived. With the gate propped open by a cast iron mouse that appeared to be pushing it, the couple got into the yard easily enough, and immediately noted a path hewed through the aspidistra leading to a side ramp adorned with multicolored spindles and handrails that matched the King Cake house. He and Jessie easily mounted the porch. No one remarked on the stained knees of Teddy's khakis or the little, brown oak leaves caught in Jessie's hair.

In less than a second, Xochi spied the ring. "You're engaged!" She hugged Teddy, then Jessie, then burst into tears. "Sorry, hormones. I'm so happy for you."

"Ai-yi-yi, we have another wedding to plan!" Corazon took Jessie's hand to view the ring. "Muy bonita. When—in spring?"

"We were thinking in two weeks," Teddy said. "Just a simple ceremony with a justice of the peace."

Nell beamed at them. "You know that won't be possible with the Billodeauxs involved, though of course we will defer to Jessie and her mother about what they want. Is there any reason to hurry?"

"We want to meet one of the qualifications that Miss Simms set for us to keep Lizzy."

Nell stopped smiling. "That first time you visited the ranch together, I thought you were perfect for each other, but I didn't expect an engagement so soon. Is it really good to rush for the sake of the child and have no time to adjust to marriage? Lizzy is fine with us for now. We all enjoy having a baby in the house again."

"You just want to keep her, don't you? Can't you understand she's my last link to my birth mother?" He failed to keep the jealousy out of his voice and knew he'd hurt the woman who raised him, but she didn't show it or strike back. That wasn't Nell's way. Yet he kept on speaking. "You and Dad started married life with Dean as a baby, and he wasn't yours. You adopted Tom and had the twins within the next two years. Why don't you think we can manage?"

"Believe me, while having a baby for a little while is nice, we have very little desire to relive the teen years. Remember, I still have two of those at home. This will all be straightened out long before she reaches that age. I won't mind skipping teething either. Certainly, I believe you can take care of Lizzy, but having a little time to yourselves might be nice. I always thought so." Nell revealed herself to him. Obviously, there had been moments she simply wanted time alone with her husband.

Xochi laid a hand on Teddy's arm. He felt her calming warmth flood his body. "You're doing your woo-woo thing on me, right?"

"You know you have to watch your blood pressure, brother of mine. Usually, you're pretty mellow, but you've been under great strain lately."

Jessie nodded. "I can agree with that. We only wanted to tell you about the engagement. My mother won't be having any say in the wedding. She's not coming. Like Teddy said, small and simple. Maybe just a ceremony at the courthouse."

"Oh, no! That cannot be." Corazon put her hand over her big heart. "You want in two weeks, we see what we can do. You got a dress?"

Jessie brightened. "I do, though I haven't tried it on in ages. It might need some adjustments and shortening to keep it from tangling in my wheels. I certainly won't need the train."

"We do something nice with that. So at the ranch," Corazon said, already making a mental list her audience could almost see.

"Let's discuss this over dinner. The men probably wonder where we are," Nell said.

"If I am not home, there is no dinner," Corazon proclaimed.

Xochi glanced through the trees of her backyard, across the bayou to the Riverside restaurant where Junior held a part ownership. "I say we celebrate with dinner out across the way. Champagne for everyone! Oh, not for me. Call Dad and Knox to bring Edie and T-Rex along and get word to Trinity. We'll get a nice takeout for Nurse Shammy and Brinsley who is sure to be lurking around."

Corazon hugged her daughter-in-law's shoulders. "With this one, always a fiesta."

Nell got on the phone. Xo continued to study her yard, shady with oaks, but bright in the sunny spots with beds of black-eyed-susans, Mexican blanket flowers, and orange marigolds. "Why not here if we don't need a lot of space? It's more intimate than the ranch. I put a small ramp on the gazebo, too, to let you use it. We can place the justice of the peace there. If Beau's Blooms can't handle this at short notice, we'll cut some of my flowers and hand tie them for bouquets. Who do you want as your attendants, Jessie?"

"You," Jess said. "Just you. Most of my old friends fell away when I had my accident. Teddy, what about your best man?"

He sorted through all his brothers. Dean had been really mean to him when he first entered the family, though he'd defended him later from teasing. Tom tended to do what Dean did back then. Certainly not playboy Mack. T-Rex, a little too young to trust with the rings. "I guess my nerd brother, Trinity. He won't show me up by being too tall, or play practical jokes like Tom or Rex might. He needs to sharpen his social skills anyhow."

"Perfecto," Corazon agreed. "Some of the boys are still naughty."

"Your dad wants to know how many pigs to roast." Nell held her phone away from her ear.

"Roast pigs, ahh…" Jessie stumbled over that one.

Teddy squeezed her hand. "Family joke. Adam Malala, our Samoan friend, had forty at his wedding on the island. It's a prestige custom there. Tell Dad one would be fine. We don't expect a crowd."

Nell relayed the message and phoned for reservations at the Riverside. "They're getting a table ready for us. Let's celebrate!"

## Chapter Thirty

Jessie hardly expected her wedding day to be like this. Out of deference for the football schedules, they'd chosen a date in mid-October when the Sinners had a bye week and UL played an early afternoon game, leaving plenty of time for Coach Mo to shower, shave, and struggle into his rented tux in order to make the seven p.m. sunset service and reception. Jessie said he could simply wear a suit, but her dad refused to be outshone by the Billodeaux men who owned custommade tuxedos because they so often attended charity affairs. Teddy, having filled out since the last time he used his, took the garment to the elderly tailor who did alterations from his tiny shop behind his home in Chapelle.

As for her gown, Corazon shortened it, and they did a trial run to make sure the fabric wouldn't tangle in the wheels of her chair, a new one matching Teddy's but in blue, her favorite color. The rest of the dress with its crystal-strewn strapless bodice posed no problems with her more toned arms, and the fingertip veil fit perfectly. Around her neck, she wore the simple pearl necklace Teddy had gotten for her birthday, recently returned along with her phone and other belongings by the Shreveport police.

Xochi purchased a buttery yellow high-waisted gown with a bodice of sparkling crystals that charmingly showed off her baby bump. She'd styled her dark hair up threaded with ribbons that matched the color and appeared in the bindings around the flowers.

Beau Regard of Beau's Blooms had clapped his hands gaily in excitement over the suggestion that they use flowers from Xo's garden in the two bouquets. "I do so love an original idea. It's always roses, roses, roses and calla lilies, but lately peonies, so out of season right now. How perfect for an autumn wedding!" He and his partner came to harvest the blossoms a day in advance to chill and suck up preservatives prior to being wrapped. A centerpiece of more substantial varicolored mums rested on Jessie's train, used as a head table drape, but the amber vases on the pale yellow cloths covering the smaller tables held more of the garden flowers with little wisps of fern.

When Jess thought about the wedding she'd planned with her mother, Dale making most of the decisions, she often felt her mom was more in love with Troy than she. And her dad, well, he'd been so proud of the young man he'd helped coach to greatness in the NFL. Surprisingly, when she'd called her brother to see if he wanted to attend, he'd said, "Can't Sis, got a game that weekend, but I think you made a good trade. I know I'm speaking ill of the dead, but Troy Gilbert was a jerk through and through. From what I remember of Teddy, you couldn't find a nicer guy. Be happy." At least one of the Minvielles had seen through the big-man-on-campus façade.

Jessie clutched her bouquet and stared out at the rented tables and chairs arrayed around the oaks, far too many for their tiny affair. Outside of the immediate family circle only Mawmaw Nadine and the Abbott grandparents were invited. She'd questioned Nell, dressed in a more subdued yellow suit than Xo's choice, about the arrangements and had gotten the reply, "Billodeauxs, you never know how many will show up," which seemed like an evasive answer. No time to worry about that. Her in-laws-to-be had footed the bill for everything. No quibbling from her.

Her dad was running late. Had he changed his mind about pushing her chair to the gazebo to keep her hands free for the flowers? She should have known when the sound of a large bus coming to a stop before the house drowned out the crickets and tree frogs just warming up for the evening. Thundering feet rounded the home, and Jessie watched from the tall windows of the dining room as the entire UL team, dressed in suits and ties as if they were on their way to a bowl game, lined up to make an aisle for her. X-avier gave her a wide grin and a thumbs-up.

"Oh, Mama Nell, we're going to need another pig to feed them all."

"Already taken care of. We have plenty of food and champagne, plus the bus to get them all back to Lafayette safely."

Jessie gauged Teddy's smile as he sat by the justice of the peace waiting for her to become his wife. The fairy lights strung on the gazebo and along the oak limbs made him glow, or maybe that was his inner light. "Did everyone know about this but me?" she asked.

"Pretty much," Xochi said. She tucked a daisy boutonniere into Coach Mo's lapel as he puffed to a stop next to his daughter.

"Sorry, honey. Some of my boys spend more time

primping than the most girlie of girls. I swear X-avier fiddled with his fro for an hour. Anyhow, we're here, your groom is waiting, and the team has another surprise for you."

"Oh, really," she said with a little trepidation in her voice.

"It's good, just wait."

"I wish Mom had come with you."

"I tried, I really tried. Nell talked to her, but your mother doesn't give in easily."

Joe came to walk Nell down the improvised aisle. Xochi followed them, and Mo steered his daughter's chair down the back porch ramp. As soon as they appeared, X-avier sounded a pitch pipe and led the Cajuns into an a-cappella version of All You Need is Love by the Beatles.

"They've seen Love Actually?" Jessie murmured.

"Some of them, but they all went along with it. Rehearsed after football practice. Some have really good voices, like X-avier who's kind of a showboat, but the others are doing the da-da-da-dums. For you, baby."

"Oh, so sweet." Glad she'd worn waterproof makeup Jessie pushed away the tears with her own smile.

The justice of the peace, a woman who clearly doted on marrying people, spoke a few words about the joyous uniting of a loving couple. Xo took her bouquet. Awkward Trinity did not fumble the rings. Jessie and Teddy repeated their vows, exchanged rings, and turned to face their witnesses, a wall of handsome Billodeaux men, their sisters and wives, plus Brinsley, the butler, all dressed as if they attended a royal wedding in Xochi's backyard. Their eyes lit upon Lizzy in

Mawmaw Nadine's arms, Nurse Shammy on one side ready for any emergency, and Nell on the other. Dressed in a sunny, ruffled dress, a white bonnet and booties, the baby watched wide-eyed, beguiled by the lights and the sun setting over the bayou turning its brown waters to gold.

Teddy whispered, "Did you see that? She smiled at us, her first smile."

Maybe not, but if Lizzy had started smiling earlier none of her caretakers gave the secret away. Jessie held out her arms. Shammy wrested the infant away from Mawmaw Nadine and propped her in the crook of Jessie's elbow. The team started another chorus of love, love, love as Mo wheeled his daughter forward, Teddy beside her. Jessie glanced up at a solitary form standing on the porch, her mother wearing the suit she'd chosen for another wedding, and dabbing at her eyes with a hankie.

"Teddy, take the baby!" She handed Lizzy over and pushed away from her father's control. "Mom!"

But the woman had gone. As fast as she drove her chair, Jess couldn't catch up, the long tables in the house for the buffet presenting obstacle after obstacle right down to a whole roasted pig with an apple in its mouth presented in a nest of ruffled purple and white cabbage leaves occupying a pedestal of its own. On the front porch, she heard the slam of a car door and watched her mother's SUV pull out of a space behind the team bus. Gone. For the second time that evening Jessie wanted to cry.

Her dad and Teddy minus the baby came up behind her. Mo squeezed his daughter's shoulder. "I guess she did want to see you in your wedding gown. Don't worry. She'll come around."

"Jessie, please don't cry. Come back outside. The team has arranged a first dance for us," Teddy said.

"A dance?" she sniffed, trying so hard not to let the tears stream.

"Yes, follow me." He led her back to the yard where champagne bottles popped, and recorded music, or maybe a karaoke machine, played in the background. Most of the team had retreated to tables, each with its own bottle of wine, but X-avier Hopkins stood in the gazebo, microphone to his mouth.

"Ladies and gentlemen, I give you Mr. and Mrs. Teddy Billodeaux." He paused for the applause with impeccable timing. "While I wish them all the best in life, I do have to say I would have liked a chance with Jessica before Ted intercepted her heart. Now, my mama says football don't last forever, so I'm thinkin' I might make a wedding singer. Don't you laugh now." He waited for the laughter to subside. "Here's my version of At Last My Love Has Come Along, no disrespect meant to the great Etta James. I figured if it was good enough for Obama and his lady, it's is good enough for this fine occasion too." He launched into the song and wasn't half bad.

Teddy held out his arms to Jessie. "Climb aboard, and put your arms around my shoulders."

"You sure this is going to work?" But Jessie obeyed, alighting on his lap in a cloud of white. When it came to the Billodeauxs she figured she'd be saying that for the rest of her life and be proved wrong.

Teddy moved his chair in a series of deft serpentines, each ending with a twirl and back again, then a series of wide circles growing smaller and smaller until Jessie laughed and threw her hands in the air. "I'm getting dizzy."

"I'm getting tired—but you are much lighter than the kicker they made dress up in a Goodwill wedding gown so we could practice."

"That's where you've been when you had to go out to do all those interviews? For a while, I thought you had a girlfriend on the side."

"Not me. This is forever, Jess."

"Yes, yes it is, Teddy." They sealed these second vows with a kiss, drawing more applause. The song ended. The kiss continued—until X-avier interrupted.

"I might be persuaded to perform a few more times after we tuck into the spread that awaits us. I hear we got two whole pigs, Junior Polk's famous crab cakes..." X-avier consulted a notecard. "Mawmaw Nadine's brisket and fabulous bread pudding, Miss Corazon's taquitos and quesadillas, all else catered by Down By The Riverside Restaurant. Family and wedding party first. Just leave some for the team."

"Wish I were as smooth as X-avier," Trinity Billodeaux muttered. He pushed the dark curls he should have had cut for the occasion out of the way of his black-framed glasses. "If there were any girls here not my sisters or married, they'd be all over him."

Teddy, just in front of him in line, answered, "Maybe he'll give you lessons, but chin up, Lorena and Mack aren't engaged or married either. And look at me, who would have thought I could be so lucky?"

After the meal, the couple cut the three-tiered traditional wedding cake edged in icing lace ordered from Pommier's bakery, a cake Jessie had considered too big when they selected it. It went fast since the football players had no desire to take any back to the dorm in little boxes. A good local photographer took traditional group pictures and candids to commemorate the occasion. Coach Mo kept a sharp eye on his team and herded them back onto the bus when all were happy but not drunk or combative.

Before leaving, he took a check from his pocket and handed it over to Jessie. "From the day you were born, we set up a wedding fund for you. Never told you about it because we didn't want any begging to use it for other stuff until we started paying the deposits for the occasion."

"With everything that happened I forgot all about it. I guess you couldn't get most of those deposits back."

"No matter. Joe wouldn't let me pay for anything but the use of the team bus. What's left is yours to start a new life. Live it well, honey." Mo kissed his daughter on the cheek. "Okay, the team is singing Ninety-Nine Bottles of Beer. I need to go before we get arrested for disturbing the peace." Jessie suspected her father's sudden exit masked a few tears.

Junior Polk took his place. "The keys to our condo in New Orleans." He tossed those to Teddy. For Jessie, he had an envelope. "Gift cards to some of the best places in town to eat, and free drinks at Mariah's Place. We all picked our favorite spots. Mariah said you'd better stop by and see her. She has to approve the bride."

"We will," Teddy promised.

Nell kissed them both. "This is a good time to leave. We'll handle everything from here. Gifts have been piling up in the bedrooms, but you can open them when you get back."

"Gifts?"

"Yes, when word got around town, people who wished you well went to LeClerc's and ordered off your previous list. You made that man ecstatically happy. Now, drive carefully. Call when you get there. Love you both."

The family lined up on the front porch, lighting the night with sparklers to see them on their way. Nurse Shammy waved the baby's tiny hand at them as they got into the van and let Joe stow their wheelchairs. As soon as his dad stepped back, Teddy drove over the bayou bridge, blocking the happy scene on the porch, but on the other side, Jessie could see the lights in the oak trees on Xochi's lawn still twinkling and reflecting off the dark water.

"We're on our way, wife of mine." Teddy took the turn that would head them toward New Orleans. "I brought the wedge." He earned a radiant smile for that.

Jessie unfolded her father's check jammed into the envelope containing the gift cards. "We certainly are. Twenty-three thousand dollars, Teddy. Enough for a down payment on a little house with a picket fence."

Chapter Thirty-One

As usual, Mama Nell proved right. Having some time to themselves to sort out living together permanently worked well. Who got which side of the bed? What TV shows to watch since they had only one set? Where to cram all those wedding gifts of china, silver, and crystal plus the more practical rice cooker and toaster oven in their small place? Who did the cooking? What should they eat that both liked and when? Teddy had gotten a little practice putting up with Ella.

Still, the highlights of every day were their daily visits to Lizzy and their nights spooned around each other, at least Teddy thought so. Jessie continued to work as a trainer for her father's team, but not on a fulltime basis, just enough hours to keep her insurance with the university to treat any conditions paraplegics were prone to suffer. He owned a personal policy to cover the same that took a big chunk out of his earnings, but knew his family would rush to cover anything he couldn't handle, a special type of security most didn't have. Teddy urged Jess to sign up for those extra psychology courses she wanted to take in the spring and work toward a counselor's degree.

Both had enough free time to do some house hunting. They'd given the realtor a list of must-haves: the fenced yard, a good school district, nice neighborhood, single story, three bedrooms, two baths preferred, but they could do with less. Handicapped accessibility would only be a plus. Yet most of the places in their price range appeared as old as the owners who had been shipped off to nursing homes. Some had sagging wooden ramps. Others sit-in baths rather than the roll-in showers they both used. Yards in the old neighborhoods tended to have lots of space, which meant upkeep in the form of hiring someone to mow and rake the leaves from mature trees in the autumn.

As they left yet another failure for a home with its ugly chain link fence, overgrown shrubbery, and turquoise-tiled bathroom, Jessie said, "I don't think we'll ever find a place in Lafayette we can afford that isn't a major fixer-upper. Maybe we should try Chapelle."

"We'd both have longer commutes."

"But less traffic and a safe, small town environment," their ever-optimistic realtor chirped. Teddy supposed those who lacked eternal optimism rarely applied for real estate licenses. Daisy Derouen, a primo pusher of houses in Chapelle, widened her red-lipsticked smile and jangled her bracelet filled with tiny house charms representing the many she had sold, including the mansion, Pecan Grove, to billionaire Jonathan Hartz who had the wealth to redo whatever he wanted.

"I'd consider it," Jessie said.

"I don't think so."

"I'll keep looking. You know I will." Daisy slipped so easily into her black Jaguar purchased with her commission on the Pecan Grove sale, wrapped a silk scarf around her blonde lacquered hair, set her sunglasses in place, and roared away as elegantly as Grace Kelly on the roads of Monte Carlo. She had no idea she'd started the newlyweds' first spat.

Jessie sighed. "Wouldn't that be nice, to just slide into a sports car and take off without a lot of bother?"

"No room for the wheelchair," her new husband said. "I've never been able to do that and don't know what I'm missing. Who cares?" Teddy, who'd used his crutches for the less-than-stellar tour of the 1950s cottage, seated Jessie in the front seat of the van, dealt with her chair, and thumped himself around to the driver's seat.

Jessie started in at once. "Don't get frustrated because we haven't found a place yet. We should try Chapelle where houses are cheaper."

"No."

"There is nothing wrong with Chapelle. We both grew up there, attended the public schools, and turned out fine. Lizzy could visit the ranch and play with Xochi's child. I kind of like the idea."

"Listen, Jess, I've spent years trying to live independently of my parents. I can't command a salary like my brothers in football do, or even Trinity who has gone to work as a computer geek at Hartz Technology and finally moved off the ranch. They all have more talent and brains than I do. We'll never be rich, and I don't want to be known as the poor brother by everyone in Chapelle. Not to mention that the family would be all up in our business trying to help. I don't stick out as much in a city the size of Lafayette. Face it, if you'd married Troy, you'd be wearing a ten-carat ring and maybe getting around in a chauffeured car instead of a van with a ramp."

Teddy should have been warned by the way Jessie's cheeks burned red. "Did I say I wanted a big ring and a sports car? No! Sometimes, I get a little down about all the things I used to do. You're the one who taught me to accept some help and move toward independence. This whole search for a house is for Lizzy, not me. I'd be content to stay in the apartment with you, but the idea of having family close by if we need them appeals to me. After all, we won't be getting any help from my mother."

Whoa, she'd used her cheerleading voice, loud and clear in the confines of the van. Too true about her mother. He'd caused their estrangement, or maybe only Lizzy had. Probably Dale would have accepted their marriage without the baby and waited patiently for pure white grandchildren to come along. They'd married in haste to give the child a home, and that might not be enough to keep them together if overcoming obstacles to adopt Lizzy failed. On his side, he loved Jessie and considered himself lucky to have her. Maybe she loved Lizzy more than her new husband.

"Listen to me, Teddy, and hear what I say. Troy was the jerk I was prepared to marry to please my parents. I doubt we would have lasted more than a few years. Instead, I got a kind, caring man who buoyed me up when I fell down and opened new worlds for me. I consider that a good trade. Lizzy is an added bonus as far as I am concerned. Yes, I love her, but if she has to be raised by your parents or Xochi, I'll accept that. We can be a loving aunt and uncle, a part of her life regardless, and have children of our own someday. Now, I want to look at houses in Chapelle. Do you have any problem with that?"

He gave the best response he could offer. "No, ma'am. You know I love you, Jess. Our marriage isn't all about giving Lizzy a home." Teddy raised her hand to his lips and kissed her fingertips.

She squeezed his hand. "Let's go visit the baby."

\*\*\*\*

Lizzy attended her first Sinners' game at the age of seven weeks. Teddy looked down upon his family from the booth. Jessie occupied his old spot on the end of the row in the reserved seats on the fifty-yard line, which Joe Billodeaux greatly preferred to a skybox, where the team couldn't hear his encouragement, or the refs his comments on their calls. Lizzy lay in a sling across Jessie's lap. As the camera panned around the Dome, they paused on Joe and his family. Teddy gave his usual announcement, "Daddy Joe is in the house!" and drew the usual cheers. He added, "Also my bride, Jessica, and the baby we hope to adopt." More cheers. Teddy swore Lizzy's blue eyes searched for the source of his voice coming out of nowhere as her picture flashed on the big screens. Once the game started, Jessie placed little pink headphones on the baby's curly black hair to filter out the more startling noises of a football game in full action, but she seemed to take an interest in the players wearing black and red who streaked up the field and down. Billodeauxs started young when it came to football, and Teddy hoped to make her one of the family soon.

Even better, they'd gotten permission from the sour Miss Simms to keep Lizzy with them the next weekend when the Sinners played away, and most of the family planned to follow them to Atlanta for the game. The fact that the social worker did not approve of taking small infants on airplanes unless absolutely necessary worked in their favor. Yes, they'd gladly babysit and prove they could handle Lizzy's care. An added bonus: Nurse Shammy said the baby now slept through the night—if waking up around five or six a.m. counted as a full night. She'd helped them gain possession of the infant for a couple of days by claiming a burning desire to attend the game as well, even though neither flying nor football were among her favorite things. Hope grew that they'd be able to keep the baby permanently, but no house in Lafayette or Chapelle seemed to fit their needs.

After the Sinners put the game away thirty-four to seventeen, Teddy met the clan in a private room at one of their favorite New Orleans restaurants. He put down his fork to give Lizzy a bottle when she grew fussy, allowing Jessie to enjoy her meal. That drew a nod of approval from Nell. With reluctance, he strapped the baby into the Billodeaux van for the ride back to Chapelle. Corazon took a place next to her, but Knox, who had been persuaded to attend the game this time around, held back a minute after withdrawing a black case from under the driver's seat of the van. "Belated wedding gift for Jessie," he muttered.

Teddy handed the case to his bride who opened it on her lap still warm from holding the baby to find a spanking new pistol and a bunch of forms. "A smaller, lighter-weight weapon for you, and forms for concealed carry papers for you and Teddy. I'm certified to instruct you, but you must have a doctor fill in the medical part since you have some disabilities. You need to get your fingerprints taken on FBI cards, two sets to send in along with the fee, and get it notarized. Then, you can keep your guns with you in those pouches both of you have on your chairs, handy in case you need them. I figure the bad guys are still out there, and you both need to be ready." For Knox Polk, quite a speech.

Nell stopped Joe in the midst of lifting her into the van with his big hands around her waist. "Put me down a minute. Do you really think they're in danger? Ella did want Teddy to keep her baby. She put it in writing."

"You never can tell about folks. They change their minds, and that boyfriend of hers signed nothing. Better safe than sorry. You remember your moves to defend yourself with crutches, Teddy?"

"Yes, sir, I do, but I'll put in some practice time."

Jessie, still staring at the pistol with the pink grips, managed to say, "Ah, thank you for thinking of me. I really would like more lessons in handling a gun. We'll set up some times when Teddy can practice with us."

"All right, then." Knox folded his long, lean length into the driver's seat since his employer had indulged in a few beers at the game and wine with dinner, while he had teetotaled the whole time to stay alert and on guard. Joe swung his short wife into their van and took the shotgun seat while Edie, T-Rex, and Trinity waited their turns, T-Rex already asking when he could get a concealed carry permit.

"When you are twenty-one and not a second sooner," Nell shouted from the interior, waking the baby.

Corazon dangled plastic keys in front of Lizzy's blue eyes to distract her from crying. All aboard, the troop drove back to Chapelle with Teddy and Jessie behind them by a few minutes. They watched the van peel off at their exit and continued on to Lafayette.

"Teddy, do you really think we need to be armed at all times?" Jessie asked in the darkness of their car.

"Knox is one of the most paranoid people I know, always vigilant. Makes him a good bodyguard, but sometimes he can creep you out the way his eyes are always looking into the shadows. I wouldn't worry. Nothing has been heard of Ella and Wyatt since they stole that car in Shreveport. I'm pretty sure they've left the state."

"I can certify her boyfriend did not want the baby if he couldn't sell her. We have no reason to worry, I guess. Hey, did you know they give a senior citizen discount on these permits, $62.50 for five years if you are above sixty-five, $125 dollars for young'uns like us?" said Jessie who had been reading the forms by booklight. She obviously attempted to lighten the conversation.

"No worries, we can afford it." At the moment, halfway through football season they could. Teddy parsed his money carefully to last the whole year, and his new responsibilities did concern him, especially if they got the baby permanently. Right now, he'd only think of next weekend when Lizzy came to stay for a while.

Chapter Thirty-Two

Ted and Jessie prided themselves on how well they were doing as prospective parents. Jess had an afternoon away game to work for UL. They agreed in advance to order pizza and salad for dinner, and after some debate to watch a rented movie both finally settled upon, one with no explosions to wake the baby. Nell delivered the child into their willing arms on her way to the airport, leaving behind a diaper bag stuffed with supplies for Lizzy. She kissed all three of them and delivered a reminder from Knox to keep their guns handy, while the rest of family waited in the van.

After Jessie left for her job, Teddy had the baby all to himself. He encouraged Lizzy to reach for squeaky toys, showed her brightly colored pictures in Sports Illustrated, and sang the Lizzy song Jessie had made up, maybe not as well as his wife, but the baby didn't seem to care. Before putting her down for a nap in the crib now returned to the second bedroom, he made sure she was dry, well fed, burped, and rocked to sleep, her gurgling stomach pressed against his warm chest. Not a bad idea to nap himself, but he had work to do on the computer.

Lizzy awoke wailing before Jessie returned home. Teddy rushed to her side to find himself dealing with a shit storm, literally—oozing from her onesie, all over her back when he removed it, and spread to her hair with small, flailing fists no matter how fast he tried to clean up the mess. The pile of used wipes mounted as Teddy held his breath, dealing with the nauseating situation. Lizzy appeared to think they were playing, splashing her hands into the poo while he attempted to clean them. He started over again just when a key turned in the lock and the automatic door swung open in the living room. He hoped help had arrived.

"Whoa, what stinks in here?" said Jessie, returning from the game.

"Lizzy and a massive loose dump. Need your assistance, please!"

His wife, entering the nursery, caught her breath too.

Jess sized up the situation. "Okay, I need to shower after being out in the sun all afternoon. Just bring her to me naked, and I'll hose her down. You can change the sheets and clean up the wipes while I'm at it."

"Teamwork, I like it." Teddy gave Jess a head start before transferring Lizzy off the soiled changing pad and onto a clean flannel receiving blanket spread on his lap. She seemed to enjoy the ride to the bathroom. Teddy enjoyed the view of a nude Jessie reaching out to take the baby into the stall, spraying her with carefully adjusted warm water, and gently shampooing those dark curls. He watched the whole time, half wishing he could join them in the shower, but he stood by with a dry towel to take Lizzy back to her room, put her in a new diaper and outfit and into her baby seat with an arch full of interesting dangles to keep her occupied. He wiped down the changing pad, stripped the sheets, and hauled the trash bag to the dumpster, cursing out an SUV that blocked the ramp and made it more difficult.

He returned to find Jessie wearing a comfortable pair of pale blue sweats as she blow-dried her hair. "Say, that was kind of sexy watching you in the shower with the baby, I mean in a sweet way. Got anything on under the sweats?"

Jessie turned off the dryer. "No and no. We are not having sex while Lizzy is awake. Maybe later…"

"Introduction to Family Life 101. Do you think she'll be sick like that again? Should we call Mama Nell?"

"She might have diarrhea again. I know we shouldn't let her dehydrate. Honestly, I hate to call Nell. We'll look incompetent."

"I still have the number the hospital gave for advice to new parents."

"Perfect."

The doorbell rang. "Probably the pizza. You take care of that, and I'll call the hospital."

Jessie moved toward the door. The whoosh of outdoor air and the aroma of tomato sauce and pepperoni helped act as an air freshener. She paid and tipped the deliveryman who asked how Ella was doing. Awkward question. "She moved out."

"Sorry to hear that. One of our best customers." He went on his way while Teddy completed the phone call.

"Pedialyte, do we have any? The nurse said to use that for the next couple of feedings, then try the formula again. Call again if it continues."

Jessie set the pizza delivery aside and rummaged in the diaper bag. "Plenty of formula, and aha, Pedialyte. I'll put some in a bottle."

"Mama Nell thinks of everything."

"She's raised a lot of kids." Jessie wheeled close to

Teddy and laid her head against his. "I think we just survived our first parenting crisis."

"Yeah, but Jessie, are we really ready for this?"

"I think every new parent asks themselves that— and they can't give theirs back. Do you want to?"

"No, but we might need more help than we imagined."

"We'll work on it. You ready to eat?"

"Not really. I've washed my hands three times and can't seem to get the baby poop smell off of them."

Jessie glanced at his lap. "You got some on your jeans, that's why."

"Changing, changing right now."

Lizzy missed their company and started to fuss. "I'll see to her. You put on something clean."

Teddy nodded. Teamwork, that's what they had. Together he and Jess could do anything.

Chapter Thirty-Three

Jessie raised Lizzy to her shoulder and patted her back. "What's the matter, baby? Lonesome or did that accident leave your tummy empty? We've got something that will taste really good. Let's go get it. After you finish, Mom and Dad can have their dinner." Using those wonderful words pleased her so much, but she shouldn't get her hopes up. Jessie propped the infant in her lap and began to turn. A long shadow blocked the light from the hall, not like her husband's shorter profile. "Teddy?"

"Wrong guy. Told you I owned a gun. Now put that baby back in her seat and get her stuff together. We're going to see her real mama." Wyatt Coffey looked the worse for wear, unshaven for days, hair greasy, clothes grimy, favoring one leg as he leaned against the doorway.

"Where's Ella?" Jessie wanted to move her hand into the pouch where her pink pistol lay loaded and ready to fire. She hated to admit it made her feel safer after the assault, but she'd relished her lessons this week with Knox Polk, right down to keeping her firearm clean. Freedom, freedom from fear that anyone would think a woman in a wheelchair an easy target.

"None of your business. Do what I told you."

"Was this Ella's idea? She wanted Teddy to raise her child. What changed her mind?" Jess spoke loudly, clearly, hoping Teddy heard. "I'll cooperate if you tell me Ella wants Lizzy back."

With his dark, feral eyes focused on her, Wyatt growled, "I could just shoot you and take the kid."

"You might hit the baby. Your hand looks none too steady. Or I could drop and injure her. What would Ella say then?" She kept her eyes on his, willing Wyatt not to hear the soft thud in the hall.

"Ella won't say nothing. I had to drop her at a hospital in Little Rock 'cause she came down with a high fever, near delirious. Aspirin didn't do no good. We had a fine hidey-hole in a mountain cabin we found down a backroad. Even had canned goods in it. I'm growing out my beard, and she was gonna dye her hair black so's we could go into town when we ran out, but then she took sick."

"Did you force her to have sex too soon? She had lots of stitches from delivering a big baby. I'll bet you ripped them out and gave her an infection." Keep him talking, keep him talking.

"Maybe I did, but I risked getting caught to find her a doctor. Couldn't go back to visit, but I called. Ella Sue is crying and crying. Says the doc told her she's all messed up inside and might have too much scar tissue to have more kids. After she mends, might be surgery will help. I don't want no more kids anyhow, so I took her key and come to get the one we already have. Hand her over or I might just hunt down the other cripple that lives here. I know he's around. Saw him take out the trash." Wyatt's eyes shifted from hers and took a nervous glance over his shoulder.

Jessie drew the attention back to herself. "In the bathroom changing his ostomy pouch."

"Gross. My grandpappy had one of those, had to shit in a sack. Good time to catch Teddy unawares like a dog taking a crap." Coffey half turned.

Teddy's crutch slammed down on his left shoulder, but the other hand held Wyatt's gun. He dropped the arm as the pain hit, but didn't lose his weapon. Teddy whapped him across the kidneys and again across the back of the neck as the man sank to his knees. Whether intentional or not, the gun went off. Jessie felt her wheelchair tilt. She thrust Lizzy, screaming, onto the bed, and found her own pistol. She didn't hesitate to shoot, higher this time, not his hip but his groin. Maybe the wound would kill him, maybe not. She didn't really care as long as he never threatened to take Lizzy again. Setting her weapon back in the sack, Jessie picked up her baby...her child, and comforted her.

"Remind me never to make you angry." Teddy knelt awkwardly and felt for a pulse in Wyatt's neck. "Still alive. I'll get a towel and put some pressure on the wound. Have your phone in that pouch as well as your gun?"

"Yes, where was yours?" Jess willed her voice not to shake, to stay calm for Lizzy's sake as she pressed the baby to her wildly beating heart.

"In the night table drawer like always. I thought he'd hear me coming in the chair, and I can't handle the pistol well when I'm up on my sticks. Call 9-1-1 and get an ambulance and the police over here." Teddy pushed to his feet.

"I know the drill. I have both on speed dial." She used a testy attitude to cover any hint of anxiety.

Teddy did the first aid. Jessie rocked the baby in her arms. Blood on the floor again. Another wheelchair out of commission. She waited until Wyatt Coffey was hauled away to request Teddy's spare chair from the closet, calm as could be. The whole scene seemed like a repeat of the first with the endless questions and the crime scene people being called in again, only it ended differently.

"Guess we should call Child Welfare again," Officer Nelson said with regret.

"No need. We had Miss Simms' permission to keep Lizzy for the weekend. Considering the mess in here, we'll take her back to the ranch." Teddy did the talking. Jessie simply sat holding the baby, noting he omitted saying all the Billodeauxs were out of town.

Officer Nelson shook his head, not quite convinced. "How about we give you an escort down to Chapelle to make sure you don't get lost on the way."

Steady as ever, Teddy said, "We have no problem with that. We'll get some things together and stay down there for a while."

The police escort got them to Lorena Ranch in record time, but the squad car stayed outside as the gates opened, welcoming them home. The lights in the oaks popped on illuminating their way, but the mansion lay dark at the end of the lane until they rounded the curve by the kitchen to see that single window aglow. From inside the house, the dogs yapped, and Brinsley opened the door.

"Welcome, Mr. and Mrs. Teddy. Mr. Polk entrusted the safety house to me in his absence, a rare honor. I did serve with the British Forces, you know, a batman to a high-ranking officer. Excellent training for a valet. I was just about to have a nightcap and a few nibbles. Would you care to join me?" The butler moved to get both wheelchairs out of the van despite the dogs milling about his feet.

"We have a cold pizza and wilted salads to share," Jessie said as Teddy helped her down and put the sleeping Lizzy in her lap. He grabbed the diaper bag and gently pushed the curious dogs aside with the tip of his crutch.

"An excellent addition to the menu. Your rooms stand ready, the nursery also." Brinsley balanced the pizza box topped by the salads on his fingertips expertly as if on a silver tray and followed them into the house.

Teddy and Jess headed straight for the elevator and put Lizzy down on her back in the nursery crib, keeping their voices and the lights low. Having downed a full bottle of Pedialyte while the police asked their questions, the baby slept soundly, worn out from her day. They scooped up a baby monitor to take downstairs.

"Frankly, I can't see Brinsley as a batman, but definitely as an Alfred," Teddy said in the privacy of the elevator.

"Not that one, a batman, like a servant to an officer."

"Where do you learn these things?"

"Same place I learned about marriages of convenience—Regency novels. And Teddy, I'm so glad we don't have one of those." Jessie leaned over for a kiss. The terror of the day faded like the sunset. Sunrise would bring a better tomorrow. The elevator door opened and closed three times before they were done.

In the short interval they'd been gone, Brinsley had set the table with small bowls of nuts and mixed olives, a basket of breadsticks, their salads now in wooden bowls and revamped with goat cheese and raisins, and a sweating shaker of martinis. The timer dinged, signaling reheated pizza on the way. The butler poured the drinks and held out his hands. "Please, enjoy."

Jessie relaxed after the first sip. "There really is no place better than Lorena Ranch."

Teddy nodded to agree. Unfortunately, he thought so too, and could never provide Jessie and the baby with a life like this.

## Chapter Thirty-Four

Lizzy woke at five a.m., reliable as an alarm clock. Jessie wheeled down the hall and retrieved her along with a bottle from the small fridge in the nursery, and a dry diaper. Teddy changed the baby in bed while she ran hot water over the formula to take the chill off. The three of them snuggled until seven.

Dressing and moving downstairs toward the aroma of coffee and the scent of cinnamon, they entered the kitchen, Jessie with the baby in a sling sound asleep. Brinsley had set out a plate of sliced bagels with tubs of smears and a pan of hot cinnamon rolls from a pop-open can, T-Rex's favorite do-it-yourself snack. Where the butler spent the night, they did not know, whether at his own home or in a spare bedroom. Teddy was willing to bet he hadn't left the premises in his care, but would not offend his dignity by asking.

"If you would care for porridge or something else hot, I shall do my best to provide it, keeping in mind I rarely cook."

"No, this is great, Brinsley. Hand me those cinnamon rolls, Jess."

"Your plans for the day, sir?"

"Maybe take a swim, then watch the Sinners play in Atlanta. I hope you'll join us for the game, but we can scrounge our own lunch and put something together for dinner. You can try Jessie's cooking. She's pretty good."

"I am sure that would be delightful."

"Sit down and eat with us." Teddy knew the butler wouldn't, but wanted him to know he could.

"I've eaten, thank you, sir. I believe if you need nothing else, I shall take the dogs outside and enjoy my second cup of coffee on this beautiful autumn morning." He and the eager dogs departed.

Jessie sighed. "Every day should be this good."

"We might as well enjoy it. If you think we were in deep shit yesterday, it's nothing compared to facing my parents tonight. We're going to be in trouble for not calling them again."

"We handled it."

"They won't see it that way."

Taking advantage of the free day, they splashed in the pool, chilly after an autumn night and flecked with curled, brown leaves from the wild pecans and an occasional colorful contribution from the chicken trees. The time approached to spread the tarp and close it down until March. Lizzy watched from her seat in the shade.

Teddy assembled peanut butter and jelly sandwiches on whole wheat with a garnish of apple slices for lunch, while Jessie poured the milk and fed Lizzy a bottle. She rubbed a little peanut butter on the baby's lips and watched her tongue dart out to taste it. "You're supposed to do that now to make sure they don't develop peanut allergies. I've been reading up."

"And Miss Simms doubts you can be a mother."

"We both know that isn't true. You'll make a wonderful dad too. Just look at you assemble that PB&J."

After the mutual admiration, they saddled old Rascal for a ride around the paddock, taking turns and watching Lizzy react to the soft snuffling of the horse. "This is such a great place to grow up," Jessie said without considering. She caught Teddy's grimace.

"Is that what you want? To move in here with my parents and let them handle everything?"

"No, I didn't say that. I never want you to think I'm like Ella, always trying to get something out of you. We'll find a house. It will just take a while."

Three p.m., kickoff time. To their amazement, Brinsley showed up wearing a black and red Sinners jersey with Joe's old number seven on it, and bearing chips and dip. Chilled beer, always in the fridge, a must, though he preferred his warm from a case in the pantry. The Sinners took a tight game, winning by a field goal off of Tom's toe in the last seconds. Sloppy chili-cheese Fritos for dinner with raw vegetables in a nod to Nell, not exactly the best of Jessie's dishes but fine after a game.

Night fell. Lizzy went to bed fed and bathed to sleep soundly after all her new adventures on the ranch. The Sunday night game came on. Teddy checked his watch over and over again. His phone rang at ten p.m., exactly the time he figured his parents would stop by the apartment to pick up Lizzy on their way home. His mom didn't even bother with hello.

"Why is their crime scene tape across your apartment door again? Where are the three of you?"

"At the ranch, safe and sound. All is well, no one hurt. Well, Wyatt Coffey is. Jessie shot him again. He tried to take Lizzy from us, and we defended her. The cops have him now."

A laconic voice near the speaker phone in the van said, "Where did she shoot him this time?"

"In the groin. He nearly bled out."

"Jessie girl, you got to aim higher…for the heart," Knox prompted.

"Who says I didn't hit what I targeted?" Jessie retorted, her ear close to Teddy's phone.

A snort and a chuckle followed—Knox Polk laughing, as rare as white alligators.

"Teddy kept him from bleeding out."

"Because Teddy is a noble kind of guy," Knox replied, implying he wouldn't have bothered. "But a good one."

A deeper voice broke in. "Team meeting as soon as we get home."

"Dad, can't it wait until morning? I know you're tired from the travel."

"Tired? Don't you bet on it, you. We need to talk."

From Nurse Shammy and Corazon, "How is Lizzy doing?"

Jessie took over. "She's sleeping. Had some diarrhea yesterday." Jess rolled her eyes at Teddy as "some" was putting it mildly. "We found the Pedialyte in the diaper bag. She's doing fine this morning, back to normal."

"I meant to warn you she'd been a little loose. That's why I packed it. Glad you knew what to do," Nell said.

"Sure did. No worries."

"The way Knox is driving, we'll be home in about fifteen minutes. Put some coffee on. We have a lot to discuss. Love to all of you."

They waited a moment to be sure the phones were

disconnected. Jessie looked at Teddy for guidance. "You've been to plenty of these team meetings. Should we prepare our case in advance?"

"Might as well make the coffee and see how it goes. By the time things get team-meeting serious, you rarely get to appeal. It's more like crime and punishment."

"How can they punish us? We live on our own. We're independent."

"By not letting us adopt Lizzy."

\*\*\*\*

The team meeting began at eleven p.m. in the den after everyone fortified themselves with coffee and Cokes for the kids. Teddy couldn't remember any such meeting being held so late or having so few members of the family present. Their roles were filled by Knox and Corazon, Brinsley, and Nurse Shammy. This was as serious as it got with Jessie and Teddy in their chairs facing the rest on the sofa and loungers.

Daddy Joe rose up. "Son, we respect that you want to live independently. You've already proved you can. Jessie is new to self-help but learning fast. You only have to win the Super Bowl once to prove how good you are, and you've done that the way you defended Lizzy, both of you. All we asked of you was to keep us in the loop, and you didn't, no."

Joe put his big hands on the rims of Teddy's wheelchair and got right in his face. "There is no football game more important than family. I had to learn that and so do you. Something this big happens, you call us immediately. No waiting for halftime or until the game is over not to ruin our fun. How would we remember that game if any of the three of you had been injured or killed, and we didn't learn until it was over?" Joe stood up again, towering over the wheelchair, and stepped back.

"Hey, Mom gave birth to the triplets without calling you because you were in the middle of a game."

"Playing a game, not watching one—and she was wrong, but this isn't about your mother."

"We took care of things, Dad, called the police and the ambulance, answered the questions, saw to Lizzy. What could you do to help?"

"Be there. Simply be there if you needed us," Nell answered. "Yes, you did well, but if you ever want to be parents you have to learn to put the child first. Where will she be safe and happy? Your pride doesn't matter."

Nurse Shammy chimed in showing some of her old starch. "The baby takes precedence over all. Nowhere is better for her than the ranch, which is secure and has knowledgeable medical assistance." She spoke of herself of course.

"This place is as safe as I can make it. Got eyes everywhere and good people all around." Knox added a rare comment.

"I know, I know! You're pressuring us to move back here. We've been looking for a small house with a fenced yard and can't seem to find one that doesn't need lots of retrofitting."

Jessie had remained silent until now, holding his hand. "Yes, my father gave us a generous check, all the money he saved on the wedding, for a down payment. It's just finding the right place where we can manage things."

Nell's soft voice answered. "This is the right place.

You can stay in the house or choose any one of the camp cottages. They are all accessible, have two bedrooms, and about as much space as your apartment."

"And if we don't, you keep Lizzy. Right?"

"It won't be up to us, though if you aren't approved we will surely provide a home for her."

Jessie squeezed Teddy's hand. "Take the cottage. Someday, we can build a place of our own from scratch after the adoption."

"About that." Joe stepped in again. "You'll need a bigger place eventually built to your needs. Choose any place on the ranch to do that. It won't be charity. I'll finance it. You pay me back, and I won't require a huge down payment. Save some money for furnishings. No bank will give you a better deal. You can use the same architect as we did for Camp Love Letter. He understands special needs. Don't go too small either. You might want your own gym and extra bedrooms for more children. Hell, I didn't build this place big enough the first time around and had to add on."

Teddy dug in again, trying to keep control of the situation. Daddy Joe could be overpowering on and off the field. "We don't want to build more than we can afford on our salaries."

Joe took a seat as if he realized he dominated the couple by standing over them. "Let me tell you something else. Connor Riley let on CBS is looking at you for their pre-game and halftime show as a replacement for old Al Harney who is retiring after the end of this season. Connor thinks they can use some diversity and youth on their broadcasting team. You know the game inside and out."

"Did you put him up to it?"

"Nope. I wasn't going to say a word until they approached you, but I want you to know a great job might come your way. It requires some sacrifice, being away every weekend during the season and lots of travel, pretty much like the Sinners do—more actually, and big bucks."

"That would place all the burden on Jessie when I was away."

"Look around you, son. I see a room full of helpers."

Corazon added an emotional plea. "So good to have a baby around the place again. Lots of arms to hold her if Jessie needs us." All the female heads bobbed.

"Indeed," added Brinsley.

"Fine, we accept. No other choice I guess." He hated the grudging note in his voice, knowing all these people had done for him and would do for Lizzy.

"No shame in doing what is best for your family, Teddy." Joe clapped his hands, the usual ending to a team meeting. "Rex, Edie, to bed. School tomorrow. We'll move your things as soon as the cops let us. Meanwhile, stay here."

The baby monitor Jessie kept in her pouch sounded. Lizzy wanted a midnight feeding. Nurse Shammy stood, then stopped. "No, you should take care of her. Call if you need me. I'll be home with Brinsley. We both miss our own bed."

Edie covered a huge yawn with her small hand. "Nice to have you home, Teddy. I can use some help on my English projects. But could you go feed that kid? Her room is right next to mine. Meeting adjourned, okay?"

## Chapter Thirty-Five

Not much to move from the old apartment. Most of the furnishings belonged to the college. The wedding gifts went into storage at the big house except for the most practical ones. Jessie made a list to get cracking on thank-you notes, many to former Sinners she only knew from the sports section of the newspapers.

At first, they thought to choose the cottage most distant from the mansion, felt churlish about that, and selected one in the middle of the oak grove just a short roll from the family. "I feel like a real Cajun now, living in my mama's backyard," Teddy remarked as they set up housekeeping.

"You are one by adoption. Now go to the other side of the bed and help me put the sheets on."

"Only if we get to use it this afternoon for some fun."

"That's a promise. Be glad we have some privacy now. The papers did get hold of our story and those iron gates keep them at bay." Jessie unfolded a sheet and sent it sailing his way.

Teddy caught his end and tucked it in. "The police reports, I guess. The paparazzi have finally discovered Teddy Billodeaux as a source for gossip. I probably shouldn't have announced my wedding at the game, or mentioned Lizzy either. They were right on that."

"Mama Nell handled it well. She released some of

our wedding pictures to the press. Disabled Couple Weds. Hopes to Adopt wasn't such a bad headline. Since we didn't give interviews, the article read pretty much like any wedding announcement: location, a description of my dress, where the reception was held, the flowers, etc. A mention that we'd honeymooned in New Orleans, all three days of it."

"I promise we'll do something else soon. At least, that was better than the latest. Handicapped Honeymooners Beat and Shoot Intruder and Don't Mess with These Lovebirds! I never appreciated how great it was to be ignored by the press. We pushed Mack's antics in Dallas to the back page. Kind of weird seeing one of our wedding pics next to Wyatt Coffey's mug shot."

Jessie tossed him a pillow and a case. His phone rang before he could stuff one into the other. He held it close to his chest without checking the number. "Want to make a wager on whether it's a reporter, the police, or someone up at the mansion calling to see if we need help? The one who gets it right picks the position and pleasure of their choice after we finish here."

"Corazon or your mom."

Teddy glanced at the number. "Wrong." He let the call go to voice mail and finished with the pillow.

"Teddy, this is Dale Minvielle. I don't know if Jessie has a new phone number or if she'll take a call from me. Please ask her to get in touch. Thanks."

Teddy raised his pale brows at his wife. She held out her hands to catch the phone and redial. "Mom?"

"Thank God! I had to learn Teddy and that baby put you into jeopardy again from reading the newspapers." Dale shouted it loud enough for Teddy to hear. Jessie's face showed all her hurt. She disconnected and returned the phone to Teddy. He barely had it in his grasp when it rang again.

Jessie shook her head vehemently. "It will be my mother again. Don't answer it."

"She's sending a text…"

"I am so sorry. Those words just ran out. I wanted to say I know Teddy is a good man. He has taken you to a safe place where you probably won't let me in the door if I try to visit. You were a beautiful bride. I wish you a happy life. If you let me into it again, I promise I will try to love Lizzy. Might take a while, not good with babies, but I will get there. Teach her basketball, maybe? Mom."

Teddy held out the phone to his wife. "You should forgive her. She's trying."

Before Jessie's fingertips touched the cell, it rang once more. This time he checked the number. "Not one I recognize. Yes or no?"

Jessie shrugged and pulled up the spread on her side. Teddy cautiously answered, "Bonjour" without identifying himself to disguise his somewhat famous voice of the Sinners. He'd been known to mimic a fairly thick Cajun accent when he wanted to get rid of annoyance calls.

"Hey, Teddy. That you talkin' French?"

"Ella? Where are you?"

"Still in the hospital, but they'll be movin' me soon. Right now, I'm cuffed to the bed. Accessory to grand theft auto—like the game. Wyatt loved playing that one. Then, there's abetting the escape of a felon, pawning stolen goods, breaking and entering that cabin where we hid out. Lots of stuff."

"I guess you'll need a good lawyer."

Jessie shook her head and mouthed at him, "Figures."

"No, I'm pleadin' guilty. They'll go easier on me and let me serve my time in the county jail here in Arkansas instead of the state pen. Wyatt will end up in Angola peeing in a bag when he gets better. My daddy said we were gonna end up in jail. Shoulda listened to him. I plan on real good behavior and gettin' out early. Maybe I can work in the kitchen and learn to feed a crowd so I can find a job when my sentence is up."

She was beating around the bush. Teddy believed he could save her a few wrenching words. "You want Lizzy when you do. Because you can't have any more, Wyatt said." He watched Jessie react to his words, her face going sad, her eyes filling with tears.

"Maybe I could if I had some surgery done. Not likely the prison system will pay for that."

He fought against making the offer, which seemed like a bribe, but it forced itself past his lips. "Maybe I could help with that surgery if you want other children."

Jessie spun around and cupped her hands over her face, turning her back to him. Her shoulders shook.

"Not sure I want more kids. Hard to believe after all this, but for once I'm gonna do something decent and let you and Jessie adopt her. Saw all about your wedding in the tabloids. Wish I coulda been there."

Teddy tried to harden himself against her wistfulness. "Thank you. That is best for Lizzy. We're staying at the ranch in one of the cottages. Later, we'll build a house here. It's very secure."

"I won't be bothering you no more so don't worry.

I won't show up at the ranch gates again. But could I ask for pictures to see how Lizzy grows up? I bet she'll be pretty no matter what Wyatt said. I didn't set him on you. He did that his own self after he messed up my insides. Make sure you get him to sign any papers for Lizzy, too. He'll come cheap, I'm fairly sure."

"What about your dad? Will he try to claim the baby?"

"Hell, no. Hates Melungeons and everybody like 'em. She's yours—yours and Jessie's child now. Like Mama always said to me about you, Lizzy will be livin' in clover. Ma done the right thing leaving you in a safe place. I'm doing the same. Have to go now. They're here for me. Just remember those pictures, huh? I'll send the address. You're a good man, brother. Bye now."

Teddy laid down the phone and went to his wife. He slung an arm around her quaking shoulders. "Jessie, it's over. She's letting us adopt Lizzy. She'll sign legal documents."

That made Jessie cry harder. "So happy," she managed to say before wiping her tears against Teddy's strong chest. "We had to give up some of our independence, but Lizzy is worth it."

"Yes, yes, she is. It won't be so bad, living in clover with you."

## A word about the author...

Once a librarian, now a writer of romance, Lynn Shurr grew up in Pennsylvania Dutch country. She attended a state college and earned a very impractical B.A. in English Literature. Her first job out of school really was working as a cashier in a burger joint. Moving from one humble job to another, she traveled to North Carolina, then Germany, then California where she buckled down and studied for an M.A. in Librarianship.

New degree in hand, she found her first reference job in the Heart of Cajun Country, Lafayette, Louisiana. For her, the old saying, "Once you've tasted bayou water, you will always stay here" came true. She raised three children not far from the Bayou Teche and lives there still with her astronomer husband.

When not writing, Lynn likes to paint, cheer for the New Orleans Saints and LSU Tigers, and take long road trips nearly anywhere. Her love of the bayou country, its history and customs, often shows in the background for her books.

You may contact Lynn at www.lynnshurr.com or visit her blog—lynnshurr.blogspot.com or send e-mail to lynn.shurr@yahoo.com